A Vast, Untethered Ocean

A Vast, Untethered Ocean

A Novel

RD Pires

ISBN-13 978-1-7347495-2-6

Cover design by Grace Han

For Alex

Author's Note

Every story I've ever written has come with an "Aha!" moment—a deciding event in which I realize, quite suddenly, "I'm going to write this book." For A Vast, Untethered Ocean, that moment came at roughly 5:45 AM as I was homeward bound on my morning run. I heard a line spoken in my ear by the main character as he addressed his husband, perhaps the most important line in the entire story which succinctly summarizes the entire purpose of our protagonist's journey. I stopped running to look around, the sun just beginning to show signs of rising, and thought, "that's it."

Not only did the line I heard make it through every round of editing (thankfully), but that experience became a theme of sorts for Brooklyn's story. Life is a flurry of events, some of which you remember because they're BIG and IMPORTANT, some of which you forget because they're mundane—and others which are so fleetingly insignificant that, naturally, you remember them forever. Everything gets muddled up and you can't recall exactly what happened when or which way you're going to go now. But every so often, you get a moment of perfect clarity (hopefully), and a few more things make sense to you.

This is a book about grief. It's also a book about figuring things out. It's about thinking you were going to be an astronaut, but becoming a machinist instead. Thinking you were always going to have someone by your side and then waking up one morning to discover they're gone forever. I don't need to tell you that life is full of the unexpected. You've probably figured that out for yourself. But I hope through all the muddled memories, the twists and turns, and the indecision; that the people you encounter in your life bring you moments of clarity which help you see the way forward.

Whether they be real people—as they so often are for most—or a voice in your head on a late summer morning.

Chapter One

Dying might solve his problems.

Brooklyn searches his brain for an argument, but nothing arrives. *Doing it* might find him that elusive peace—not only a reprieve from the pain but an end to it. It's a tempting possibility he can't shake.

Heart racing, he stares out at the bridge illuminated by his headlights. Just below the idling of the engine, he can hear the Schoharie Creek splitting around the bridge's center support. The river has swelled from all the autumn rain. Maybe soon the temperatures will drop low enough for snow. He might be gone by then.

Brooklyn has pulled the truck onto the grass off the side of the road. If he rolls forward, there's nothing to stop him from hitting the water. No barriers or railings to keep him on land.

A voice shatters his ruminations.

"What are we doing here?" Oleander asks. In the rearview mirror, his face is hidden by shadow, although Brooklyn can picture it perfectly. Ollie still looks twenty-eight and not thirty-three as he should. Time doesn't appear to affect him.

Knuckles white on the steering wheel, Brooklyn doesn't answer. He's still listening to the river. The chill has made his skin rigid and dotted it with goosebumps. Beneath the jacket his body shivers. He's now aware of every minute detail of his form. His cells, the atoms that compose his cells, make themselves known to him. They are animated, vibrating with energy. They rip themselves apart and replicate, constructing the components of his being: the pores in his skin, the creases in his brow, the mounds and valleys of his face. Every hair on his arms stands like the blades of grass beneath the Ford Ranger. His heart pumps blood through the network of narrow veins beneath his skin. Why does he now fully realize that he is indeed helplessly and unmistakably alive?

"Brooklyn?" Ollie says.

The truck feels much too small, just like the home he'd left behind only minutes earlier. Every aspect of his world has shrunk, leaving Brooklyn to wonder what happened to his vast expanses. What happened to the empty corners of the map, the idea that he was but a dot on a wide canvas? By the time he'd left the house—taking only a bag of clothes and the damn box he can't seem to remove from the back of the truck—he'd been suffocating from the lack of space.

Now he contemplates suffocation of a different nature.

Bridge or river?

The sky is beginning to lighten, though the sun has not yet risen.

"Did I ever tell you I wanted to be an astronaut?" Ollie says. Though the question might appear out of place, Brooklyn knows what Ollie is up to, and he's overcome by a reluctant smile.

"I think I remember you mentioning something *maybe* once."

"I doodled all the time. I drew planets in my notebooks during class: little spacemen landing on the moon with their footprints stretching out in a line behind them, rockets soaring among the stars." Ollie's chuckle is melancholy, but fond all the same. "Everyone in my family knew about my obsession."

"Yeah?" Brooklyn says, encouraging.

"Every Christmas and birthday, my stuff was all space related: my cards, the toys I got. My mom would even try to decorate the cake with a space theme."

"Try?" Brooklyn's lines are scripted, but he could run through the dialogue a thousand times without it feeling old.

Ollie laughs, a full laugh that fills the Ranger like warm air. "She wasn't the best artist." The laugh fades.

"What happened to that dream?" Brooklyn goes off-script. Through the rearview mirror, he watches Ollie's gaze lose its focus. Perhaps there is no answer to this question, or at least not one that Ollie cares to admit. Instead, the question dilutes like smoke out of a cigarette. Ollie's hair, fine and soft, is almost as dark as his pupils. The strands are long enough that they curl just a bit at the ends where they frame his angular face.

"It was just one of those things," Ollie says finally. "A kid wanting to be an astronaut, you know? I left it behind eventually. These things happen."

Left it behind.

Brooklyn thinks of garnet shutters, sheer hanging drapes, and a writing desk against the back wall. An ornate grandfather clock, and a large square bed with a chip carved out of the footboard from an assembly mistake. These memories are all relics of the house he's left behind. Their house. Absentmindedly, he kneads the heel of his fist against his breast, easing a knot that's causing him pain.

"Are we going, Brooklyn?" Ollie asks.

Brooklyn is listening to the water again, his mouth dry. He imagines the river is icy, painful to touch. The kind of cold that suffocates from the moment of entry, even if he takes a large breath right before the plunge.

"Yeah, we're going."

He chooses the road.

Chapter Two

The lights on the runways look like stars. On the windows, the glare from the fluorescent lighting reflects the throngs shuffling by in various states of dis-belonging. Through the muffled announcements of airlines opening their gates, a motif is building—though it is vague and just beyond the palpable as of yet. It hustles by in hurried cellphone conversations, misunderstandings and mistimings, and also sits alone on the tandem chairs, waiting with bereavement and apprehension.

To Brooklyn's left, a woman clutches her purse with both hands, one at the shoulder strap and the other around the bag. She does this not because she's afraid that someone may come along and try to snatch it from her, but because it's the only source of comfort she can hold to at the moment. That and the scrunched newspaper sticking through her fingers with the *TURN OF THE CENTURY* headline screaming from the top of the page. She tries to scan the crowd with forced nonchalance. Her shadowed eyes rove and then dart back to a spot high on the far wall. Light makeup softens the lines on her face—or maybe it's hope that does this—and mollifies the residue of the years of worry, though she is obviously tense to anyone who takes a second glance. In truth, everything inside her is riding on this meeting, this reunion. It's apparent in the absolute stillness of her feet. But where is he? He should've been on that last plane; God knows she checked the flight itinerary more times than she cares to admit. But the crowd has thinned, and the faces passing by are no more recognizable to her than the people on the bus ride here. Any of them might be the last passenger to disembark. What will that mean when nobody's left?

There he is. The newspaper falls from her loosened grip. Now he comes to her. Now the muscles in her huddled shoulders can finally relax—

"They're going to call me soon." Ollie's voice is strained from inactivity. He clears his throat.

How long have they been sitting here? Brooklyn nods and looks down at the paper coffee cup in his hand. He's ripped a jagged V where the spout was, rendering the plastic lid useless. The fingernail on his left thumb is still black. He scratches lightly against the cup's waxy interior. His nail may be bruised, but it doesn't hurt anymore.

The man who has just arrived hesitates for the briefest of moments before putting his arm around the woman's shoulders. She folds into him seamlessly, as if she hasn't waited years to do this, merely moments. The ease of their integration forces Brooklyn to rearrange his mental image. They may have parted ways only a week previous, maybe only a single night for that matter. The instant they walk away, the waiting woman's story is happily resolved. He feels a stabbing pang of envy. Or maybe it's melancholy.

He has said this before, but maybe it won't hurt to suggest it one more time. "You don't have to go, you know."

Ollie sighs. "I know." He is hugging his carry-on with loose arms. "I know I don't, but I think it's for the best."

Brooklyn reminds himself that he must stay calm; he must keep his voice down. "Well, I don't." He wants to take Ollie's arm, turn him, and stare him in the eyes. But Ollie has not looked at him once in the past hour. "Look, I'm sorry—I really am. I can change, I promise."

Ollie sighs again. "I can't keep having this discussion."

"Well, I'm going to ask you to do it one more time, because I'm not satisfied. I'm not going to let you go easily."

"It's not about letting me go easily."

Why can't Ollie look at him? It's as if a solid and opaque wall exists between them. Oleander has stopped trying to see through to the other side.

Brooklyn stops fiddling with the empty cup. He sets it down on the plastic seat beside him. Above, the vaulted ceilings threaten to disappear into the heavens. All the walls and beams and flooring are a sterile white that does little more than alienate and diminish the soul. He feels anything but welcome.

"It's not permanent." Oleander lifts his hand and it hovers, shaking, for a multitude of unbearable moments. Eventually, he places it on Brooklyn's knee, squeezing.

The gesture is foreign, laced with restraint and regression. How long has it been since he last touched Brooklyn?

"I think we need time away from each other," Ollie says.

"How long?"

"I don't know." Ollie pauses for a moment. "Long enough."

He will stay with his parents in the house he grew up in. The house he moved out of many years ago when he agreed to share a home and a life with Brooklyn. On this evening, Ollie will board a plane, taking with him the vast majority of what Brooklyn knows of himself. This piece of Brooklyn sits remarkably well in the corner of Oleander's suitcase, tucked between collared knit shirts, thinning blue jeans, and a jacket or two. Oleander will be a different man when the plane touches down—one who is not a part of a greater being but instead a separate and independent entity of his own. He will land not only as the man who Brooklyn has willingly given himself to but also as a thief, with this stolen part of Brooklyn's life. And he will be too many thousands of miles away.

A woman's voice comes over the speakers in the huddled waiting area. Her words are shards of glass, slicing through their conversation. She enunciates with the utmost precision, even when threatened by the low quality of the sound system. "Good evening, all passengers, and thank you for choosing Antheia Airways. Flight five-seven-zero will be boarding in just a few moments. If I could have all passengers in rows twenty-five to thirty-two begin lining up, we can get started boarding as soon as possible."

Around them people in the waiting area stir, gathering themselves and their belongings to begin their respective journeys. Brooklyn feels his heart leap, though Oleander is not in any of the rows mentioned. Those passengers who do stand wander forward in a slow daze, either still entranced by their books and magazines or caught in their own foggy thoughts. A few travelers exchange goodbyes that spread themselves across a spectrum of emotions.

"I suppose you don't want me to contact you. No letters or calls . . ."

But Oleander smiles gently and takes Brooklyn's hand in his own. This gesture means much more than the hesitant touch a few minutes ago. "Of course I want you to," he says. And perhaps he does feel some pain at this, the threshold of separation. He whispers, "We'll have to figure out how much or how often is okay, but I could never cut you out completely."

Warmth rises in Brooklyn and clouds his eyes. His vision blurs. He's holding back with all the strength he has, but maybe this will be one of those lost battles. The woman who spoke over the intercom is letting people past, and the line moves slowly forward. One by one the travelers step into the sloped hallway and disappear into the unknown. They might not be at their destination yet, but they're no longer here.

"It's only for a little while," Brooklyn repeats, and Oleander nods. The woman speaks again, though the sound slides past Brooklyn without registering. Seeds of hope have taken root inside him, and for the first time since Oleander announced his departure, Brooklyn considers that there may be a second chance for them. It might be possible. He can see himself entering through the doors of the airport once again, coming to wait at this very terminal with a hand resting over his chest and the other in his pocket. He can see the shadow of goodbyes all around him, while he has come to reclaim what he'd lost. This is a specter to him, but he welcomes the vision.

For now, Oleander is standing.

"No." Brooklyn stands as well, looking around for any excuse to present itself. Some portion of his mind recognizes that he's going to make a fool of himself, but that awareness has been diminished by his grief and his greed. He wants more. He's not finished. "You can't go."

"Brooklyn." Oleander isn't looking at him anymore, his eyes set firmly away.

"Please—"

"Don't make this harder than it needs to be."

"But, Ollie—"

"You have to let me go." The travelers in line continue to file out, one by one. "Let me go."

Oleander remains out of grasp, and Brooklyn doesn't reach for him. For a moment they are silent. Then Oleander begins to walk away.

"I love you," Brooklyn says.

Their eyes meet. "I love you too." And in the next few moments, Oleander is gone.

The strings of Brooklyn's hood hang uneven. Without significant weight at the ends, they retain a wave-like material memory as they dangle down the middle of his chest. The surface of the sweatshirt expands and contracts periodically in time with his breathing. Is he breathing? Yes, and it hurts. He has never felt so belabored in his life, so very aware of every ounce of blood pumping through the chambers in his heart. Reminding him that he needs the circulation in his veins, needs oxygen in his lungs.

Brooklyn drifts over to the windows and stares out at the stars, the lights. He can see the plane clearly even though darkness has engulfed everything else. From here, he is shielded from the harsh realities. From here, he cannot see the stewardess welcoming each individual guest aboard the aircraft. He cannot see the passengers shuffle into the cabin and move their way in a single-file line down the aisle. He cannot see them slide into their seats, preparing to be taken to their new destination and leaving behind whatever remains here.

From inside the airport, he can see nothing.

But Brooklyn knows all this is happening. He can see it in his mind. He can see Oleander walking in jilted strides down the rows and rows of seats, nodding with a half-smile at some people and being ignored by others. He can see the warm cotton sweater hugging Oleander as he passes number after number until, finally, he stops. He has found his seat. He shifts his bag so it sits against his hip, and he reaches up to the overhead compartment. There's a spot just for his belongings. It's beside the red backpack and the worn black duffel. His bag fits neatly between them, almost as if the space had been left there specifically for him.

Then Oleander politely asks the woman below to let him by, and she complies by tilting her knees to the left. She already has a magazine out, the glossy pages swimming in the dim artificial lighting. She smiles at him, though her eyes say that she hopes he's not one of those chatty or, heaven forbid, fidgety types. She needn't worry; he's not. She has a good seat partner. Oleander doesn't ask for her name, nor does she ask for his. They have entered a silent agreement, one that will last until the landing gear touches down on the tarmac on the other side of their shared journey. The plan is that they enter this plane as strangers and leave as strangers, never to meet again.

Then, Oleander will stare out of the porthole at the dark landscape. By now, only a few passengers are left to board. They do so quickly— far too quickly—and already the captain is speaking to them and the stewards rove the aisles with plastered smiles. It won't be long now.

Yes, Brooklyn can see the tow pulling them back from the terminal. All seatbelts are buckled, all trays in the upright position. The interior lights have dimmed. As the plane turns, Oleander will be treated to his first real view of the airfield. He's content now. He cannot change his mind; even if the decisions he's made might not be the right ones, he has cast his lot and will take whatever comes his way.

Maybe Oleander sees another place in his mind. Maybe he sees a dark blue well-worn couch with an ivory throw and brass-plated buttons along the seams of its arms. Maybe he imagines tiles the faintest shade of mint green, made noticeable only by the white lines of grout.

Maybe he sees their apple-red pickup parked under an ochre sun and swathed in humidity.

Brooklyn is losing sight of Oleander's plane now. Its minute windows are impenetrable from this distance. He sees nothing but the lights on the outside of the aircraft.

He doesn't watch the takeoff. He turns away, facing the mass of people streaming in every direction. In his mind, each person is indistinguishable from himself. Each one controls as much of a share of his body as he does.

His eyes are dry. His hands are cold. And his heart is numb.

Chapter Three

The Ford Ranger is a lustrous deep red, the color of apples in animated films. Brooklyn purchased it thirteen years ago—not new, but shining like he couldn't believe. He likes that the black leather on the steering wheel has peeled, resembling amorphous continents on a map. He likes that it has only an AM/FM radio and a temperamental tape deck in the dash. He likes that the brake pedal is a little too sensitive and that he can always get the cabin to the right temperature without even trying.

A cool sun climbs its way through the windows, turning the black dashboard pale.

Once he crossed the threshold out of Schoharie, Brooklyn found everything became much easier. Or at the very least, easier than it had been. Before, everything had seemed monumental and paralyzing. The hows and whats and whens had cornered him, throwing doubts like darts against the weaker parts of his mind until the idea of leaving became insurmountable. And now . . .

Now there's a sense of liberation, a feeling of finality. It's in the spinning of the wheels beneath him, the miles of road he has traveled, and the miles of road he has yet to travel. Why had leaving ever seemed so difficult?

Already, he's passed through Sloansville, where Highway 30 melted seamlessly into 162. The world awakens. Other vehicles materialize beside him on his once-solitary road. Everything is new to him: the road, winding to and fro among the last true green of the year; the trees, waving to him now that they can see his confidence; the sky, littered with gray-spotted clouds billowing on an otherwise uninterrupted canvas of the purest blue. Maybe he is not yet free, but Brooklyn can feel himself hurtling toward freedom.

"Haven't seen one of those in a while," Ollie says, pulling himself forward to rest on the console between Brooklyn and the passenger seat.

"What's that?" Brooklyn asks.

"A genuine, happy smile." And Ollie is wearing one too. The air is thick between them as it always is, but for now it's also clear. That's something that cannot be ignored. Brooklyn feels stirrings of excitement for this clarity. He laughs.

"Laughing at nothing already?" Ollie says. "You can't go crazy yet, Brooklyn. You only just started."

"Yeah, yeah." Brooklyn lets the laugh die amicably. "If I do, it's only going to be an improvement."

A cloud passes over the sun, and Brooklyn's reminded again about darkness. Beside them, fields made of straight lines and harsh angles border the highway. The stalks of grass are lean and tall, desperate for a drink of sunlight.

"Did you say goodbye to anyone?" Oleander asks.

"No." Brooklyn rests his hands at the ten-and-two position on the steering wheel. He wastes little time being dishonest. "I didn't want any awkward questions or for anyone to try and stop me." He looks at Ollie in the rearview mirror and huffs. "I didn't want any of the pitying looks they all give me nowadays."

"You know it's because they care about you."

"Yeah, well, I've had enough of them caring about me." Brooklyn isn't angry, but his voice has gone deeper and gravelly. "I'm not a charity case."

"Kathryn won't be happy."

Kathryn. Not saying anything to her was hard, but she'd forgive him. She always did. "Do you remember going to Coney Island with her and Adam?" Brooklyn's smile is back, but it's different than the one before.

"Of course," Oleander says, grabbing the seatbelt around his waist absentmindedly. Brooklyn can tell the boardwalk is materializing in front of Oleander in the same way it does for him: the saccharine smell of blueberry cotton candy, the mustard on corn dogs, and the chorus of a thousand people talking in unison as they wander a river of asphalt and wood. The amusement park rises around him, games and rides surging upward like skyscrapers. "Everybody else canceled because it was supposed to rain that day."

"The sky cleared up around eleven in the morning, and the temperature warmed to a perfect mid-seventies," Brooklyn adds.

"And that man with the red glasses gave Kathryn a ride wristband because his daughter ditched the family to go hang out with her friends." Ollie has his hands outstretched as if he's gone blind, feeling a world around him that he cannot see. They're laughing again. "She was convinced he had an ulterior motive. Poor man was just trying to do something nice."

"I don't blame her. He looked a little unsteady."

"I'm still surprised Adam didn't swoop in and grab it himself."

"I think he'd already bought his, otherwise I'm sure he would've." Why hadn't Brooklyn said goodbye to Kathryn—or Adam, for that matter? Perhaps it was to create a sort of tether, to make sure he was coming back. But if he doesn't?

The idea that he might not see anyone again becomes a stony weight in his chest. The distant pain pushes outward from his ribcage, bursting to be felt. He tries a laugh again, but it's halfhearted. "You were incredible at that shooting game."

"Ah, the old-time shooting gallery." Oleander puffs up his chest with stoic pride as though he'd been waiting for Brooklyn to bring it up.

"Sharpest eye in the West."

"And don't you forget it. I'll bet none of you sorry sods had ever seen a man with such natural-born talent."

"Never had, never will again."

"I could've shot each of those targets with my eyes closed."

"I bet." Brooklyn clouds the authenticity of the statement with cynicism. "What was the nickname we gave you?"

"The nickname?"

"Yeah, the one we called you for the rest of the day."

"I don't recall . . ."

"You were a big fan. Might've come up with the name yourself."

"Oh, that nickname!" Ollie exclaims, as if suddenly understanding. He touches his fingertips to his chin. "It was a great title. Really exemplified my solid mastery of my craft."

Brooklyn rolls his eyes.

"I believe it was Eagle-Eye Ollie."

Brooklyn emits a low whistle. "Greatest sharp-shooter these United States ever did see."

"Cheers to that." Ollie raises an imaginary glass.

Brooklyn shakes his head with a smirk, leaving Ollie to drink his imaginary toast on his own.

Ollie smacks his lips. "I must say, though, no amusement park was ever as near and dear to us as the Santa Cruz Beach Boardwalk—"

Then the music on the radio changes. It goes from an acoustic love ballad to the eager strumming of steel guitars and the earnest howling of musicians having an unmistakably good time. The heart behind the tune is infectious and grabs hold of them both in an instant, raising their spirits above the horizon. Brooklyn knows Oleander's reaction is instinctual. Ollie closes his eyes and sings along to a melody he has known since before he can remember, one that is as ingrained in his soul as the knowledge of love and happiness and loss.

"Turn that up!" Ollie commands, managing to speak between verses, and Brooklyn willingly complies. For a moment they are not who they are. They're travelers on their way to a mythical kingdom ever just beyond their reach. They're not on a road in New York but traveling between snow-capped mountains where people know each other by the flowers in their eyes and the songs on their lips. *Shambala*, sung by Three Dog Night.

Brooklyn doesn't sing along, but he watches the way Ollie's lips curl and part and come together again as he sings with a voice Brooklyn has never stopped clinging to. His own heart dances because Ollie's dances. His own face smiles because Ollie's smiles. And Brooklyn *is* happy. Ollie has released himself completely; he has always been this way with music. He sings with his eyes shut, his face turned toward a sun he knows is just beyond the roof of the truck. He sways along with the jubilant rhythm and never once falters over how silly he might look.

They stay this way until the song is finished. The music fades while the chords repeat, still in full swing and leaving the impression that maybe the musicians went on playing this way forever. Maybe they're still playing their song somewhere, spreading this infectious joy. Ollie settles back into his seat with satisfaction. The radio volume is lowered into background noise, fading to where it sits just above the level of the tires rolling over the asphalt.

Brooklyn's smile dwindles again. It has a habit of doing that. He's back on the road, driving away from the place he calls home. There are no diamond-capped mountains surrounding him, like in the song they just heard. No mythical kingdom with people extending peace to one another. He is back in the state of New York with a pressing weight on his mind, and he can't help but let his worries stumble forth. "Do you think they miss me?" he asks.

"What do you mean?"

"Kathryn, Adam, Jeanice, any of our friends?" Brooklyn pauses, wondering why he has a habit of destroying any positive mood. "Do you think they miss me?"

"Why wouldn't they miss you?"

"I don't know."

"Then why would you ask that?" Ollie's tone is firm.

"I'm not sure. Just a thought."

"Well, why would you think that?" Ollie spits the words now, almost annoyed. "Of course they miss you."

"I don't know," Brooklyn repeats. "I distanced myself. I haven't talked to them or seen them in so long. I wouldn't blame them if they didn't miss me. I know what I did."

"Well, you're wrong." Is Oleander angry? His tone is sharp, as are his movements, but he looks more hurt than livid. "People don't just forget someone so easily, especially someone who was that important to them."

"I know."

But Oleander doesn't respond to this. He stares out the window across from him with his jaw set. Brooklyn knows he has upset Ollie; he can tell from the absence left by the departed conversation. The vacated space where their dialogue hangs is like the darker square left behind on a wall when a painting is removed. This reminder, the knowledge of where the artwork used to hang, makes the wall seem much emptier than before the painting had ever been hung.

The knowledge turns into regret. And still Brooklyn takes this conversation, picks it gingerly from the air, and sticks it in his pocket.

Chapter Four

By the time the scarlet truck enters Brockport, the sun is nearing its zenith. Trees arch over the road like great doorways, and the brick buildings line up along the sidewalk like school children. Brooklyn has never been to Brockport. It's existed all this time, completely separate from him. Yet, now their paths have crossed. Brockport is newness. Yesterday afternoon, he dropped his finger on a map, and there it was: his first stop. The only defined stop on his journey.

Driving along East Canal Road with the water on his right, Brooklyn feels a small sense of pride. He has made it to the end of the first segment.

A sort of mysticism paves the road, and a romantic sheen glosses the sidewalks. People trundle alongside the buildings, their lives running adjacent to his at this particular moment. They dress in thick sweaters, wool coats buttoned or tied at the waist, and black or brown boots with buckles and fur peeking over the tops. They grin as they walk, talking and laughing and breathing the late morning.

He parks the truck beneath the grand spire of a Gothic church on State Street. For a while he just sits there, letting the blood pump through his veins and the breath circulate through his lungs. What will the ground feel like beneath his feet? How will the air taste?

Ollie doesn't say anything, but Brooklyn snaps his head around to look at him. The Ranger doesn't have a proper back row but includes two moderately sized cushioned seats that fold down from either side of the cabin. They face inward like chairs at a café table. Jump seats, Brooklyn thinks he's heard them called. Oleander could sit up front, but he never chooses to, instead relegating himself to a place in the truck just behind the forefront.

They exchange a knowing look. "I'll be back," Brooklyn says, trying not to sound apologetic.

Ollie nods.

Brooklyn steps out of the vehicle. The air tastes like rain and sun. It fills his lungs, and he feels inflated, his back becoming straighter and his head higher than usual. The soles of his feet bounce on the pavement, carrying him across a path that—though he walks beside a blank brick wall—feels exciting.

He pauses only once, at the corner where the road meets Main Street, to glance back at his truck. There's a spot by the top-left corner of the grille where the paint has thinned and the hood is beginning to rust, but he can't see it from here. Neither can he see Ollie seated inside for the glare cast by the sun over the windshield.

Then Brooklyn turns the corner, and they are out of sight.

Brooklyn walks all the way down Main Street until he reaches a pale green bridge that stretches over the wide canal. The water below is calm and patient, flowing past at a gentle pace and catching the sunlight as often as it can. When he turns back, he enters a small blue candy shop, where he indulges himself in the aroma of sweets. One woman leads another around the store. He watches them, wondering. They could be related; they have the same face, although the one leading is a few years older. The other might be her visiting sister from out of town, coming to Brockport for the first time to mend a bond strained by distance and differing worldviews. They had been close before—he can see it in the way they share the same laugh—but that time together drifted to the wayside once their adult lives began. None of that matters anymore, though. Now the sister is here, sharing a house with her older sibling once again—however briefly—and meeting the niece she's never taken the time to get to know beyond superficial birthday checks and Christmas toys. They are family again, and maybe this rekindling will last. That is, if Brooklyn believes such things can truly last. Maybe the younger sister already regrets coming, alienated by the strict restraint with which the older one and her family live their lives. The way they excrete judgments on other people in hushed tones masked by their pointedly humble demeanor aggravates her. The older sister had hopes she might convert her sibling, but the younger is as stubborn as their mother, taking every opportunity to give sly, ill-disguised remarks about the drabness of their simple life. In the end they will hate each other. People always do.

The woman leading swears by the candy shop's ice cream, giggling girlishly at the thought of her guilty pleasure, but the cold is enough to fight Brooklyn's temptation to take this overheard recommendation.

Ollie would enjoy some of the chocolates. He loves them, and is never one to deny his sweet tooth. Brooklyn picks up a box of assorted squares. After a moment he decides against the gesture, sets them down, and leaves the shop.

Outside, he passes a number of eateries before spying a brick storefront with a white sign down a side street. Brooklyn crosses the road feeling excitement for something that is generally mundane but has grabbed hold of him anyway. Light filters out of the windows through the gaps between posters of book covers, local author meetings, and book clubs.

How fortunate, Brooklyn thinks with sarcastic enthusiasm, *they've just opened.*

He pulls the door open and enters, breathing the smell of printed pages, glued bindings, and lushly illustrated dust jackets. The bookstore is warm on the inside, the kind of warmth that seems to come naturally to places of great contentment. The warmth of welcome.

His eyes wander over the innumerable shelves carving paths through the shop, which are lined with more stories than he could ever hope to lose himself to. His feet carry him along the aisles, no particular destination in mind. The NEW FICTION titles, dressed in oversaturated covers ranging from abstract art to detailed illustrations of fantastic worlds, pop out at him. Faces from biographies smile or project the serious nature of their tone.

And then Brooklyn does something he does not *ever* do. The thought never fully coalesces in his mind; it remains a patch of fog hovering idly over a bank. And yet, the compulsion carries him through the rows and rows of printed volumes. He reenters fiction and combs the bindings with his eyes and his finger. Duiker, Dumas, du Maurier. Durant.

He stops. This is not the first time, but the feeling is just as surreal and inescapable as ever. To think that this bookshop a hundred miles away would have it—it's an idea that floors him completely. With shaking hands, Brooklyn picks up the novel. It feels fragile in his suddenly large and inept fingers. A light turquoise color sweeps monochromatically across the paperback save for a subtle, shaded geometric design below the title: *This Peace of Mine*. He doesn't need to read the summary; he knows it by heart. This was his first. His most successful one, too.

Brooklyn raises his eyes above the shelf. There are more people now, maybe fifteen or twenty. They wander the aisles much like he had before, their eyes downcast to skim the book spines. To his left is a man with dark glasses and chestnut skin, a large overcoat pulled around his slim shoulders. Off to the right a couple peruse in unison. Already she has three books held close to her breast.

Have any of the people in the store or in town read it? Did they enjoy it? Maybe someone has the book in a house with wood siding and a rust-colored fireplace tucked away in a corner. Maybe it sits on a shelf in its designated spot beside other stories its owner has enjoyed, lit by the sun every morning around ten o'clock and surrounded by the smell of dark-roast coffee.

And then Brooklyn's chest hurts, and he has to clench his teeth and inhale sharply, fighting the stinging in his eyes.

He slides the book back into the open slot. He looks around again, but nobody has moved very far from where they were before. He backs away from the shelf, saddened and embarrassed that he should be overcome with emotion by such small things. Maybe one of these people will come along and pick it up while they shop, but they will not know he was here or who he was. It will make no difference.

Brooklyn wanders the rest of the street, dipping into stores here and there along the way. When he returns, he finds Oleander reading the paperback copy of *Beloved* he keeps in the truck. Seeing Brooklyn at the door, Oleander puts the novel out of sight.

They drive away from Main Street, saying a word here and there to break the lengthy stretches of silence. Brooklyn follows a local map he got from one of the stores, winding his way through the unfamiliar town—stopping only once at a general store to grab a few things—until they arrive at a modest inn painted white with rose-colored trim. All of the curtains appear to be drawn, though the curled wrought-iron railings at each windowsill give the building an elegant, welcoming look. Paint peels at the corners of the windows, but this is hardly noticeable given the humble presence of charm.

With the engine off, Brooklyn gives Oleander a forlorn look. He wants to beg Ollie to follow—of course he does, he always does—but he knows what the answer will be. He knows it never changes, and maybe it cannot change, but that doesn't stop him from wanting to ask. Instead he diverts his gaze and picks for a while at a stiff patch of upholstery on the passenger seat. He once spilled vanilla crème frosting while transporting a cake, the first he'd ever made, without a cover. It was meant to be a surprise for Oleander's birthday—though the real surprise was that they'd never been able to get all the frosting out of the cushion. Maybe it was a sign Brooklyn's homemade frosting wasn't all that edible or healthy. This had happened at a time when they could laugh about things like that. Even now it brings a small smile to Brooklyn's lips—just a flicker.

They exchange goodnights. Brooklyn grabs his sack from the store and his bag of clothes before stepping outside. The wind has started to carry a deeper chill again. There are still a few more hours of sunlight left in the day, but already he can feel gooseflesh on his arms.

A radio plays "Amazing Grace" in a room off the lobby. The tinny notes, which move farther and farther toward the sky-colored ceiling, help Brooklyn ascend the staircase. He's aware that the sounds fade when he reaches the third-floor landing, but the melody repeats airily in his head. Without words, the song feels mournful.

Then he's in his room, alone.

This is no special room. A lone queen bed sits in the center of the left-hand wall. On either side are old cedar-stained nightstands with a matching dresser across the way. On this rests a fairly large television and a white binder stuffed with tourist guides and restaurant coupons. Beige-and-scarlet-striped wallpaper completes the scene. The room is dripping with symmetry.

Before long Brooklyn has ordered a movie on the television, an action film where the main characters exchange clever quips and ride away from every encounter unscathed because the producers don't want to distract from their actors' good looks by marring their perfect features—although he will admit the protagonist is quite handsome in a generic Hollywood sort of way—and he wishes the score wouldn't bounce so theatrically through every fight sequence and wonders how these movies make so much money. Oh, but he's just bitter and sad because it's getting later and the sun is going down and he's still alone, though this shouldn't be a shock to him because why would things be different in Brockport, but maybe just a small part of his mind had been hoping that something would change, though he can't imagine what, and he's not paying very much attention to the film—someone always double-crosses the hero near the end—and knows he's supposed to be feeling sorry for this handsome man because he lost the girl when he was supposed to keep her safe, but this is all typical film stuff, so why are there warm tears rolling down Brooklyn's face?

He realizes at some point that he's forgotten to eat because he was much too distracted by the film, though he can't say exactly what happened in it.

What's happened to *Brooklyn* is that the room has gone dark. The pale glow from the television washes over his face, and it's entrancing. The credits slide past, tiny words barely readable, as if to say, "We know you don't care about these names." He's not hungry and so he instead reaches into the sack to collect his liquid prize.

The bottle is heavy in his palm. Brooklyn watches the gap of air travel as he tips the bottle sideways, and heaves a heavy sigh when it's righted again. It makes a satisfying thud when he sets it on the dresser.

This room in the quaint and charming hotel is no special place to be. Brooklyn is alone, just as he ever is when he locks himself in his room at night. He knows he shouldn't care what anyone else might think, since he is the only one around to notice. He's not going anywhere soon; he's not entertaining. The room is empty.

So why does he feel like judging eyes are watching him? He brings his right hand to his hair and then his face, feeling the rough beginnings of a beard taking shape around his jaw. His skin is sandpaper, and it grates his palm with hundreds of pinpricks. Then he twists off the black bottle cap, his nostrils detecting the wooded odor almost immediately. It's just a spot of whiskey to wet the throat; there's nothing wrong with that. And who cares if he should get a bit drunk? He's a grown man, for fuck's sake, north of thirty. To hell with the staring eyes he can't seem to find.

Brooklyn melts into himself, listening to his own breathing and the *glrrp* of whiskey as he swallows. He takes care not to look at the red numbers on the alarm clock by the bed and stares instead out the window. He can't see anything from where he's sitting. It's all a void, a black void peering in at the room and at his diminutive, sorry state.

No. He needn't answer to a soul. He's where he belongs, and if he hasn't had a drink in ages—it's got to be ages since the last—then he's earned this. It's his plight, his reward, his torment. *It's that damn desk clerk's fault, that's what it is*, Brooklyn thinks. The man knew—with his smug grin and his trendy, asymmetrical haircut. He probably sought this job so he could pontificate over mild opioids about the vagabonds who frequent the inn. He and his friends most likely get each other off complaining about the inanity of the consumerism everyone else participates in. If only they understood the world like Brooklyn did. Pretentious little shit, judging Brooklyn just because he reserved a room for one and bought himself an unopened bottle of whiskey. It doesn't matter that the bottle was hidden in Brooklyn's duffel bag. The man must've seen him put it in there. And now Brooklyn's worried about guilt because the man couldn't keep his goddamn judgment under control.

THUD.

Brooklyn is aware that he's a cliché: a writer tormented by his darkness and taken to drink. He doesn't care anymore. After all, clichés are grounded in truth. Much like stereotypes. Much like jokes.

When Brooklyn decides he's had enough, he lifts the bottle—much lighter now than it was before—and drops it into the waste bin even though about half of the drink still remains. That should keep the eyes off his back.

Brooklyn slides his hands into the back pockets of his jeans. He saunters over to the blinds, which cut the black void outside into wide strips. The moon isn't visible, but he can see the tops of balding trees. He's sure that somewhere not far from here, the water in the canal drifts along, cold and deep, but welcoming and beautiful just the same.

Chapter Five

The six-foot truck bed will never be clean. It has sand from sunny beaches, dirt tracked in from foggy mountain trails, and dust from arid hills. The minute particles collect in the grooves of the plastic interior, fill in gaps, and dry over rougher textures. Brooklyn has cleaned the bed many times, but the dirt manages to hide from even his best attempts at extrication. He cleans the particles away, and then they return. The amount of detritus is neither decreasing nor increasing, but constant.

Brooklyn leaves much later than the morning before, having to drag himself out from beneath the covers. While combing his thick and coarse hair with his hand in front of the bathroom mirror, he briefly wonders if maybe he should turn around and go back to Schoharie, to the house with garnet shutters. Maybe this journey is just a stupid idea.

The thought is enticing but ephemeral. He then gathers his things and leaves.

Brooklyn's breath crystalizes in the crisp autumn morning. Absentmindedly, he pulls the sleeves of his jacket down over his hands. At the rear of the truck, he tips his bag through the hatch door in the camper shell, though he's careful not to hit the box still resting inside.

Ollie is awake and ready for him. He seems content, if not happy; interested, if not enthusiastic.

The highways rush to meet Brooklyn again. Byways cut lines through a never-ending sea of green fields. On this second day of travel the novelty hasn't worn off, but he now considers himself a sort of veteran to his journey. He has a confidence he lacked before, however slight it may be.

Brooklyn forgets the minutes. Maybe he hums along with the tunes on the radio, but certainly he and Ollie don't talk. They share an old silence like a familiar meal—they know the taste of it and which hungers it satisfies. Brooklyn was aggravated by the silence before, but now it is something they both understand.

How did it get to be this way?

In his mind Brooklyn sees shuffling, huddled bodies: a party at one of his friends' flats many years ago, back in the earliest days of his and Ollie's relationship. Cheap plastic lanterns hung from wires over the patio, spilling green light onto uncomfortable furniture and dying ferns. Music blared from inside the building, only slightly muffled by the sliding glass door. The air was sweltering and thick with the mixed odors of summer—shoddy beer, ocean sand, and the remains of sunshine. He can see ruddy faces, happy with alcohol and youth, but none was more radiant than that of sweet Oleander Rhodes. Ollie, who has eyes green enough to shame the grass.

They sat in their corner of the patio the entire night, in a world of their own, blanketed by the colored lights of the lanterns above. Brooklyn might have felt bad afterward for stealing Ollie's time and attention from the many people who wanted to chat with him—he doesn't remember. Ollie was, after all, much more friendly and likable than Brooklyn, certainly more well known that close to his hometown. Brooklyn also can't remember what they talked about, but he can remember wondering what on earth he could possibly do to keep those stars in the sky from disappearing.

Maybe they talked too much. Maybe all the questions have already been asked.

Brooklyn can see a parked vehicle sitting off to the side of the road: a midsized SUV, silver and worn with a dent in the back bumper. The right front tire must be flat too, because the entire thing's tipping unmistakably in that direction. He doesn't have much time to look as he drives past but gets enough of a glance to tell there's no one inside.

"Wonder where they've gone," Oleander muses from the backseat as the vehicle shrinks in the rearview mirror. He's turned around to stare through the back window and that of the camper shell.

"Dunno," Brooklyn responds, disinterested. But no sooner has he spoken than a small figure appears in the distance, walking close to the edge of the road. At first glance they might've been mistaken for a tree. Soon, however, Brooklyn can tell it's a person trudging along with a bag on their back and a duffel on their hip.

"She looks like she could use a lift," Oleander says.

Much to Brooklyn's dissatisfaction, he can't help but agree. She might be handling her baggage fine now, but she's a long walk from the next town. Still, there are any number of other people who might pass this way. Surely one of them will feel helpful.

"You should give her a ride," Oleander says when Brooklyn doesn't reply. Brooklyn can feel Oleander's hand on the back of his chair by the way the fabric tugs in response to his touch.

"What am I going to do for her?" Brooklyn asks, sighing. His hands are white on the steering wheel; he hadn't realized he'd tensed up.

"Give her a ride, that's all."

"We're probably not going in the same direction once I get off this." Brooklyn gestures vaguely to the highway. Picking up another person means having to make conversation about the weather and road conditions. It means having to act overtly polite and welcoming. Having to deal with someone unfamiliar, who doesn't function exactly as he'd hoped. It means putting himself on guard, even if he doesn't mean to. He doesn't need someone to make the silences awkward.

"You can drive her to an auto shop faster than she can walk to one."

"She's not going to want help from me."

"You can't know that," Oleander replies, frustration creeping into his voice.

"It's pretty likely."

"You're just like everybody else driving by." He's practically in Brooklyn's ear.

"Well, what if she's crazy? What if she's a thief?"

"You don't have anything she'd want to steal."

"I've got a working car."

"How is she going to get you out of it?"

"You don't know what people are capable of."

"I know perfectly well what people are capable of," Oleander says with harsh finality.

Brooklyn takes a mental step back, knowing full well that he can't argue this statement with good conscience. Oleander releases his chair and sits back against his own seat, quiet now.

"Why do you want me to help her so badly?" Brooklyn asks. He reminds himself that Oleander is trying to get him to commit an act of kindness. Brooklyn doesn't know why Ollie's insistence makes him angry, but he can't stop himself, which infuriates him even more.

"Why don't you want to?"

The traveler has on a stretched light orange cardigan, and the parts that aren't pinned down by the bag on her hip or her backpack flap behind her in the breeze. Her brightly colored scarf unfolds like sunflower petals, the patterns shifting and rearranging themselves as the cloth flutters. Her tan leather boots look as worn as her car had, which suggests that maybe they've seen just as many miles. Thick, tightly curled hair wraps around the back of her head. As Brooklyn pulls level with her, she turns and lifts her thumb, and for the briefest of moments they lock gazes. Her eyes are ochre, like clay.

Then she's behind him.

Oleander sighs, though he doesn't speak. Brooklyn feels his own shoulders sag. In the mirror, he looks just like what he is: a man at war with his nature. He could continue on this path—one that is neither urgent nor fragile and will require all the time it needs—and leave her until another traveler passes by who is more giving and open than Brooklyn.

But what would this prove about himself?

The truck slows, decelerating until he can pull over to where the grass rushes to meet the gravel shoulder. Then the vehicle stops altogether. He shifts into park but leaves the engine running. Ollie says something as Brooklyn exits, but his words—soft-spoken and invisible but certainly real—are lost in the wind. Brooklyn doesn't catch them fully, but they sound like "There he is."

He hasn't gone too far past the woman, maybe a hundred yards or so. Seeing him stop, she picks up her gait, brilliant spirals of untamed black hair bouncing behind her. Her wrists are adorned with more bangles, bracelets, and strips of cloth than he can count from this distance. They rise up her arms like tattoos, and he wonders if they're almost as permanent.

Brooklyn sighs. Then, when she is within earshot, he says, "It looks like you could use a ride."

She smiles as widely as the sky. Once at the back of the truck, her hand reaches out to brush the scarlet side. "Thank you, sir," she says, nodding.

"You can put your stuff back here." Brooklyn pulls open the bed of the truck, and the woman graciously shoves her duffel bag through the slot. She keeps the pack with her.

"Oh, it sure feels good to take a load off. People always saying how I pack too much, but even having less than normal was breaking my back." She laughs, a rich, deep sound that makes him think of honey and lemon tea. "Thanks again. I don't know how many people just passed me by, but I knew when I saw you. I knew you were going to help me."

Brooklyn can't help but smile back, feeling a twinge of shame at her certainty. "You need me to call anyone for your car back there? I have a cellphone. That was your car, right?"

"Yeah, that thing." She waves her hand behind her as if swatting a fly. Then she looks at Brooklyn—*really* looks at him—square in the eyes, and flashes of mischief pass through her stare like lightning. "I don't need it. It was my ex-husband's, after all. Damn thing never worked right anyway." She brushes a stray strand of hair from her face and sticks out a hand. "I'm Zinnia, by the way."

Brooklyn takes her hand and wonders if maybe she can see things about him when she looks at him that people normally can't tell from just a glance. Honesty—yes, that's what comes to mind when he speaks to her. She feels like honesty. "I'm Brooklyn."

"That's a beautiful name," Zinnia says with a wink.

"Should we get moving then?" he asks. Now that he's thought these things about her, he feels vulnerable. He wants to be back inside the truck.

"I think so," she agrees, and moves fluidly around to the other side of the vehicle.

Chapter Six

Brooklyn fills the glass much higher than usual, keeping his eyes fixed on the red wine. Oleander stands by, arms crossed over his chest defiantly. He doesn't want to be the first one to speak. Brooklyn knows this game and he's content to play it.

When he stands the bottle in the back corner of the counter, it clangs loudly.

"I bet you're pleased with yourself," Oleander finally says, unable to contain the accusation any longer. Brooklyn wouldn't be surprised if Ollie started tapping his foot on the floor and posing with his hands on his hips, the way they demonstrated annoyance in old films. "Makes you real happy to embarrass us like that, doesn't it?"

"I wasn't embarrassed," Brooklyn says, perhaps too truthfully. He's already had a few glasses with dinner. This one's just to keep the buzz going.

"Yeah, well, you should be."

"I can be whatever the hell I want to be." Brooklyn rotates the glass by the twisted stem, eyes still fixed on the unblemished surface of the cabernet sauvignon. The gold monogram letters are barely visible anymore.

"I'm guessing the answer, then, is yes. You enjoy being an ass." Oleander's words are imbued with spite. "They're our friends, Brooklyn. Or maybe now I should say *were* our friends."

"I know."

"Then why don't you act like it?" Oleander gives an exasperated sigh that says he's just as frustrated by Brooklyn's disinterest as he is with what Brooklyn has done.

"They're my friends, yeah, but I don't need to see them every other fucking day."

Brooklyn is about to finally lift the full glass to his lips when Oleander's voice raises another few decibels. "We don't see them every other day."

"It feels like it."

"Well, forgive me for trying to give us a social life. For trying to keep us—to keep you—from being holed up all the time. To give us *someone* to talk to other than each other. We're going to go insane if we don't." Oleander's standing up taller now, and Brooklyn senses weakness like an animal senses fear. Oleander is afraid of the point he's really trying to make, the opinion he really has. Yes, he's angry, but he doesn't want to say exactly what's on his mind, or it might tempt the storm.

"You mean me, don't you? Don't you—*Don't try to shake your head like that*. I know you. You think I need to talk to people." Brooklyn licks his front teeth. He's won this small battle by seeing through the "we" ruse.

Oleander stammers for a moment and then regains his composure. "I—well, you—yes. I do. I go to work every day. I work with people. Even if they're not friends, even if I don't see them outside of work, I do *see* them and *talk* to them. I interact with others."

"I talk to people."

"Arnold dropping by for a half hour or calling every couple months doesn't count. Going to the grocery store once a week doesn't count, Brooklyn."

"It's not like I'm just lying around here. I'm working too, you know. Who paid for these countertops, huh?" Brooklyn slams his open hand on the granite, making Oleander flinch. "I did. And the floors too!"

"Don't put words in my mouth. I'm not saying you don't work. I'm saying you don't socialize."

"I don't need to socialize."

"You do at some point."

"I don't need to do it *all the fucking time!*"

"We don't see them all the time!" Oleander lifts his hands as if he might be able to squeeze the frustration out of the air. He mouths words that never come out as if struggling to keep control. "We barely see anyone! And even if we did, that's no excuse for you to act like an ass when we're around them!"

"All this going out just keeps interrupting me," Brooklyn hisses. "How am I supposed to get through my work, keep everything straight, when I've got to put on a face all the time and go *hang out* with other people? That's why the last one had shit sales. Arnold said it was all over the place. I need some damn peace. I'm working on something!"

"You are always working on something!" Oleander's voice tears like fabric over the last syllable. "I appreciate what you do, really. I get it. But you are always lost in your worlds. If it's not one, it's another. And every night it's 'No, it's too late' or 'No, I'm just getting somewhere,' 'No, we just saw them two weeks ago,' 'No, I'm too tired to do anything else, and I can't stop now.' Yet you've only finished three novels in how many years? Well, maybe it's not you, Brooklyn! Maybe I'm the one who needs to see people, to see our friends. I'm tired of being cooped up in here."

As if he wants this to be the end of the conversation, as if he can no longer talk on this subject without betraying himself, Oleander turns away, his hands clenched into fists. For a moment he seems lost, lingering between destinations. Between leaving and staying. Then he begins to organize the space around them in a fury, putting away dishes that have sat for too long on the drying rack and collecting the leftovers they'd taken from Kathryn's house. Brooklyn may have once found this impulse endearing, but now heat rises in his face.

"You don't want to be here?" he asks.

"Don't twist my words."

"That's more or less what you just said. You're tired of being cooped up. Is that what you want? You want to go places? You want to see people? We can have friends! We can have all the fucking friends you want, and we'll have fun little dinner parties every day, and we'll talk about how fun our little fucking jobs are, and they'll say, 'Oh, I wasn't really feeling your last one, Brooks, you were trying too hard with the irony. Maybe if you have a little more action next time . . .' We can do whatever the hell you want!"

"Don't try to turn this on me. I'm just trying to say that we can't be the only people we talk to. It's unhealthy." And now Oleander is the one avoiding eye contact. He's moving busily back and forth across the kitchen, making every excuse not to get near or even look at Brooklyn.

"This life isn't enough for you?"

"I didn't say that—"

"'Cause you seemed pretty content with it—"

"Always have to make this my fault—"

"—but now it's every damn day we're at each other's throats—"

"—can't do anything without you ruining it for me and everyone else—"

"—that's what's driving me insane! *Would you fucking stop and look at me?*"

Oleander freezes, standing against the counter with his hand on the open door of the cabinet. He is breathing heavily, winded as if he's been running back to Brooklyn all the while. For a moment they are both still, ire burning into their skin and turning the air between them sallow. This is where the game leads, where it always leads, and where neither of them has truly won. This is where the night begins—a night inundated with silence and isolation. A night consisting of walking back and forth within the confines of the home, trading rooms but never sharing spaces, while they fume silently with anger, sorrow, stubbornness, and guilt. A night filled with wordless goodnights and hours of uneasy, ineffectual sleep.

Then Oleander says, "I can't."

He moves to shut the cabinet door. Brooklyn lunges forward, his hand outstretched. He doesn't know for what reason, but at the sound of those words he knows he needs to stop Oleander. This is not the way the game is played. This is not the next step Oleander is supposed to make. And this is a move Brooklyn has neither prepared for nor even begun to consider. It is a move to end the game.

The cabinet door connects with Brooklyn's thumb, catching it between the two faces of wood with a loud crack that echoes in the kitchen and through the hall beyond.

"*Shit!*" Brooklyn stumbles back, holding his thumb with his other hand. For a brief moment he traverses empty space, and then his elbow collides with a smooth, cold object behind him. He turns on his heel, and he and Ollie watch as the wine glass flies from the counter and falls. The crash is deafening. Burgundy liquid paints the tiled floor like blood.

Immediately Brooklyn grabs a towel and is down on the floor, mopping up the mess at their feet and pushing the shards of broken glass into a pile near the center of the kitchen. His thumb throbs excruciatingly; he needs to inspect it, put ice on it. But for now, he needs to soak up the wine with this towel.

Oleander is slower to meet him, sinking to the ground on tender soles. He plucks the larger shards from the pile with his bare hands and cradles them in his palm. It's then that Brooklyn realizes he is crying.

"There're a couple tucked away still; that wasn't the last of them," Brooklyn begins, but Ollie is shaking his head.

"We can't do this anymore," Ollie says, but the words don't make any sense. "I think we need some time away from each other."

Brooklyn can feel the glass pieces scraping beneath the towel.

Chapter Seven

Zinnia glances around as she enters the truck and starts in mild surprise with a hand to her chest. "I didn't know anybody else was in here."

"Oleander," Ollie proclaims with a warm smile. "Most people call me Ollie."

Zinnia slides into the passenger seat, fanning her face comically. "Damn near had a heart attack. Couldn't see you from outside with the camper shell on and all." She laughs in good humor at her fright. Then her eyes widen, and she turns in her seat to face him. "I don't mean to take your seat, if you were up here. I really wouldn't mind sitting in the back there."

"Oleander always sits in the back," Brooklyn says, sliding in behind the steering wheel.

"Really?"

"Yeah," Oleander says. "I don't want to sit next to that guy."

Zinnia laughs again. "No, I can't—"

"Honestly," Oleander says. When Zinnia looks to Brooklyn, he nods in agreement.

"You sure?" She still sounds skeptical.

"Yeah, I like it better back here—I'm not just being polite." Ollie shrugs.

"Well, all right." And with that, Zinnia slips her bag to the floor between her feet. The movement seems to send a wave of relief over her, as if somehow that pack was an incredible burden. Brooklyn is certain it can't weigh more than five pounds. She leans her head back against the chair, her hair fanning out behind her, and closes her eyes for a moment. "I can't explain it, but I am so, so happy you all came along."

Don't mention it, Brooklyn wants to say, but he doesn't. Instead he disengages the parking brake. The familiar low rumble of the tires over the asphalt fills the truck's cabin. Brooklyn wonders if Zinnia is going to fall asleep. He doesn't know how long she's been traveling, but she can't fall asleep now. He doesn't know where she wants to go.

"So, where you headed?" he asks.

"That depends on where you're headed, Mr. Brooklyn." She keeps her eyes shut.

Is she trying to be easygoing, or does she expect a longer ride from him than he anticipated? Brooklyn isn't sure whether he wants to divulge his destination to her. She is, after all, a complete stranger. And though he doesn't *own* the place he's headed, some part of him doesn't feel comfortable telling anyone else its name. This journey is his, and although Zinnia may be in his truck, she was not part of his plans.

"West coast," he says.

"Beautiful strip of land," she replies dreamily. "What brings you folks over there?"

The road is a little less manicured; Brooklyn has to drift back and forth in the lane to avoid the worst potholes. "Open wounds." He doesn't know why he says this. Cryptic responses generally lead to prying.

"That's an intense explanation." She smirks until she sees the serious look on his face. "Well, what're you going to do out there?"

"I've got an idea, but I'm not completely sure yet." Brooklyn keeps his eyes dead ahead, hands at ten and two on the wheel. He's said too much; his throat constricts. Yet it's far too late at this point to take the words back. Oleander has been quiet through all of this. Brooklyn spies him staring in the rearview mirror.

"Illinois," Zinnia says, opening her eyes now. "I'm trying to get to Illinois, but I'll go as far as you'll take me."

"And what's in Illinois?" Brooklyn asks.

She winks. "I'm not completely sure yet."

Far above the world, the sun has planted itself at the pinnacle of the sky. Brooklyn rolls his window down just a tad to let the cooler air from outside blow in, and Zinnia does the same, her sheer scarves dancing like petals in the wind. She tilts her face to get the full brunt of the gusts, enjoying every moment of it. Perhaps she would have walked the entire road without complaint had she not been carrying baggage with her. Maybe she would have walked farther than the eye could see, to where the hills on the horizon turn a pale violet and disappear into the sky—no, beyond that. Maybe she would have walked all the way to Illinois.

"How do we get to Illinois?" Brooklyn asks, words whipping around in the wind.

"Haven't you got a map?"

"Nope, I didn't think that far ahead." This is partially true, but the main reason is that he hasn't needed to use maps in nearly ten years. Only now does Brooklyn realize how small a square of the world he's been relegated to.

"Well, you head west and keep going west until it's time to go a little north," she says, pantomiming the directions with an outstretched hand. "It's real simple then, isn't it?"

"Thank you," Brooklyn replies with the faintest hint of sarcasm. "I'd forgotten my United States geography."

She giggles. "Don't mention it."

Brooklyn steals another glance in the rearview mirror. Oleander watches the grassy hills go by in silence.

"I promise I'm not kidnapping you," Brooklyn begins, and Zinnia gives him a look of mock reproach. Her expressions are so unguarded, she must be one of those individuals who believe in the general goodness of people. Perhaps this freedom of spirit means she won't mind if he continues his journey after all, in spite of her presence. Realization jolts him then—he's *not* antagonized by her. Granted, he's only known her for a handful of minutes, but usually that's all the time it takes. He feels daring; he might actually suggest what's on his mind. "I promise I'm going to take you in the right direction, but there's somewhere I want to go first, and it's not exactly along the way. It's kind of a stop on a trail of places I've thought about visiting."

"By all means." She seems rather comfortable in his Ranger already. "Indirect paths are often more beautiful."

In many ways, it frustrates Brooklyn that New York is most often thought of as a solid city. The uninitiated envision a dense Manhattan stretching out across the thousands of square miles of land. They think of tall, thin buildings reaching up toward a heaven that is far out of reach. Tightly bordered streets stretch long and straight, carrying a continuous flow of hundreds of thousands of people every hour. These hordes move along avenues lined with shops and pizza parlors and lights that hypnotize the senses. Everywhere they look, there is something new and exciting to distract them.

But this is not the New York Brooklyn knows best. His buildings are humble and wide rather than boasting and tall. They greet people like a grandmother taking a child into her bosom. The streets he knows are bordered by trees and grass. Mostly quiet. Where the streetlamps are the only source of light at night, but there's not much to see once the sun goes down anyway.

The series of highways Brooklyn has so far driven are much the same as the New York he knows. And though he's glad he left his home, he's also thankful that the world around him has not yet changed too much. These trees might be the same ones that grow beyond his bedroom window. And this air still tastes the same as it did when they—the two of them—would sit outside while the sun went down, Brooklyn writing in his notebooks and Ollie reading. Perhaps this is how Brooklyn keeps the longing at bay, how he staves off the stinging waves that wash over him usually in moments of solitary contemplation.

As another hour melts away, Brooklyn finds himself listening to his new passenger rather than speaking. She is vibrant, talking with more than just words. Talking with movement, with her hands and her shoulders. She doesn't tell stories so much as recreate them. From a less eloquent tongue, her stories might come off as inane, but from her each one emerges multi-dimensional and engaging. Brooklyn doesn't mind that he's not expected to do much more than listen and say a few words here and there.

"—but I knew that I could. I was—well, I guess *am*—a photographer. I know it's not extraordinary, glamorous, or *edgy* as a whole, but I have done a few cases with PIs. Let me tell you, though: not my preference. I always felt grimy afterwards. Watching people sticks to your skin like syrup, and you've got to wash it away. But when you're trying to build a resume, you take everything that comes at you into consideration." She says this all as if reminiscing about a life that is barely connected to the one she lives now, as if this is all far behind her. "Jasper loathed it—that would be my ex-husband, by the way. Said it wasn't a *real* profession because the money wasn't regular. I don't know what he was talking about though; I never went two weeks without a client. And dammit if I didn't pull my fair share."

"How long have the both of you been together?" she asks, drawing Brooklyn—and Oleander, who'd remained even more in the shadows than before—into the spotlight.

Brooklyn steals a glance at Oleander, who sits up.

"It's over fourteen years now, isn't it? Almost fifteen?" Ollie says. He pats the shoulder of Brooklyn's seat.

Brooklyn nods. "Yeah. Married ten years ago this past September."

"No way." Zinnia seems genuinely impressed and excited, her eyes widening so that they're almost perfect circles. "That's really beautiful. You must've been real young too, both of you."

"I guess we were," Brooklyn admits. "I was about twenty-three."

"Everybody always talks about how young love doesn't last, but I think it has every chance to be just as strong as older love. You got to start somewhere," Zinnia says. "Hell, maybe young love's got a better chance. It's great that you've stuck together."

Brooklyn's eyes are trained intently on the road again. His heart sags. She doesn't know any better, but he won't tell her. He sits in a remote silence now, wondering why he can't remember the last time he'd told Oleander he liked the way his hair curled a bit at the ends, or that he thought it was nice that Oleander would plant things he knew the animals around their house liked to eat.

"Not saying that couples who get married young don't make it, but you know, it's nice to see two people who are still together," Zinnia continues. Brooklyn's glad she hasn't looked over at him in a while. "That said, I don't wish Jasper and I had stayed together, though—no sir. I should've seen it sooner that we weren't meant to last."

"Why's that?" Brooklyn prompts.

"He didn't see the world same as I do. Sometimes that works out, but we were just *too* different. He spent his time trying to control me. We were always planning for the future—there was no time for anything that wasn't efficient and didn't help us financially. 'You always want to spend our money'—but why are we going to save every single penny and not spend the excess when we've got the chance? Experience things while we've got the energy?" She's still smiling—it seems she never stops—but something else lingers behind it. Brooklyn still has no real words to describe what that something is. "It got worse the longer we were together. He used to take me to the lake, and we'd go swimming. I loved swimming. But we stopped that a *long* time ago."

Now she goes silent, but her silence is just as full as her sentences. It draws itself out of her like water and fills the holes left by the absence of her voice. Then they pass a road sign that calls her attention, and she briskly grabs hold of a new direction in the conversation.

"You know we're driving toward the center of Pennsylvania." It's not a question.

"Yes, I do," Brooklyn says, and tries to swing Zinnia back into lightness again by offering a smirk.

She raises her eyebrows. "All right, just checking."

"I told you, I had to take us somewhere first."

"I'm not complaining. Just wanted to make sure you knew where you were headed," Zinnia says, shrugging. Seeing her relax eases Brooklyn's strain. He can tell she doesn't really mind—yes, even he who is normally so bad at reading other people. She's not regimented like most. She's free, floating on a carefree wind. And when she lands, she'll call this new place home and be content.

They turn off the highway in a modest town. The sign says BRADFORD. Brooklyn navigates swiftly through the quietly populated avenues. The town thins into strings of houses and forestry.

Before the homes disappear into the rearview mirror, Brooklyn steals another look at Oleander. Ollie is watching the trees slide past with contentment on his face. A small smile has relaxed the corners of his eyes and softened his brow. His hands are clasped lightly between his knees. He looks happy.

And this makes Brooklyn smile as well.

Chapter Eight

Brooklyn tries listening to Zinnia—she is talking with Ollie, who is giving her more attention than Brooklyn has seen him give anyone in years—but his mind has been yanked by Allegheny Forest as if caught on a fishing line.

Autumn has drenched the beech trees and the black cherries, spilling warm colors across an expanse that's already given way to falling temperatures. Golds, oranges, and reds appear, and he wishes he could pluck the leaves to save them before their fragility and transience take over. On the other side of the hills, the road takes them down into the valley. Brooklyn wonders how the three of them can possibly be alone today when the forest is alight in such a beautiful and impermanent state.

"—and why don't you?" The question is followed by silence, and it takes a few moments for Brooklyn to realize that Zinnia is waiting for him to answer.

"I'm sorry, I wasn't listening." His voice is gruff after a period of silence, so he clears his throat.

Zinnia laughs, and Brooklyn thinks of the colors outside. "Ollie"— *She called him Ollie*—"was just saying you don't like to do things. That this is the first time you've been out in years."

"Well, he *used* to like to do things, but all that's changed," Ollie says.

Brooklyn feels a sharp stab of irritation, but it reduces to a twinge of discomfort and guilt almost instantly. "It's not that I don't *like* to try things anymore. I was never very adventurous." His tone is a bit more defensive than he'd meant it to be.

"Not adventurous?" Zinnia seems aghast at the prospect. "Why, adventure is the steam that drives the train. I make sure I do at least one adventurous thing a week, or I'd go mad from monotony."

"Every week?" It's Brooklyn's turn to be bewildered. She can't really mean this, can she? "That seems exhausting."

"Well, you can't look at it that way!" Zinnia rights herself in the seat to face them both properly. "You can't think 'That's too much for me to handle, I don't have time for that.' Because then it's always going to be too much. You got to be willing and let it happen. Sure, if you're feeling bold, you can decide to climb a mountain—set out on a Saturday morning with nothing but a sleeping bag strapped to your pack and a can of trail mix—the one with the most M&M'S, of course, only way to do it—or maybe you look at your backyard and decide you need a few more bushes and trees so it feels a little bigger and not all so empty. Maybe that's not adventuring in the vein of Indiana Jones, but it's trying something new. A winding path is a lot more interesting than a straight one. Life would be nothing but bland if you don't add your own spices."

Zinnia seems content with her speech and watches Brooklyn expectantly with a gleam in her eyes. Oleander seems pleased as well, smiling to himself with satisfaction. Only Brooklyn is unmoved.

"Maybe," he says, though he knows this isn't really a response. "But maybe there isn't always room for all that. Sometimes you just don't have the energy. It's not for lack of trying, though. I'm out here now."

"That's true." Zinnia nods. "But you're making the trip because you realized your life was missing that daily spark, aren't you?"

Brooklyn doubts a daily adventure could cure him. This trip is meant to be a one-time shock to his system, not the groundwork for a new frame of living.

While they've been speaking, a wide river has appeared before them. Just off a bridge is a marina and a parking lot with four cars spaced far apart. Brooklyn guides the truck into a spot and sits in silence for a few moments before turning off the engine.

"This place is incredible," Zinnia says, surveying their surroundings with wonder. "Allegheny, it said?"

"Yeah." Brooklyn finds himself again at a sudden and unexpected impasse. He's seen this place before in photographs, and though he thought he might find himself wandering to this destination, to actually be here is another thing entirely. The trees extend all the way down the hillside, flocking to the river's edge to dip their branches in and drink. Underbrush gathers at their feet like playing children. Sometimes, the beauty of the world is reason enough for joy.

"It's nice and all from the car, but I'd much rather be in it, if you don't mind," Zinnia says. She opens her door, and cold air tumbles into the cabin like water through a spillway. She bounces out, but reaches back in for a sweater. "Are you coming along?" she asks Oleander after she's found what she wants from her bag.

He smiles toothlessly but shakes his head. "I'll wait for you guys to come back."

"Really? After that brilliant speech I just gave a moment ago?"

"Yeah, it's fine," Ollie says. "I want to stay here."

"But it's so beautiful! I don't understand."

Oleander's smile is melancholy. He doesn't reply.

Brooklyn steps out, his own sweater pulled over his shoulders. He closes the door and walks around to Zinnia on the other side. "He doesn't leave the truck," Brooklyn says, offering an explanation for Oleander.

"What, like ever?" Zinnia asks, confused now. "That's not possible."

"He's comfortable in there. He feels safe. He doesn't like to leave."

"But—"

"He'll be there when we get back."

Oleander is staring out the back window again, through the truck bed and the camper shell. Maybe he hears them, and maybe he doesn't.

"Oh, okay." Zinnia still seems doubtful and obviously doesn't understand, but she lets Brooklyn shut the truck door and walks with him toward the line of trees. "He going to be all right?"

"Yeah, he'll be fine." Brooklyn waves away her worry with a hand. "You learn to get used to it."

"But why does he do it?"

"I couldn't tell you."

They walk in silence until they reach the edge of the lot and head up the path that parallels the road. The atmosphere immediately changes once the forest envelopes them. They are in a smaller place and feel like giants compared to when they were out in the open air beside the water. Brooklyn and Zinnia travel at a steady pace they've both wordlessly agreed to. Only once does a car pass them, heading in the opposite direction, down toward the river and the bridge and the marina, which have now fallen out of sight. Otherwise they're alone, and it's very easy to imagine that they're the only people in the entire forest.

A trail opens up off to the right; they agree to it instinctually. "Can I ask you something, Zinnia?" He's surprised that he's the first to talk.

She looks over at him, and he can see that she's still worried about Ollie. Even so, she nods.

"Your car—it looked like it only had a blown tire," Brooklyn says. "Why'd you leave it there? Why not ask me to take you to a tow company or someplace to call for help?"

Zinnia is silent for a time, walking with her eyes on the ground but focused on a distant place. He notices now that her hair is not really black but a very dark brown, the color of walnut tree bark. And it doesn't just flow freely but forms tight curls around itself.

"There were many things wrong with that car, not just what you could see. Right from the get-go." There are traces of spite in her tone. "My ex-husband stopped helping me pay to fix it even before we split, and after . . . well, there was no chance of getting help after.

"Don't get me wrong, I don't blame him for stopping. He bought it for me after we married. But it was *his* car even then. I could never get that out of my head, and he never let me forget it either. Neither would he take it back when we split. So, while it was given to me, it carried this weight with it, this guilt. This attachment to him that I couldn't shake. I drove it out of convenience because it was easier than finding another way to get around, but when it broke down back there"—she points behind her, though the highway where they'd met is far off in another direction—"and you stopped to pick me up, I decided, 'Why not? Why not take this opportunity?'" She goes quiet, and Brooklyn thinks that maybe she's done, but then she speaks again, and the words are much softer. "Maybe when I get where I'm going, maybe in . . ."

"Illinois?" Brooklyn offers, and Zinnia laughs like he's told her a joke.

"Yeah, in Illinois. I'll call someone, let them know to pick it up and impound it or something." She shakes her hands in front of her. "I'm not one to let unfinished business hang, but sometimes you just need to step back from things. Otherwise it'll drive you crazy, I tell you."

"Those are good words to live by," Brooklyn says.

"And what about you?"

"What do you mean?"

"Well, Ollie was telling me stories in the car, and for a while I couldn't believe he was talking about you." Zinnia seems to say this out of concern. Brooklyn buries his hands in his pockets. "Granted, I've known you for all of a few hours, but, you know, first impressions and all that."

Brooklyn shakes his head. "Oleander likes to pretend," he says. His voice isn't angry, but it is hard. "He likes to remember things not as they were but how he would've liked them to be. Unfortunately, it's a habit of his."

"He's a romantic."

"He's persistent. And sometimes beguiling."

Zinnia pauses, and her brows crease. "I didn't realize there was animosity."

Brooklyn sighs and softens just as quickly as he'd frozen over. "There isn't. There's just . . . It's hard to explain."

"Did you want to try?"

"I don't know."

"It may help. Take it as an adventure." She winks.

The leaves rustle above them as if the trees are hoping he might respond. Brooklyn and Zinnia have been climbing steadily all the while, and the breeze up here is a bit stronger.

"We're not really together," he says, and then wonders why he's telling this woman. By definition she's still a stranger—he doesn't even remember if she told him her last name. Yet he can't help but speak to her. She's so honest with him. He wants to reciprocate, even though the subject matter collects heavily in his chest and weighs him down. Even though it pains him to think about these things. Maybe he can relinquish some of this weight to her for the time being because she won't be around long enough to force him to reconcile with it. "Things are complicated."

"Aren't they always," she says.

"We're making amends, of a sort," Brooklyn continues. "At least, that's what I'm hoping. When this is all said and done, things will be different for the both of us. Better. I'm sorry, but I think that's all I want to say."

The path becomes wooden planks where the dirt trail ends. All around them thick tree roots breach the ground, creating convoluted waves that border the path like moss-patterned railings. RIMROCK OVERLOOK, a sign says, and this is enough to make Zinnia gasp in delight. She glances back at Brooklyn with a look that says "Keep up with me" and then leaps down the wooden steps.

"Wait!" Brooklyn calls, though it's much too late now. The steps are steep, and he takes them one at a time as he tries to hurry after her, though Zinnia has disappeared around the bend. He curses silently. As he navigates the curves in the boardwalk, his footfalls create deep thumps, like hammer strikes on a massive marimba. The tangle of trees and moss and undergrowth builds a labyrinth out of something that should be much simpler. It unbalances him, threatens to topple him over the sides of the path. Zinnia is like a child, running off, unable to contain herself. If she injures herself on this unkempt path, of course he'll have to be the one to get her help. If he doesn't break his own neck first. She is—

And then the world opens up again: a brilliant, textured, meticulous, and infinite landscape that is untameably vast and inexplicably intimate all at the same time. He sees the river coated in sunlight beneath a blue but spotted sky. The hills are aflame with tongues of dancing golden and orange treetops. Below the observation deck the earth drops down so that he is not only gazing out at the fire but submerged in it. A part of it. Alight as well.

"It's even better up here." The voice comes from behind and above Brooklyn.

Confused, he turns slowly on the spot, still in awe. There is nobody on the deck with him. But he's certain she called.

"Brooklyn!" She's in the trees.

He sees Zinnia above. Her legs are wrapped around the thick limb of a tree. With one hand she holds on to the branches, but the other is spread wide in the air, open and outstretched above her. She laughs and screams in delight, and for a moment Brooklyn wonders if maybe he's picked up someone who might be insane.

"What the hell are you doing up there?" he asks, and the void beside him threatens to swallow his words.

"Sitting on top of the world! You should try it, it's amazing!" Zinnia stretches out the last word so that it soars over the edge of the cliff. Now Brooklyn knows she's crazy.

"Get down from there, you're going to get yourself killed," he calls.

"Nonsense! I'm getting myself *born*."

"That doesn't make any sense."

"What doesn't make sense is that you're down there when you could be up here." Zinnia gestures around her, dangerously close to falling.

Brooklyn takes a step back, wishing now he'd never listened to Oleander. On his own, Brooklyn never would have picked her up. He could've arrived in Allegheny and had a peaceful walk with a beautiful view that would have satisfied and comforted him. Instead, he is here with a mad woman who climbs trees and tries her best to get herself—and him—killed. She is adamant and deranged, and stubbornly confident that she can do whatever she wants. Brooklyn could turn around though, leave her here. Someone else could help her the rest of the way. He can't deny that the idea flickers inside him. But he shakes his head, closing his eyes to what he knows is better judgment.

"I'm pretty sure you're not supposed to be up there," he says, his feet planted. His hands have balled into fists.

"I'm not leaving behind trash, I'm not cutting anything off, and I've no intention of killing anything." She laughs again, and Brooklyn is amazed at how much she finds funny. "Least of all myself. Sometimes it doesn't hurt to do what others tell you not to."

"That's a real nice sentiment—"

"I'm serious, Brooklyn. As beautiful as the view is from down there, it's all the more spectacular up here." She punctuates every word of her next sentence. "I am sitting on the edge of the world."

Brooklyn opens his eyes and looks up at her. She is unafraid, audacious, and satisfied with herself. Arms trembling, he turns on his heel. He doesn't allow himself to think—or at least is trying not to—listening instead to the soft thud of his shoes on the hard ground.

Brooklyn means to leave, intending to head back up the path through the labyrinth of moss and roots, but instead he finds himself at the base of what looks like a thick maple tree. It looms directly above him, taller than he wants to imagine, with intimidating, outstretched branches.

"That's the spirit!" Zinnia calls. In his mind Brooklyn can see her waving her hand in the air. All that stands before him is a vertical trunk. He isn't sure he knows how to climb trees. Maybe he had climbed them as a boy. He thinks he remembers vague havens made in canopied hideaways, but he can't be sure. Memory is such a fickle thing, and he could be lying to himself. But what difference do memories make when what's in front of him is very real and so very tall?

Brooklyn reaches up and grasps at the lowest knot, where the tree must have once been trimmed. It's the only thing he can reach, but he is determined now that he must climb this particular tree. If he steps away to go to another, he might lose his nerve. The bark is coarse on his palm but forgiving enough from a season of rain. Mustering strength, Brooklyn pulls himself upward, ascending as far as he can go. For a brief moment he can feel his soft hands slipping off the short knob. Instinct takes hold of him, and he lifts his legs, squeezing the trunk between his knees—

And falls.

Brooklyn hits the ground with enough force to knock the wind out of his lungs. He hadn't climbed very high, and the leaves protect him from any real damage, but humiliation and frustration rise red in his cheeks. "This is stupid," he says, batting leaves from his hair.

"Come on, try again," Zinnia calls from her spot, already perched above him.

"That's easy for you to say." Brooklyn refuses to look up at her. "You know how to do this. I can't. I don't even want to."

"Brooklyn."

"What?"

"Nobody's going to make you."

Brooklyn breathes, taking in the scent of the trees: the sap, the bark saturated with water. He shakes his head, frozen between the urge to march back to the truck and the disappointment of what it would mean if he does. *Now you're crazy, just like her.*

"You can do it," she says. "Keep going."

So Brooklyn steps up to the tree again, grasping the top of the knot with both hands. He pulls himself off the ground and squeezes the thick trunk between his thighs to gain support. He counts down quietly to himself and lets go with both hands, quickly wrapping them around a branch above his head. His arms slide over the moss and bark. It feels childish, but he tells himself to think like an animal—a cat or a sloth that might climb without a second thought. He pulls himself up onto the branch, his arms shaking from the strain. Over one branch he ascends, and this is the hardest, but now he goes for the next one and the one after that. His mind goes from animals to a single word, which repeats like a mantra inside him. *Up*, he thinks. *Up*.

If the wind was cold on the ground, it's nothing compared to what it is now. Now it's like submerging his face repeatedly into a river of icy water with each gust. Yet somehow, Brooklyn doesn't mind it as much as he'd have thought. His torso is warm from exertion. He looks up, and the branches have begun to thin, shrinking quickly in diameter to a size he believes cannot support him. He has climbed as far as he can go.

"Look around you," Zinnia calls.

For a moment Brooklyn is unsure of which direction he is facing. Before him stretches the hillside, climbing above the tree on which he sits. Slowly, very slowly, for he doesn't want to lose his balance, Brooklyn turns on the branch. He bears the pliant bark in his intent gaze, not wanting to look away. He lies low on it, swings his legs around to face the opposite direction, sits up, and looks out.

Brooklyn feels something crescendo in his chest, but it's not the pain he usually feels. It's a rush of excitement, a rhythm that builds faster and faster until it's pulsing in his ears and making his head feel light. Zinnia calls out again, crying things he can't understand. She laughs, and he can't help but laugh too. He's no longer looking out over a golden-soaked valley; he is soaring above it, casting a shadow over a sea of red and orange and yellow hues below him.

Chapter Nine

The Allegheny River passes beneath the bridge, close enough that by glancing out the window, Brooklyn can trick himself into thinking he, Ollie, and Zinnia are floating on the water. And maybe they are. After all, he still feels the wind on his skin. He wonders when the sensation will leave him and hopes to delay that moment for as long as possible.

"You should have seen it!" he says. "I climbed a tree, Ollie. A tree! I'm thirty-two fucking years old, climbing like—I don't know. From way up there, it was exhilarating." He's beyond the ability to form coherent sentences.

"Truly gorgeous," Zinnia agrees, stretching her hands to the ceiling of the truck.

"I wish you could've been there."

And just like that, the river is no longer beneath them. Instead, it follows them to their left.

"Sounds incredible," Oleander says. There's no contempt in his voice, but it lacks a certain enthusiasm.

Reluctantly, Brooklyn admits to himself that they should drop the topic. He and Zinnia returned to the vehicle less than ten minutes ago, but he can already see their nonstop talk about their walk in the woods is having an adverse effect on Oleander. Ollie stares straight ahead with an expression of vacant contentment on his countenance. Brooklyn looks over at Zinnia to give her a sign, but he can tell by her body language that she's already come to the same conclusion.

She stares out the front windshield, watching the line of the hills. She seems composed, relaxed but still teeming inside with energy. Brooklyn can feel it because he's experiencing the same inner effervescence.

"I saw you were reading when we got back to the car," Zinnia says.

Oleander nods, but she's not facing him. "Yeah, I pass the time that way."

"Do you go through a lot of books, then?"

"There are walls of them back at our house in Schoharie."

"How many would you say?"

"At least five hundred."

Ollie is not exaggerating. Brooklyn can see the small corner room at the back of the house, its white-and-scarlet wallpaper peeking out through gaps between the bookshelves they'd inherited from Ollie's grandparents. A black floor lamp stands in the only available corner. The window is too narrow to provide enough light during the day, but on spring evenings the room is awash with brilliant yellow sun.

"Have you brought all your favorites?"

"No, just the one." Oleander shrugs.

"I always tell myself I'm going to read more, but I'm horrible with that kind of thing. It's not that I don't enjoy it—I really do. I just always make excuses about what I should be doing with my time." Zinnia smirks at her own irresolute tendencies.

"You shouldn't worry about it," Ollie responds. "You keep yourself busy. Sounds like you do plenty of other things that are way more interesting."

"But some books can be just as fantastic." Zinnia turns her head to one side, though she can't see him without turning all the way around. "Some of the best adventures are in books. They're damn sure better than regular life, I'll tell you that."

She may not be able to see Ollie, but Brooklyn can. He watches in brief spurts between following the road, waiting for the reluctant smile to break over Oleander's face. It's there for only a flash, then it's masked again. Gone, as quickly as it came.

"They're not as great as a real experience, but I suppose they're better than nothing," Ollie says quietly.

"All right, well, let's get you to Illinois," Brooklyn says. "A promise is a promise. I dragged you through Allegheny National Forest, and now we're going to get you to your destination."

"Oh yeah, so much dragging," Zinnia says, facetious.

"Do you know where in particular you're headed?" Oleander asks, his head appearing between their seats.

"I'm still thinking about it," she says, all but waving off the question. "I've got things mulling over. I'll know sooner or later. We're not driving the rest of this thing in one shot, are we?"

"I don't know if I'll make it that long, but we can try," Brooklyn says.

"I'm not saying we should, I just wanted to know how crazy you are." She winks at him.

Before long the forest recedes to one side of the road, though the river holds strong beside them. Buildings materialize up ahead; a town creeps out of the woods, split by the river. The signs say SOUTH WARREN.

Widely spread homes share fenceless lots, their plots spilling seamlessly from one to another. Brooklyn feels a passing urge to stop here for a peek, but the urge does not outweigh his desire to keep ambling toward bigger destinations. He clears his throat. "I'm guessing that I need to take Interstate 80 pretty soon."

Zinnia puts a finger to her lips and ponders this a moment. Maybe she has a map in her head. "You should go the other way," she says as they pass a road sign with exits and highway junctions listed. "Take I-90."

"Any particular reason?"

"It's shorter."

"Shorter? It's definitely not shorter." Though he just passed the sign, Brooklyn struggles to recall the names on it. "There wasn't anything for Illinois on there. How can you tell?"

"I've passed through here before with my sister. Long time ago. I helped her move out to Indiana—which is far too quaint and safe for her, if you ask me, but I haven't heard a peep from her about moving back since, so, hey, you can't know everything. Regardless, we took I-90. I think we should go that way."

"You *think* we should go that way," Brooklyn repeats. "Have you ever gone this way on I-80?"

"Not exactly," Zinnia says.

"Not exactly?" Brooklyn raises an eyebrow. "To think I believed in you. This isn't a nostalgia trip, is it?"

"Do you have many siblings?" Ollie asks.

"Only the sister," Zinnia replies, ignoring Brooklyn's last comment. "My family's originally from Maine, but that wasn't boring enough for her. Decided to get out as quickly as she could. Got a summer job in high school so she could buy the car from my parents at eighteen and everything. I drove out to Indiana with her, which was a blast. Then I took buses home."

"Do you see her a lot?"

"We call and send postcards every once in a while, just because. She comes around during the holidays." She smiles with the side of her mouth. "I suppose we stayed pretty much as close as we could over the distance. I just sound bitter because she never looked back after she went.

"I could've moved around, but when I married Jasper—he was from one town over in Maine—we stayed in the area. He wasn't going anywhere for anything, let me tell you. No sir." She shakes her head. "I thought I could handle it, but I ran out of metaphorical cliffs to dive off of and fake smiles to put on for all his posh guests."

"You don't want to stop in Indiana to see her?" Brooklyn asks, curious now as to why she'd want to cross over into Illinois when she had a sister, who she seemed to miss dearly, along the route.

"No, I couldn't do that. At least not right now," Zinnia says, and shrugs in a noncommittal way. "I'm sure Johanne would love to see me, and it'd be great to see her, but I've got to go somewhere on my own for a while. I mean, I'm not old—dammit, I'm only thirty-five—but I feel like I've already lived a whole life as someone else. Now I've got to start over as someone closer to who I actually am."

"You don't think you'll miss it all?" Oleander chimes in.

"I'll miss some parts." She sighs, as if images of these things immediately come to mind. "Of course, the rest of my family is back there in Maine, and . . . I know I make him sound terrible, but my life with Jasper wasn't constant torture. I just need this too." She gestures out the front window to where the sun has begun its long fall back toward the western horizon. "When I get where I'm going, I'll make sure I get along just fine."

They arrive at the junction where Interstate 80 splits off to the left. Instead Brooklyn keeps on, following the wide curve of the highway as it carries him through an invariant backdrop of greenery. Although these roads he's traveled since yesterday morning have been saturated in sameness, he cherishes their color. He would rather have it this way than the monotony of a more urban environment.

Brooklyn, Ollie, and Zinnia settle into the role of travelers, staring out of windows without truly watching anything that passes. They speak in short bursts, strings of conversations that weave in and out of the landscape like threads in a blanket. At infrequent points, Zinnia directs Brooklyn on where to turn, though the signs are not always entirely clear. He wonders how she can remember these things, whether she has a secret destination in mind. She is without a doubt a restlessly charming woman, strong in her convictions yet untouchably gentle. She smiles with the sun and frowns with thunderclouds.

Then, when the city of Erie, Pennsylvania has briefly appeared before them, the road meets the interstate.

"I know I said you could tell me when we were going to stop, but I *did* actually mean that I wanted to stop tonight," Brooklyn says as he turns onto a sloped on-ramp. "I'm going to have to call it soon."

"No! Just a little farther," Zinnia says, trying to hide the urgency as an afterthought.

"I'm beginning to think this is a large, roundabout way for us to get somewhere," Brooklyn teases.

"It is actually the fastest way to Illinois," Zinnia replies, and then clicks her tongue against the roof of her mouth.

"Really?"

"Yeah, cross my heart and hope to die." She lifts a hand in oath.

"You sure?"

"Sure as I am sane."

"That doesn't strike a whole lot of confidence in me."

"And you're a picture of sound foundations." She pops a couple of almonds from her bag into her mouth. "But I guess I'll admit I'm leading us somewhere."

"Just when I was starting to trust you."

"Yes, well, you took me somewhere, and now I want to take you somewhere in return." She grins mischievously. "It's only fair."

"Where are we going?" Ollie asks.

"I can't tell you that," Zinnia says, as if it's obviously out of bounds. "I want to keep it a surprise."

"Can we at least find out where we're going to stop for the night?" Ollie says.

"And whether we're going to get to eat something before I die and one of you has to take over driving?" Brooklyn mumbles.

"Yeah, yeah, okay." Zinnia waves off their complaints like a well-practiced mother of whiny children. "I want to stop off in Sandusky."

"Sandusky?" Brooklyn asks.

"Yeah, it's in Ohio. Past Cleveland a ways. A kind of coastal place off Lake Erie." Then, when there's no response, she says, "You think you guys can hang with that?"

"I suppose I'm going to have to. How much farther past Cleveland, exactly?"

~

By the time they pull off the highway and turn onto a street called Cleveland Road West, the sun is almost gone. They enter a sleepy Sandusky amid the reddish-blue tint of twilight, when the sky seems to lower itself directly onto the city streets and the streetlamps flicker to life. The truck ambles faithfully down the road, shuddering in a way that suggests it, too, needs a fill. Brooklyn is hushed by the time of day as they roll past a shimmering bay.

"I suppose we should drop our stuff somewhere before we eat so we're not pushing for time afterward?" Brooklyn asks.

Zinnia nods. "Anywhere is good with me."

So Brooklyn pulls off at a chain motel. Cracked pavement covers the parking lot, and a logo he's almost certain he's seen but never paid much attention to before hangs over the road. The place is friendly enough. The roof isn't missing any of its navy asphalt shingles and the all-white exterior is only mildly weathered. He can see a few lights on behind the standard sheer curtains. Air-conditioning units being used even in the cool night drone beneath the evening.

It takes less than ten minutes to purchase a pair of rooms. Afterward, they find themselves at a small diner.

"You coming in?" Zinnia asks, turning around to Oleander.

He smirks with one side of his mouth. "I'll be here when you get back."

She shrugs this time. "Just thought I'd try."

Then she and Brooklyn get out of the truck and go in. PETE'S DINER, the sign says.

"You know what I really want?" They are seated immediately, and Zinnia pulls open the menu without hesitation. She scans the pages with fast eyes. "Usually places don't—Oh my God, they do breakfast all day!"

Brooklyn snickers and shakes his head.

She says, "I'm getting me some Belgian waffle."

"Personally, I would have gone with a stack of hotcakes." He winks.

"Who in their right mind chooses pancakes over waffles?" she asks, and he can't tell if her outrage is a joke. "There are pockets specifically designed to cradle your syrup."

"I don't know, pancakes just do it better for me."

"The answer of a sociopath."

"Doesn't matter anyway. I'm getting bacon and eggs."

Zinnia's eyes narrow, and for a moment she stares into Brooklyn as if judging his past decisions. Then, coming to an apparent conclusion, she says, "All right, that is a worthy alternative. Bacon trumps all." She nods her head with approval. "Any man who joins me for breakfast dinner is a man after my heart."

"You might not be my type."

She laughs. "A minor detail."

"Do you often have breakfast for dinner?"

"No, but this is a special occasion."

"Really?"

"Yes, without a doubt."

"And what occasion is that?"

"Adventure." Zinnia places her hands flat on the Formica tabletop. "We are celebrating the spirit of adventure."

Brooklyn traces a line in the patterns on the menu's cover. Beside Zinnia he can see the rear of the apple red truck reflecting orbs of light from the parking lot lamps. The curve of the arched restaurant window blocks most of the Ranger from sight, but the camper is there. The tires sit patiently on the asphalt, resting until needed again.

"To the spirit of adventure," Brooklyn agrees.

Zinnia smiles. "May every obstacle be a tree we can climb."

Chapter Ten

The food is mediocre: the eggs are underdone to the point that they can scarcely hold their shape, and the bacon is dry and burned. Yet Brooklyn's twinge of irritation fades quickly. Perhaps the cook doesn't get many requests for breakfast food at this hour and he's not used to preparing it. Maybe there's a family emergency occupying his thoughts. Brooklyn makes these excuses in the back of his mind while he chats with Zinnia, unsure why but unable to stop himself. What matters is that Brooklyn's not angry and feels no reason to be.

He glances behind Zinnia out the window again, making certain for the umpteenth time that the truck is still there.

"It's the first time I can really remember getting into trouble," Zinnia says, setting her fork down. If Brooklyn had been asked under oath, he would've sworn that a delicious-looking, golden, crisp, much-more-appetizing-than-a-plate-of-soggy-eggs Belgian waffle had sat whole on her plate less than a minute before. But now there are few signs that the plate had ever been occupied, only a left-behind stripe of maple syrup along one edge and a fleck of waffle crumb near the center. "For whatever reason, my seven-year-old self was completely behind throwing a cup of yogurt into the air in the middle of my parents' living room."

"A bunch of stupid things always seem like a good idea when you're a kid," Brooklyn says.

"Yeah, I guess so. And it was only when it was on the way down, full freefall, that I thought, 'Hmm, maybe I should've thought this through a bit more.'"

"I'm guessing it splattered—"

"Everywhere. All over the beige carpet, a bit on my dad's armchair. It was like the volume of strawberry yogurt had multiplied threefold." Zinnia's laugh fills the dining room easily. "I was practically swimming in it—or at least that's how it felt."

"What'd you do?"

"Oh, what kids normally do at that age: I stood there staring at it for a while, realizing how much trouble I was in. Then I bawled my eyes out until my dad felt too sorry for me to give me the spanking I deserved." The laughter simmers beneath her grin.

"The power of mercy." Brooklyn pokes his eggs with the prongs of his fork, watching the pieces slide lethargically over each other. Was there cheese mixed in?

"You ever get in trouble?"

He laughs a little and shakes his head. "No, not really."

"No?"

"I was a real quiet kid."

"I would have never guessed." Her words are flecked with sarcasm, but they go down more easily than his scrambled eggs.

"Yeah."

"And you never did anything wrong?"

"Nope." Brooklyn takes another mouthful after his mental preparation. The initial taste of each bite is never quite as bad as he remembers it, but once he swallows, something less enjoyable lingers. He contemplates getting a waffle like the one Zinnia's inhaled, but his deeply rooted dislike for wasted food doesn't allow him to.

"I ran away from home once," Brooklyn admits. He surprises himself with the words.

Zinnia makes as if to say something but thinks better of it. He continues.

"Well, not really. I mean, I wanted to. I wanted to see what would happen, but I couldn't. I don't know, I was too scared or something. See, I'd just gotten really angry at my parents—of course, now I can't remember why. I don't even think they knew why. I was nine or ten." He's rambling, mumbling some of his words, and he feels more nervous than he knows he ought to be. "There was a hatch in the ceiling outside my bedroom door that led to the attic space—not a real attic, just the beams and the A-frame of the roof. I went up there and sat in the darkness with the fluffy pink insulation that I knew made you itchy if you touched it and a couple of cobwebs that nearly made me panic when I ran into them.

"I sat on one of the beams, trying not to touch anything and listening to what my parents were doing. My dad was watching some cop show, and I think my mom was in their bedroom on the phone with one of her friends. I sat there for the longest time. I don't know how long—had to have been at least a couple hours. I just remember I got really, really antsy waiting for something to happen.

"Finally my mom left her room and went into mine. I could hear her calling my name and then, when I wasn't there, going to ask my father if he'd seen me. That's when they started the hunt. I could hear them checking everywhere—our house wasn't very large to begin with, but they opened every cabinet, every closet, and looked under every piece of furniture over and over again. Their calls for me kept getting louder and louder. I heard my mom start crying. 'George, we have to call the police,' she said. And she kept saying it over and over again. And here I was right above them, listening the whole time.

"I realized that what I was doing wasn't going to make me feel better. I wasn't going to get satisfaction in the way I'd hoped. Instead I just felt more and more terrible the more distressed they became. So, finally, I opened up the hatch and climbed out. I found them in the kitchen—Mom with tears on her face and my father speaking with the police."

Brooklyn pauses, staring down at the mint Formica surface as if he were looking down at the floor of the kitchen in his childhood home, hanging his head in shame. "I was in trouble then. But my parents' anger was laced with anxiety and relief. The feeling I got just before I came out of hiding stuck with me more than any punishment I received."

Zinnia matches his thoughtful silence, watching him with her wide ochre eyes. They don't show sympathy, or empathy, or pity, or even concern for that matter. They are full of understanding. He cannot hold her gaze for long.

"Well, I bet, as a whole, your parents felt very lucky to have you as their son," Zinnia says. "You know it's all right when the child feels loved enough to only pretend to run away."

Brooklyn nods absentmindedly.

"We should probably go," he says, standing.

Zinnia does the same, leaving money on the table for their food. As soon as they've reentered the night, she turns around, smiling again and looking at him expectantly. "We have one more stop I'd like to make tonight."

Brooklyn fights the urge to look at his wristwatch. "I thought you might," he says. "Are you going to tell me now why we came here?"

"Not yet. I'll lead the way." She walks to her side of the truck, and Brooklyn has no choice but to follow, fighting with himself about where he should draw the line. A voice inside him is convinced he's had enough surprises for one day, not to mention he's tired and a bit drained from all the interaction. He doesn't mind having Zinnia around—she lightens the mood—but her energetic presence is a bit taxing.

Another side of his mind reminds him that he wasn't looking to make this drive in a straight line, that following Zinnia will be good for him. He must force himself to say yes more often. So he gets into the Ranger and follows her lead, turning here and there as she dictates. His blind confidence isn't complete, and after a few directions he wonders if she knows where she's leading them, but he says nothing.

Oleander watches inquisitively through the front window and asks only once where they're headed. Zinnia is quick to let him know that she's not going to say anything until they get there. He resorts to watching in silence, just as curious as Brooklyn.

They drive along a narrow road with square houses to the left and a vacant landscape to the right. For a moment Brooklyn is lost, wondering how on earth they found their way to the ocean. He searches for the smell of saltwater and sun-washed sand. But when he cannot find it, he remembers where they are. This couldn't possibly be the ocean; it must be Lake Erie.

After a few miles, Zinnia tells Brooklyn to stop and turn the car around to park in the opposite direction, "just in case." The road doesn't have much of a shoulder to park on, but there's a long, recessed section of pavement before a grand home, where the residents' circular driveway meets the road. He maneuvers so that the truck is obscured from the house by one of the trees in the front yard. It's rather late at this point, though, almost eleven, and Brooklyn hopes they've all gone to sleep and will be none the wiser about the visit.

"We've got to leave the car here. We won't be gone too long, I don't think," Zinnia says in a low voice, a mischievous grin still on her face. "Sorry about that, Ollie."

He shrugs, though is obviously curious about what they're going to do.

"And where exactly are we?" Brooklyn asks, though he knows what the answer's going to be.

"I can't tell you. It'll ruin the surprise!"

Brooklyn is quite sure that knowing their destination will do little to ease the tension inside his stomach. He wonders if he's going to end up reliving the cheese-eggs tonight.

"C'mon!" Zinnia hisses, and opens the truck door.

"We'll be back," Brooklyn assures Oleander unnecessarily.

The rush of the black water over the shore is louder now, and the wind carrying over the waves is cold and steady. Brooklyn pulls the front of his sweater over his chin. Overhead, the myriad stars twinkle like the eyes of curious spectators. Hands in their pockets, the pair make their way down the lane, and though Zinnia doesn't say much other than "We're almost there" and "I'm so excited," Brooklyn can feel his pulse quickening. He breathes through his nostrils, forcing deep, slow breaths.

"Just up ahead now," Zinnia says one last time. "Just around this bend."

Brooklyn strains his eyes, but he can't see anything other than faint city lights ahead and the road turning quickly after the last home. He wonders if she's leading him to the low apartment-looking buildings straight ahead.

They round the bend and are immediately greeted by a massive, flat expanse of pavement—one of the largest parking lots Brooklyn's ever come across. His mouth drops open when he reads the sign.

"Cedar Point?" he asks in a husky whisper.

"Yeah, Cedar Point amusement park," Zinnia responds. "One of the best and biggest amusement parks in the world."

Brooklyn realizes then that the faint city lights he had seen before were actually spotlights and ride lights left on during the night. He also realizes that the parking lot before them, which must allow for an awful large number of cars, is almost completely empty save for a few small vehicles all the way at the other end, near the park entrance.

"I hate to break it to you, Zinnia, but I think we missed closing by a few hours at least." Brooklyn scans the area, but his eyes are not deceiving him. He can't imagine there are any visitors left inside.

"Perfect," she says. These two syllables cause Brooklyn the most anxiety. A surge of sudden nausea grips him.

"What do you mean perfect?" he asks, hoping he's misheard her. "The place is closed."

"Well, we can't break in if the place is open."

Now Brooklyn is certain Zinnia is crazy. He halts. "You want to break in? To that place?" He gestures at the structures at the other end of the asphalt lot. "I'm not looking to get arrested, Zinnia."

She shakes her head, dark curls bouncing around her face. Swiftly, she grabs him by the arm and pulls him to the edge of the road so that they're beneath the overhanging limbs of a tree. "We're not going to get arrested, because we're not going to get caught. We're not even going to do anything harmful."

"But you just said we were going to break in," Brooklyn hisses. "I think most places would count that as harmful."

"All right, I used the wrong word. We're going to hop the fence. We're not going to break anything."

"I think you're missing the point. That doesn't really make it any better!"

"You've got to keep your voice down. Look, I just want to go inside for a minute."

"I don't think the length of our visit is going to matter to security."

Zinnia makes a shushing motion with her finger, and Brooklyn struggles to keep the volume of his whispers under control. "Why do you want to break in anyway?"

She thinks about this for a moment before answering, as if contemplating the many different responses she could give. During Zinnia's momentary speechlessness, Brooklyn feels a heavy shiver run down his spine, instigated by a gust of wind off the water nearby. He should have denied her this trip. He should have told her back at the diner that he was too tired and wanted to turn in because there was more driving to do in the morning.

"I went here once with my sister. Our uncle took us. This was a long time ago. I don't remember much, just that I had a really great time." Zinnia grabs Brooklyn's shoulders to look him better in the eyes. She's not pleading, but again he's reminded of the honesty she carries with her. He feels his resolve ebb the slightest bit, though she hasn't given him much reason yet.

"I love these places: these meccas for excitement. People come away feeling as though they've braved terrifying beasts and lived to talk about it," she continues. "The rides can create such a transparent happiness. Places where that kind of beauty happens—I don't want to believe the feeling goes away when the people are gone. There's a residue that hangs on. I want to feel the park when it's empty. I want to feel what it's like to be inside when all the people have gone home, to see if I'm right about the atmosphere. I want to know if the happiness still exists there even in their absence."

Can't you do that by coming on a random weekday? Brooklyn wants to say, but he doesn't. Instead, he watches Zinnia search his face for a reaction. Can she tell what he's thinking?

"I am not trying to do anything dodgy here, I promise," Zinnia says. The moon has risen high above them, gray as dust.

Zinnia's excitement at the prospect of trespassing on private property, of hopping the fence to get into the theme park at night, is unnecessarily risky. There are a hundred other ways the two of them could experience an adventure, if that's what she's after. Yet she stares at him with conspicuous hope that he'll agree, that this will satisfy the hunger in her. Perhaps she's done everything else. Perhaps this is one of the few things left for her to feel.

Brooklyn is also certain, though, that Zinnia will back down. If she sees he's against this plan—that he says no and means it—she'll follow him back down the lane to where the Ranger waits patiently for their return. Maybe she will do so with some measure of disappointment, but she wouldn't complain aloud. She wouldn't be angry at him for saying no. She'd let it be. He doesn't know what he's basing this assumption on, but it feels correct.

He taps his fist against the side of his thigh. "So, where exactly would—I mean, how would we even get in?" he asks, against his better judgment. His mind is already racing madly, deciding what the worst outcome could be. He adds, "In case we were to try this insane plan of yours."

Zinnia does a little bounce on the spot, which makes Brooklyn consider rescinding his suggested support. Turning around, she begins leading him along the road again, walking close to the edge where the trees border a grassy belt.

"Well, it looks like there's a road just over there. We'll look for a good place to jump."

"You don't think they've thought of that?"

"I'm sure they have." She shrugs a little, her hair bobbing to accommodate the movement.

Brooklyn shuts his eyes and shakes his head, as if doing so might change where they are and what they're about to do. "This is beyond a bad idea," he says, though he keeps walking beside her.

"I won't force you to," she says simply.

They reach an intersection in the road. The main gate to the parking lot is pulled closed for the night. To their left are what look like tollbooths—small cabins oriented in a row beneath a tall awning that arches over the road. The light in one of the cabins is on, and Brooklyn can make out a man slumped inside who is thankfully facing the other direction. Although Brooklyn doesn't believe they've broken any laws yet, he's not too keen on raising suspicion.

To their right he can see the road Zinnia's talking about. It extends alongside the parking lot and heads off in the direction of the park. Without hesitation Zinnia begins to follow it, keeping a brisk pace that forces Brooklyn to jog to catch up with her.

Although quick, Zinnia's step is casual and silent.

Brooklyn tries his best to match her, minimizing the noise his shoes make on the asphalt as much as possible. They move like this until they are at least halfway down the side of the lot and have put enough distance between them and the tollgates that Brooklyn can no longer make out the security guard.

A marina appears on their left, and with it comes the gentle lap of water against the docked boats. Orange lights glow in the dark. Brooklyn watches the boats bob up and down in straight rows, no two quite at the same time, though they somehow have the same cadence. He thinks of a dance where untrained people move unsynchronized but to the same rhythm. This calms him.

Brooklyn and Zinnia follow the curve of the road, the unlimited rows of boats unfolding before them. Many of them are blue and white. The soft waves slide over the smooth underbellies.

And then Brooklyn looks to his right. A powder-blue wooden structure stands almost directly over the two of them, reaching into the empty space above. Spotlights from below spread bright fans of light, like peacock tails, over the base, while tiny white bulbs line the railings that follow the track as it curves up and down in a row of bell-shaped hills. Bright clattering from flanged metal wheels flying wildly along the track fills Brooklyn's ears, though a train hasn't run on this ride for a few hours now. He can smell the grease used to lubricate the axles and chain motor, and the release of air brakes hisses through the wind. He knows all of these things but experiences none of them. For a moment he can only stare, vaguely keeping up with his companion.

Noticing his distracted behavior, Zinnia whispers to him, "The Blue Streak. We're not there yet."

They keep walking, and Brooklyn lets the roller coaster retreat slowly behind them. Where exactly is "there"? Perhaps the night is skewing his perception of height and distance. He cannot begin to compare what Zinnia called the Blue Streak to, say, the Giant Dipper at the Santa Cruz Beach Boardwalk in California or even the Coney Island Cyclone. Surely the wooden coasters are all similar in size, but standing directly beneath the blue structure, he is dwarfed. It's hard to imagine that there might be something even bigger that Zinnia's looking for. But she's determined and powers on without a backward glance.

"I don't know how good I'll be at this," Brooklyn whispers, jogging again to keep pace with her nimble gait. "I don't think I've climbed a fence in at least ten years, let alone one with barbed wire on it."

"We'll find a way," she says, waving away his concern. "I haven't climbed a fence in a couple years either, but I have complete confidence in us. It's got to be easier than a tree, right?"

"I don't know if I'd agree with that."

The road winds on. They pass another ride on the right, this one less awe-inspiring than the first, with almost no lights to speak of and thin steel scaffolding for supports. Brooklyn fights the urge to ask whether they're almost at their destination, telling himself it doesn't matter either way. They're going where they're going, and Zinnia will stop when they get there. His heart is racing again though. The farther out on this peninsula they get, the farther away they are from the truck.

Past a few buildings, the marina is beside them again. Brooklyn can feel his palms sweating, beads of perspiration forming on his back, his teeth clenching together. They have to be close now; he can sense it, feel it in the way Zinnia's steps have slowed and her gaze has redirected. She's staring up to their right.

Zinnia stops. Brooklyn stops too, forcing himself to look up at the steel behemoth on the other side of the concrete barrier topped by an iron fence. The coaster is lit from below, but it's so tall that the crest of the hill disappears in the darkness above where the light dissipates. He can only imagine where the ride ends, somewhere up in the cloudy atmosphere.

"Here?" he asks.

"Here," Zinnia says. There are no cars in sight; the road is quiet and empty. Still, Brooklyn feels eyes watching. He imagines someone jumping out and shouting, "Hey! I know what you're about to do, and it's illegal!" But, of course, nobody does.

Brooklyn notices now that Zinnia stopped at what looks like an access gate for maintenance vehicles to enter the restricted area. The gate is significantly shorter than the rest of the fence but will still require some vaulting.

Zinnia wanders forward until her hands wrap around the square bars. She stares at the world on the other side, and Brooklyn looks with her. In addition to the paved access road, there are train tracks running along the base of the massive structure, just on the other side of the gate. They come around a bend to Brooklyn and Zinnia's left and disappear into the darkness on their right. Beyond the tracks is the station for the roller coaster, a prismatic structure of corrugated steel. And beyond that, all Brooklyn can see are the silhouettes of trees.

"All right, so we just jump this fence and have a little look around—it doesn't have to be for long, just enough to feel it," Zinnia whispers, looking back at Brooklyn. He can see her creased brows and pursed lips, pleading with him through the darkness, asking for his solidarity and his loyalty. And quickly he sees that this adventure means much more to her than she's let on. She's not simply indulging in reckless fantasy; this has real significance for her. A significance that, even should she explain it as best she could, he'd never truly realize or feel in the same way. Though they're doing the same thing, their experiences will be entirely different.

Brooklyn nods.

Zinnia counts down from five wordlessly. Then the two of them hoist themselves over the top.

A moment later they are on the other side. Zinnia skirts out of sight of the gate.

"Zinnia!" Brooklyn hisses, but she is twenty feet from him now, walking off toward the dark trees. His heart racing, Brooklyn stumbles after her, feeling exceedingly vulnerable out in the open but also insanely small beneath the gigantic structure beside him, over him, behind him. "Zinnia, wait for me!"

"Come on!"

There are more fences, and Zinnia walks alongside them. Brooklyn keeps near to her as she darts in and out of shadows in front of him.

"Can you smell it?" she asks.

"Smell what?" he responds, wondering if maybe he can't smell anything because he's too focused on sensing approaching visitors.

She stops at a chain-link fence behind a stout unlit building. "It still smells like they're all here."

"What are you talking about?"

"Corn dogs, french fries, and cotton candy. The wind coming off the water, greased gears, pine needles swept off paths and onto wood chip flower beds. Sunlight on asphalt, music playing on hidden speakers, laughter. Indecision, all decisions, going where the roads lead."

Brooklyn wonders if she can really smell all these things. Or maybe she's just hoping, but that's enough for them to be real. Either way, he keeps quiet, watching her close her eyes and breathe in deeply.

Then Zinnia starts laughing, and Brooklyn steps back. Her laughter is soft, but it's enough to fill the space around them and filter through the trees into the shadows.

"Zinnia," Brooklyn hisses again. "What are you doing?"

"I'm laughing!" She keeps on doing so. "Can't you see I'm laughing?"

"Yes, I can see that, but why? This isn't exactly the best place."

"I can't help it." She throws her arms wide, as if the breeze might pick her up and carry her away. "I haven't felt this vibrant in years!"

She spins on the spot, her head thrown back and face upturned toward the summit of the steel hill lording over them and the dark sky disappearing above the treetops. "You should spin with me."

"Zinnia—"

"Please?"

"I don't think I—"

"You're thinking about it too much!"

"Zinnia, someone should be keeping watch."

"You're already out here. You might as well spin with me." She's still laughing.

Brooklyn's eyes dart about. He expects a great beam of light to fall on him and Zinnia at any moment, to corner them and force them to endure whatever punishment comes from trespassing on a closed amusement park. This doesn't happen. The branches around them rustle, but everything else remains immobile. The tubular metal beams, the chain-link fence, the grass, the plain stucco building, even the silhouettes of the trees are all as silent as the moon, staring at the two trespassers with a paralyzed curiosity.

Letting out his breath, Brooklyn begins to turn on the spot, keeping his eyes trained on the surrounding landscape as he does so. The world slips by him, the shadows melding with pools of light from the distant streetlamps. Grass, gravel, tree trunks, steel supports, and concrete rotate around him unceasingly amid a cool air that washes over his face and whispers in his ears with voiceless rushes.

"Not like that," Zinnia says. "You've got to put your arms up when you do it."

"Are you telling me how to spin?" Brooklyn shoots back, but he hears a bit of a smile in his voice. The words are as ridiculous as the sentiment. And he *feels* ridiculous, standing beneath a roller coaster in a closed amusement park and spinning while his new friend tells him about smelling sunlight and indecision and laughter. He supposes this is the point.

The world slips by faster.

Brooklyn does not know when he started to increase his speed, but now the sights around him are nothing but flashes of scenery. Snapshots that appear between the stretches of blurred gray-and-blue patches. He is losing his sense of balance, so he digs his toes into the ground to give himself something on which to pivot without twisting an ankle.

Zinnia's laughing again, and while Brooklyn resists it for the first few seconds, he finds himself laughing with her soon enough.

Chapter Eleven

Brooklyn and Zinnia spin for a few moments longer before the absurdity gets to Brooklyn and he has to stop, though his toothy grin is still etched on his face. He realizes then—maybe too late and maybe too slowly—that he's never met anyone quite like Zinnia. She exists on a thin borderline between insanity and a creative fanaticism steeped in the culture of personal freedom. She thinks mainly in possibilities, and her honest nature gives her no options other than to explore them. He can't see how she'd ever been married to a man who muffled that enthusiasm.

Suddenly she's at his side, grabbing his arm and pulling him away. Reflexively Brooklyn starts to protest, but her grip is firm. When he comes to his senses, he goes along willingly.

"What is it?" he whispers, but she doesn't respond.

There's another access road a few yards away, at the end of which is a gate similar to the one they'd hopped to get in. Initially, Brooklyn believes he and Zinnia are making a break for the gate, but at the last second they dip behind a row of electrical boxes.

Brooklyn looks at Zinnia, who presses a finger to her lips. He hadn't noticed anyone coming, but she must have. She keeps the finger there, her grip still firm on his arm, and stares back at him. Behind the index finger against her mouth, she's struggling to suppress a giggle.

For a moment Brooklyn hears nothing but the breeze rustling tree branches and the water lapping ashore beyond the fence. But while his heart races and sweat beads on his upper lip despite the refreshing night air, a tremor of something spellbinding exists. His usual frustration and anger at being caught unawares has not come. Instead, he experiences something he can't help but enjoy. He feels excitement. He is without control here. He can only crouch next to Zinnia and listen to what the night filters through to them, but he is invigorated. Perhaps this is a side effect of being next to someone who radiates so much energy.

The sound of hard shoes on pavement, walking swiftly.

Someone has drawn level with the fence that separates the understructure of the coaster from where the guests are allowed to roam. Brooklyn knows who this is, can see the person in his mind's eye: stocky, dressed all in dark blue, a badge pinned to the front of a stiffly starched uniform. They probably carry with them a flashlight and a walkie-talkie.

"They know we're here," Brooklyn mouths, and even though it's not a question, Zinnia shakes her head. "They do! They have to, we were so loud!" He is drunk with this unfamiliar feeling and can begin to understand the addiction to it.

Neither Brooklyn nor Zinnia can look without risking being seen. So they remain crouched, listening to the faint creak of unoiled hinges as the investigator opens a gate in the wooden fence. It sounds like the groan of bending tree limbs. There are no footsteps. Have they been seen? Or is the guard just making their rounds? It takes all of Brooklyn's effort not to jump out now and start running or, at the very least, peek from his hiding place. He can hear his heartbeat drumming in his ears.

Light. The beam of a flashlight flickers in the space, illuminating an oblong patch of grass beside the access road. Brooklyn and Zinnia watch it sweep slowly back and forth. It crosses the grass, the loose pavement, and the faces of the trees. But as long as their visitor does not enter the enclosed area to peer behind the box, they will not see

Brooklyn and Zinnia. The beam from the flashlight sweeps over the control box, but it never pauses.

Brooklyn holds his breath and tries to remember the last time he was this tense and this excited. *You can't see us*, he thinks to the guard, as if maybe he can persuade them. *There's nobody here.*

Then the light switches off, and the sound of the gate closing penetrates the dark. The hard shoes *click, click, click* away, and then Brooklyn and Zinnia are in silence once again.

Zinnia lifts her arm, but this time she's counting down slowly with her fingers. *Five.*

Are they going back out into the clearing? Brooklyn can't tell.

Four.

Surely Zinnia doesn't mean to do anything truly insane. If she asks him to climb the ride, Brooklyn will draw the line.

Three.

Zinnia gets off her knees and crouches on the balls of her feet instead, getting ready to move. To run. Her voluminous hair bounces around her face.

Two.

The stubborn smell of drying sweat on his upper lip suffuses Brooklyn's nostrils. He prepares himself to move as well, watching Zinnia's eyes.

One.

Then they run, flying through the darkness like nocturnal creatures. Brooklyn follows Zinnia toward the gate, the untamable mass of her thick, curling hair billowing out behind her. The wind whips past his face, wrenching warm teardrops from the corners of his eyes.

Then they jump, gripping the gate's vertical metal bars and pulling themselves over. They land on the road with the streetlamps and the marina and the dancing sailboats, but Brooklyn and Zinnia don't stop there.

At first Brooklyn follows Zinnia, turning when she turns, stepping where she steps. He is always a few paces behind, following where she leads and keeping up as he can. But then he is even with her, and they run together.

Down the lane they fly: past the Blue Streak, past the parking lot. To Brooklyn's mild surprise—though he falls only slightly out of step—they don't turn toward the road leading back to the truck. Instead they continue straight, past the tollbooth where the cars line up in the morning. He doesn't even care if the security guard is still in the booth or not.

Though they are not being pursued, Brooklyn and Zinnia continue running into the night. Running until they are by themselves and even the land has dropped away, the road bordered on either side by the gently bobbing surface of the black water. The waves urge them on and give chase along the rocks.

Only when Brooklyn's heart feels like stopping, when the cold of the night has etched itself into the lines on his face, do they slow to a jog, coming up on the mainland where the soft lights of the town greet them. Brooklyn falls into step behind Zinnia beside a smaller marina, and she leads the way onto the strip of land meant to protect the marina from waves. Both of them are breathing hard now, their chests heaving and pulses pounding, but they break out into laughter in unison. Brooklyn collapses to the ground,

"Thank you," Zinnia says. "That was everything I had hoped for."

"Not a problem. I was just thinking to myself it's been a while since I broke and entered somewhere," he says facetiously between heavy breaths. "I'm good for a couple more years now. That was fun, though."

Zinnia sinks her fingers into her hair and deftly combs them through the curls. "All it ever needed to be."

"I thought for sure that guard was going to find us. I thought for sure they'd heard us carrying on beneath that ride."

"Well, if they did, they didn't put much effort into looking around. If it really nags at them, they'll probably see us on a camera somewhere."

Brooklyn shakes his head. "Then we're lucky they didn't care too much."

"Ah, well, we didn't do anything harmful." Her laugh is present, immediate—but then it peters out to somewhere distant. "I've never met someone like you, Brooklyn . . ." She raises her eyebrows at him. "Brooklyn . . ."

"Durant," he replies, realizing what she's waiting for.

"Brooklyn Durant." She curtseys. "You are pretty unique."

Brooklyn flinches. He was certain, *is* certain, that he's a fairly average human being. He lingers in the company of self-pity far too often and for too long. He has never done anything remarkable or bold. His life has meant something to a few people, but should he vanish . . . well, he has always concluded that most things would continue on as they had when he was around. Why shouldn't they? As for tonight, he only followed along with the plans she concocted. But when she says this simple statement to him—though he does not agree—an unwillingness to contradict her stops him from responding. Instead he silently takes his own self-judgment as fact, concluding she's wrong.

"Not many people would have done that with me," Zinnia continues. "In fact, nobody I knew before would have done that with me—let me tell you, because I am completely certain of that. I hope you understand what it meant."

Then, "Thank you."

Brooklyn props himself up by extending his arms behind him. The gravel sticks into his palms, cutting into his hands, but he doesn't mind. He stares out at the lake, vaguely seeing Cedar Point across the water in the darkness. When had they run so far? When had they put so much distance between themselves and the park?

Why are some words harder to find than others?

"Maybe I only did that because I was too timid to say no," Brooklyn says. He can feel Zinnia examining him, though when he looks at her she's still staring across the undulating water. The black mirror paints a night sky filled with distorted stars and barely-there clouds. The moving starscape is streaked by nebulae where the swells break. Zinnia has the universe above and below her.

"I don't think that's true," she says after a long moment of consideration. "I think that if you had really been against the idea, you would have said no."

Brooklyn stares down at his shoes.

Then—completely without warning—Zinnia reaches to her waist, grabs the end of the shirt and pullover she's wearing, and yanks them over her head.

In the pale orange glow of the marina lights, Brooklyn can see her exposed skin, which is smooth and dark but already rippling with goosebumps in the frigid air. "What the hell are you doing?"

"There's only one thing left to do," Zinnia says matter-of-factly, crouching down to undo the zippers on the sides of her boots. She slides them off and removes the white socks beneath and then her pants, all without any self-consciousness.

Embarrassed, Brooklyn turns his head to look the other way. He can't fathom what goes on in her mind. Zinnia doesn't seem to have the slightest problem stripping naked in front of someone who, only the day before, was a complete stranger—in a public place, no less. She has to be freezing.

"And what's that?" he asks. He hears a clasp slip open as the last of her garments go.

"It's a lake, Brooklyn," she says. "We've got to jump in."

Then he sees her run over the sparse grass, the sand, the dirt, and the tide-polished rocks. Once past the lamplight, her lithe figure is silhouetted by the moon and the reflections over the water's surface. She throws herself beneath the surface. The lake swallows Zinnia, encompassing her in the painting of stars. For a long moment she is gone from sight completely. Isn't she afraid? She can't know where the shore drops off, whether the ground is littered with broken glass, metal shards, or fishing wire. The water is as black as the sky, and just as unfathomable.

Zinnia surfaces again, calling out into the night with her unbridled enthusiasm. She's as crazy as he feared. A wildflower. And in spite of himself, Brooklyn smirks again.

"*Now* I have everything I want," she shouts back to him, running her hands through her hair. The curls have retained their volume.

"You're going to freeze to death in there!"

"You sound like a grandpa. Didn't you just break into the world's greatest theme park with me?"

"I was younger back then." Brooklyn brings his knees to his chest, hugging them with his arms. He is strangely awake given the hour. When was the last time he was out this late?

"You're as young as you feel."

"Yeah, yeah. 'Age is just a number.'" He struggles against the smirk, which is trying to widen its way into a smile.

"Mr. Durant, you're as sassy as my grandma was."

"All right, that's two remarks about my age. It's starting to get a little old."

Zinnia goes under again, and when she resurfaces she's a little closer to the shore. "I'm waiting for you to get in here, by the way," she says, lowering her voice to below a yell.

The statement hooks Brooklyn by the back of the navel and yanks sharply. He raises his eyebrows. "I'm not going in there."

Yet, in the true spirit of Zinnia, this response seems to have almost no effect whatsoever. She continues to tread in place, her arms carving a circle in the water around her. "It's our last step in the initiation, though!" she says, sounding like a pleading child.

Brooklyn shakes his head. "Our initiation into what?"

"The Adventurer's Club."

"Haven't we had enough adventure for one day?"

"No," she says without hesitation. "There's always room for more. Kind of like dessert."

"I don't think those are really the same thing."

"Yes, I suppose one is healthier than the other." She winks, her arms still carving those graceful arcs. The pale moon soars overhead, and its reflection swims with her.

"You couldn't pay me enough."

"It's just a lake," Zinnia says. She splashes some water at him, though it doesn't quite reach. "Just a little water."

Brooklyn shakes his head again, glancing around at all the dark windows in the buildings along the shoreline. He's sure that inside some of them—probably most of them—people sleep comfortably in their comfortable beds. Their comfortable blankets are pulled up under their chins, hiding what's most likely very comfortable sleepwear.

On any other night he would have been one of them. Had he not stopped to pick up Zinnia this morning—had it really only been this morning?—he would have found a hotel, said good night to Ollie, and tucked himself neatly away between white linen sheets. Under any other circumstances he would have treated this night like any other—routine and unremarkable, but comfortable.

This night had become anything but comfortable.

Brooklyn loosens the laces of his white tennis shoes, feeling the tight knots come undone in his fingers. He knows that Zinnia can see what he's doing, because she hasn't said a word; she instead watches him while she treads water. He pulls off the shoes, then the socks, and stands up.

"Well, you've got to get undressed first," she says.

Though the order sounds more like a suggestion, it's not one Brooklyn's about to take. "No," he replies. "Why would I do that?"

"Do you want your clothes to get wet?"

Brooklyn sniffs impatiently, then sighs. She's right. If he wants to jump in—and *wants* is a term only lightly applicable to the situation—he'd rather have dry clothes to get back into once he's out. *You're being positive*, he says to himself. *You are trying new things, you are adventuring. You want to do this.*

He unzips his sweater. The sound is incredibly loud and conspicuous. He folds it messily, not wanting to take too much time on any one task, and places it over his shoes and socks. Next is his T-shirt. The neck of the shirt goes over his head first, temporarily swallowing him in an opaque tent of solid color, and then the rest follows.

Already, he feels the cold digging its way under his skin. Gooseflesh ripples the hair on his arms. He wants to cower near the trunk of one of the low-hanging elms, to hide in a shadow.

"You're taking too long," Zinnia says, and splashes water at him again. "You're only making it worse. Peel the Band-Aid, and all that."

Brooklyn wishes she wasn't staring at him. He had given her the luxury of privacy, and she hadn't even asked. The added pressure of an audience is at odds with his modesty about his body.

His fingers linger at the belt. *Be more than you are.*

Before he can reconsider, Brooklyn unbuckles his black leather belt and undoes the button of his jeans. He slides them down past his knees, hairs already standing on end, and steps out of the legs with only minor difficulty. Then he's jogging to the water's edge, feet making muffled footfalls on the moist dirt. His heart pounds maybe harder than it had when they breached the top of the park fence only minutes ago. The dark world tips beneath his feet, and the tide rushes up to meet him.

The water is cold as ice. Brooklyn's feet are the first to enter, and his body tells him that he's in pain, but he has built far too much momentum to stop now. The water is somehow considerably colder than he imagined, but he rushes full speed into it, crying out in shock. He wants to throw himself back onto shore, back where it's still cold but manageable. Back where the rest of his clothes and comfort lie in a heap on the graveled ground.

But screaming helps. Yes, screaming eases the pain, the horrifying cold that bounds up his legs and grabs him by the hips and waist— soaking through his underwear, which he's left on—until it's over his navel. Before he knows it, the resistance against his legs trips him, and the world spins. Then he's crashing under the surface, his sense of direction vanished. He can't breathe, he can't scream. He kicks.

He breaks the surface.

Water rolls off his head and runs down his face, neck, and shoulders. It's so terribly cold; how can this lake not be frozen over? The static of churning and rushing water fills his ears. Only then does he realize that Zinnia is laughing beside him, whooping as she did when she ran into the lake on her own. For a moment he can't find her, his vision blurred from the submersion. He wipes at his eyes, and there she is, treading water only a few feet away.

"That was brilliant," she says. "One of the top five running belly flops I've ever seen."

"That good, huh?" Brooklyn means for the words to be sardonic, but the mental picture of his tremendous entrance prevents him from keeping a straight face.

"Yes. My one regret is that nobody else was around to see it. I am the sole witness."

"I'll have to thank my lucky star then." Brooklyn's teeth chatter loudly. "Can we get out now? It's freezing in here."

Zinnia pushes herself in a circle around him, using her arms and legs like squid tentacles. "You got to move around more. If you stay in one place like that, you'll be cold. But if you keep yourself moving, you don't feel it too much."

"I'm starting to think you're not human," Brooklyn says, watching her glide.

But in the water they stay. It's been a long time since Brooklyn last swam, long enough that he decides to stick slightly closer to shore than Zinnia. They move back and forth in the dark water, no more than reflections of stars themselves when the entire lake is taken into account. They let the ebb and flow carry their minds out of their bodies and into the body of water as they ride the bobbing surface like the boats in the marina.

When they decide to go back to shore, Zinnia emerges first, stepping lightly onto the land. The water catches the glow from the lights as it runs off her body, spilling from her skin. Brooklyn notices how tall and confident she stands. Again, he wonders how she could have ever been contained, even for a moment, by a single person.

Brooklyn stares past Zinnia, wishing he could ask her to look away as he gets out of the water, even if he isn't naked, but not wanting to draw attention to his timidity. While she uses her scarf to dry herself, he lumbers out onto the grass and quickly stoops to pick up his clothes. He doesn't have anything spare to dry himself off with besides his jacket, so he uses it to pat himself down before shoving his clothes back on. Despite this, he's still wet and shivering.

"We best get back to the car before we catch pneumonia," Zinnia suggests, and she moves toward the mainland. Brooklyn doesn't ask how she knows her way back to the Ranger. He follows silently, his clothes uncomfortably soggy and sticking to his skin. Their footsteps fall in time to an innate rhythm. He realizes for the first time this evening that he is tired and wants nothing more than to slip beneath the sheets of his cheap hotel bed.

Will Oleander be able to forgive me?

The thought materializes quick and harsh, coming from nowhere. Oleander has told Brooklyn multiple times that he's not there to stop Brooklyn from doing anything. But even so, Brooklyn can't shake the nagging guilt every time he leaves the man alone in there. When had he started forgetting to think about Ollie?

Brooklyn and Zinnia turn onto the road where they parked the Ranger. The lake is to their right again on this side of the peninsula. The square houses to the left are just as sleepy and undisturbed as before, sitting back from the pavement behind short fences, a house number lit here and there. Brooklyn wonders how long he and Zinnia have been walking. At least half an hour, if he's to judge. The rubbing of his damp clothes against his body is aggravating.

Finally, he makes out the shape of the Ranger parked where he left it. Brooklyn can't see the figure inside due to the darkness, but he knows Ollie is there, waiting like he always is.

"I was beginning to think maybe you guys had gotten lost," Oleander says when Brooklyn opens the door.

"We took a little detour," Zinnia responds, "after breaking into the theme park." She winks.

"After what?" Oleander asks, incredulous. "And are you soaking wet?" He's turned to Brooklyn, whose clothes—especially around his thighs and waist—are dark and waterlogged. Walking through the cool night has done little to dry them off.

"Yeah," Brooklyn says. "We jumped in the lake after running away from the park."

Oleander's eyes portray astonishment and confusion; he seems unable to piece together two events that, out of context—and perhaps even in context—seem ridiculous and arbitrary. Most of all, he looks at Brooklyn with a light gaze that suggests he doesn't quite know what to think of the man. "I didn't realize you were so wild," he says. The words are tinted with detectable reproach.

"I didn't either," says Brooklyn.

He puts the key in the ignition and turns it. For a long three seconds, the Ranger sputters but doesn't come to life. Brooklyn backs off, looking at the steering wheel and dashboard as if he might be able to see something wrong. He tries again, and the engine reluctantly sputters but doesn't roar to life as it normally would.

"It's broken?" Zinnia asks.

"It was fine before. It just—Hold on," Brooklyn mumbles to himself. Gripping the key firmly in his fingers, he tries again. The engine sputters as before. Just when Brooklyn's about to release, it ignites, and the satisfying turn of the motor rumbles through the cabin.

A barely audible sigh of relief escapes them all.

"Back to the motel?" Zinnia says, though the question is unnecessary.

"Back to the motel," Brooklyn confirms. They pull away from the curb.

Chapter Twelve

Morning light comes far too quickly. It seeps through the gap in the curtains and tiptoes across his bed. Before long Brooklyn has half a mind to get up, pull the curtains tighter, and go back to sleep. But as his eyes flutter open and he stares up at the ceiling, he decides to remain awake rather than chase the dreamless sleep he's left behind.

Brooklyn slides out of bed and traipses across the rose-colored carpet to the small bathroom. He'd thought about washing off the lake water last night before going to bed, but removing his sopping clothes and brushing his teeth had depleted all the energy he'd had. He barely remembers crawling under the covers. Now he lets the concentrated streams of hot water drum rhythmically on his scalp. Steam billows out into the room like fog. He shaves in the bathroom mirror, scraping away the dark, scraggly mass collected over the past few days.

After he's dressed, Brooklyn makes his way to the promised complimentary breakfast, a spread that consists of a few cereal dispensers with whole and two-percent milk and sliced bread beside a chrome toaster. He spreads his toast with packets of Smucker's grape jam. This mundaneness is satisfying. Then he walks back to his room, tracing the mint-and-peach floral designs on the wallpaper as he goes. Brooklyn is at peace this morning.

He stops short of his door and knocks on Zinnia's. There's nothing for a moment, then a flurry of movement. The door opens, and she peeks around it with a toothbrush shoved between her teeth.

"Hey," she says. The word is muffled by her mouthful.

"Just seeing if you were up yet."

"I'm up." She continues brushing her teeth. "I should be ready to go in fifteen."

Brooklyn nods and goes next door to his own room. Again, it doesn't take him long to gather the few things he's brought in with him. He slings his bag over his shoulder and drops the keycard off in the lobby before taking one more trip to the dining room.

"I brought you something," Brooklyn says, climbing into the cabin of the Ford Ranger. Frost covers each of the windows, but Ollie doesn't seem to mind. He's wrapped himself in a blanket Brooklyn kept in the bed of the truck. Brooklyn hands him buttered toast. "Sorry, they were already out of jam."

"It's all right," Ollie replies, taking a bite gratefully. "You didn't really need to get me anything, but thanks."

"Did you finish your book?" Brooklyn asks. He keeps the door open and sits sideways in his seat with his legs dangling outside. This way, he can still feel the crisp air washing over his skin while the sunlight shines directly on his face.

"Not quite. Almost," Ollie says between mouthfuls.

"And how is it?"

"Just as good as the first time."

"Do you want me to get you another? When you finish, I mean?" Brooklyn cranes his neck to look at Ollie, who's got only a quarter of the toast left. The blanket has been pushed to one side and lies crumpled on the floor. "I'm sure we'll run into another bookshop on the way."

"Maybe," Ollie responds vacantly. Perhaps Brooklyn's attempts to make up for what feels like abandonment—for yesterday's events, for leaving Oleander behind—are transparent. The corner of Ollie's mouth turns upward. "I'm fine with this book for now."

They listen to the faint sounds of the city: cars driving past on the road, the low chatter from a group of people exiting the lobby. Brooklyn watches. They're the remains of a party, perhaps family members who've gathered in Sandusky for a relative's wedding. How gratifying to know they've all made the trip; they're not from this area. One of the girls is wearing a sweater from the University of Cincinnati. She and two younger men trudge out of the building—hazy and not yet awake—into the morning light. The wedding festivities are clearly not over. The celebrated is perhaps a relative they seldom see, and so they've prolonged their stay in order to spend time together. This is what keeps them bound.

"Are you happy?" Brooklyn asks.

Ollie has folded the blanket and placed it back into the truck bed through the sliding window. The bluntness of the question brings him stumbling back. "What?"

"Are you happy?" Brooklyn repeats with precisely the same inflection.

"I don't think you really need to be concerned with whether or not I'm happy."

"But I am."

"I told you before, it's not really—"

"I don't care what you said before. I just want to know. Are you happy or not?" Brooklyn has turned completely in his seat so that he's facing Oleander.

"I . . ." Oleander struggles to hold his gaze. In the end, he gives in and instead stares at the back of Brooklyn's chair. "I'm with you, Brooklyn. I'm as happy as I can be."

Zinnia appears at the passenger door. The approximated fifteen minutes are over, but Brooklyn doesn't mind.

"Decided I wanted something to eat after all. I tell you, hunger hits before you see it coming," she says, wiping curls of hair out of her eyes. She slides into the seat and shuts the door behind her, dropping her bag at her feet. She's oblivious to the interrupted conversation, mumbling incoherently to herself as she gets situated. "Good morning, Ollie," she says, flashing a smile his way. Oleander returns it, but the expression seems reactive.

Brooklyn shuts his door and starts the truck. There is no hesitation from the engine this time. "To Illinois," he says, and they pull out of the parking lot.

In the light of day, Sandusky is a shade livelier. Steady trails of cars continue in all directions, though the sidewalks are all but bare. Brooklyn vaguely recognizes landmarks from their drive into town. Night had been setting and the city was lit differently. The way in which settings morph between day and night is a subtle magic that often slips by unacknowledged. Great stories are built upon the misunderstandings of nightfall. He had imagined suspicious eyes watching him and Zinnia last night, but in the light he can see that no one gives them a second thought.

The three travelers leave Sandusky in the rearview mirror. With the workweek underway, traffic on the highway is light at this midmorning hour. Today, the sun is reminiscent of a warmer season, though many trees have already almost completely exchanged their summer greens for melancholic hues.

While Ollie had been quiet during the drive back to the hotel last night, he now wants a full report. Zinnia paints the picture for him, her tone exuberant.

Brooklyn attempts to gauge Ollie's reactions through the rearview mirror. He looks for flickers of envy or malcontent—Ollie would never admit something so petty aloud—but either Ollie is more adept at hiding his frustrations than Brooklyn has thought him capable or he feels neither. He reacts to every bit of the story as one would expect. Only when Zinnia is done and the conversation peters out does he look out the window with a lost stare in his eyes and a lone, vague smile on his lips.

For a few minutes they listen to the hum of the vehicle and watch as I-90 slides by. While the individual miles seem to pass unchanging, subtle shifts in scenery transpire.

"My uncle had a truck like this," Zinnia says after a long pause, "I think a few years earlier than this model. Although I remember his was really cool because he had a CD player in the dashboard."

"Really? I didn't know they'd started putting CD players in cars that far back," Brooklyn says.

"Oh yeah. I'm pretty sure they became an option in the late eighties if you got one of the fancy versions." She raises an eyebrow. "It was top-of-the-line stuff. I think he loved that thing more than anyone. More than me or my sister. He never had any kids or a wife, but even if he had, I think he would have loved it more than any of them too."

"I'm guessing he's a car guy?"

"Through and through. He was always talking about it. Always going to 'do this' to the engine or 'spice her up' by changing some part in the suspension. He always kept it running nice, and we took to thinking about that truck like a member of the family.

"Recently I started thinking about why he didn't make a living off working on cars," she says, then shrugs. "I suppose he never did it because that would have changed the way he enjoyed those things."

"What do you mean?" Brooklyn asks.

"People always wonder why other people don't make their passions their living," she says. "What if it changes how you feel? You know? That's the difference between a job and a hobby: wanting to do it or having to do it."

"I feel like working at something you like would make a job more enjoyable," Brooklyn says.

"That's probably true most of the time," Zinnia says. "But maybe he might've felt it took away from the enjoyment—working on someone else's car other than his own, I mean. Either way, it baffles me too."

"Maybe you've got to be into cars to understand," Brooklyn jokes.

Zinnia laughs. "I've always found it funny how people can attach so much meaning to a car when it's not even alive."

"Well, that's just like any other personal object, isn't it?" Oleander says. "You give something a bunch of your time and energy, and it becomes a part of you. It *becomes* meaningful."

"Just like places," Brooklyn continues. "The memories you have there or the things they remind you of."

"Well, when you put it that way." Zinnia chuckles softly. "I've never understood people's obsessions with their cars, but I can't picture my uncle without his. And I suppose that's why I'm talking about it now."

"I'm guessing he had to get rid of it?" Ollie asks.

"He died, actually—No, no need to apologize. Really, it was a long time ago. Nobody in the family had any room for the truck. I wasn't old enough to drive yet, or I probably would've fought for it. So it was sold to an auction lot."

"You miss him?" Oleander doesn't really need to ask the question, but Brooklyn understands why he does. That's what Zinnia wants, why she's bothered to bring up her uncle in the first place. For her, he's with them in this truck, a living person whose vivid memory she carries. Enough that maybe she can feel things like the rough stubble of curling black hair on his chin and the deep thunder of his voice in her chest. Brooklyn senses strains of him building too. A burly man, a storyteller. No tale is off limits when he's around. If she wants to hear anything about her father and her uncle growing up, there's not a moment's hesitation. He'll tell her all she needs to know. Of course, the stories end with a moral. There never was a story that she couldn't learn something from. That was the truth. And if anyone told her otherwise, they hadn't figured out the lesson for themselves yet. Yep. He's here all right, going on about never letting a goddamn *moment* slip away, because how else is Zinnia going to exchange them for memories in the future if she hasn't experienced them in the first place? It no longer matters how many years ago it was when she last saw him. Her uncle's every bit alive. Brooklyn doesn't need to see him to believe it.

"I do," she says. "I miss him very much, and I still love him, but I'm not sad about his death anymore."

"No?" Brooklyn asks.

"Grief comes in waves, and those waves are strong at first," Zinnia says. "They knock you off your feet and drag you out to sea. Sometimes you feel as if you're never going to breathe again, as if you're never going to resurface. And that's terrifying. It makes you want to give up—at least, that's how it was for me.

"But at some point, you got to get on your feet again if you don't want to drown. You back away a little farther up the shore, not so far that you can't see the waves break or listen to the swell, but enough so the waves won't reach you anymore. Sometimes you stand a little too close. They get you again. So you back away a little farther. Eventually you find the sweet spot. The water can still get loud and threatening, and you think they're going to come for you again, but they don't.

"I think it's important to remember what you have, what you're capable of, and who you still have in your life. I anchored myself to the present, and that was how I found my way back."

"What about afterward?" Brooklyn asks.

"Afterward? After you find your way back? You move on."

Brooklyn is tempted to ask how long it took her to find this special place where the waves of grief don't reach her anymore. Instead he trains his eyes on the highway and drives onward.

They cross over into Indiana as the sun nears its peak, and stop briefly to get gas and sandwiches from a grocery store. Zinnia is tempted to visit her sister, but in the end she convinces Brooklyn that she doesn't want to, citing it as "an adventure for another time." The state flies past as a slideshow of road signs, on-ramps, and exits. Brooklyn, Ollie, and Zinnia argue over radio stations and sing along to songs—the latter carried out mostly by Zinnia, with ample help from Oleander in the backseat—and sometimes they sink into stretches of silence that are neither uncomfortable nor unnecessary.

Then they enter Illinois, and the conversation changes when Zinnia reads a name on one of the highway signs.

"Exit at Tinley Park," she says, then adds a "please" as an afterthought.

Brooklyn does what Zinnia asks, and the car slows for the first time in hours. Down along surface streets Zinnia leads them, though her usual confidence shows signs of cracking—it appears as though she's leading him based on memories that are not all too solid. They pass signs telling them they've entered a town called Orland Park. This encourages Zinnia, but doesn't make her memory of the place any better. More than once she asks Brooklyn to double back, taking them through side streets between rows of cookie-cutter homes.

When at last the novelty of the search begins to wane for Brooklyn and Oleander suggests they look for a map of the town, Zinnia tells Brooklyn to stop the car. She holds out a hand, peering over the dashboard as if afraid she might see somebody and will need to duck into hiding.

She rummages through her bag and produces a small but fat envelope, stamped and with an address scrawled across the front. She holds the envelope firmly in her fist as if afraid it might get away should she loosen her death grip. Although he cannot see the entire address, Brooklyn can make out the words *Orland Park*.

"I was going to wait and mail this when I'd gotten to my destination, but the temptation is too strong," she says. "This is where his parents moved—Jasper's, I mean. I wrote a letter to them because I wanted to let them know everything that happened between me and their son. They hate me. Always did. No matter what, I was always in the wrong. Their precious boy was simply enamored by my 'bohemian' ways."

She smirks. "My intention was for the letter to be snarky. Congratulate them, you know, for finally getting through to him. I had every expletive in the book crammed into one eight-and-a-half-by-eleven-inch piece of paper."

"I'm sure that'll be fun for them to read," Brooklyn says.

"It probably would've been." Zinnia softens. "I crumpled that one up and threw it in the trash last night."

"What? You did?" Ollie asks.

"I did." She sighs. "I realized that if I leave those words with them, then I will carry those words with me for the rest of my life. I will always remember where we left off, because it isn't closure. I wrote a new letter using the notepad in the motel room. It's more of an epitaph for our marriage. I explained to them why they were wrong about me. I explained to them why I've forgiven them, though."

"You're not going to assault them now, are you?" Brooklyn asks.

Zinnia looks at him with dark humor, as if contemplating the idea. "No," she says finally. "I'm going to leave it on their doorstep and ring the bell. I want to watch them pick it up, to have the satisfaction of seeing it in their hands and knowing they're going to read it. That's all."

Brooklyn doesn't know whether or not to believe her, but he doesn't move as she opens her door. Through the windshield he and Oleander watch her walk up the block. She enters a garden through its wrought-iron gate and traipses up the path before stooping to place the letter on the porch.

For a moment Zinnia hesitates, her finger hovering in front of the doorbell. But then she presses it and retraces her steps unhurriedly to where the red truck is parked.

"Let's go," she says, pulling herself into the passenger seat.

"I thought you wanted to see them grab it," Oleander says.

"I've changed my mind again," she replies, buckling her belt. "They'll find it, and they'll read it. I don't have to see them to know that." She leans against the door's armrest, staring purposefully outside as Brooklyn turns the car around and heads back the way they came.

Chapter Thirteen

Brooklyn, Ollie, and Zinnia continue the drive in a silence impregnated with finality. Brooklyn ponders the events of the last twenty-four hours—he can scarcely believe it's only been that long—and wonders if they could have all been part of a dream. Perhaps the product of imagination, cruelly constructed to give him the false sense that he's someone who can be bold.

At the same time, the events must be real. Zinnia is sitting beside him, and she is proof. Yet now they are hurtling toward the place where she intends to separate from Brooklyn and Ollie. She has every right to leave them, of course, but the thought is somewhat frightening.

Brooklyn wonders whether he'll revert to the man who departed Schoharie almost three days ago. A voice somewhere inside him surmises that this isn't altogether a bad outcome. He has had his dose of adventure, and now he must continue forward. But which way is forward?

Maybe he has already begun to regress.

Brooklyn doesn't want Zinnia to leave. Despite his initial reluctance to help her, he can't overlook the excitement she's brought to his journey. A spark of hope flickers inside him, and he dares to entertain the idea that maybe she'll want to continue with him, even if just for a few more miles or one more state. He has so far to go, and she's reminded him of how it feels to make friends.

As if she knows what he's thinking, Zinnia gives Brooklyn a brief, sad smile and gestures toward the next exit. Without a word in protest, he complies. They enter the surface streets of another town. The sign says JOLIET.

"So what does this one mean to you?" Oleander asks, leaning forward through the space between Zinnia and Brooklyn.

She runs a hand through her thick curls, pulling on loose strands. They spring back into place when she lets go. "You know, this one doesn't mean anything. I've never been here before."

Brooklyn glances sideways at her. "Honestly?"

"Honestly," she says, and he believes her. "That was kind of the point. When I set out from my old place and got in that car, I picked a little spot on the map that I'd never heard of. That's where I wanted to be. That's where I would start over. And here I am."

"Are you sure that's what you want to do? You don't have any friends around here? Any family?" Oleander asks.

"Nope, I don't know a single soul." She winks at him. "But that's what makes it exciting. It's going to be an awfully big adventure."

"What are you going to do, though?" Brooklyn understands her words, but he can't wrap his mind around them.

"I don't know."

"Where are you going to live?" Ollie asks.

She laughs her deep, mirthful laugh. "I don't know that either."

"And you want me to just leave you here?" Brooklyn asks.

"You both are chock full of questions all of a sudden, aren't you?" Zinnia sits back in the seat for a moment, looks around, and gestures for him to make a turn down a random street. "I *want* to be left here. *I* want you to drop me off and go on your way. But it's up to *you* to decide what you want to do then. Just know that I'm not afraid. Sure as hell nobody is making me do this. This is what I need. I've got some money, so I won't be homeless—at least not for a while. By then, I'm sure I'll have figured something out."

Then, "Stop here."

Brooklyn pulls up next to a small square park shaded by wide elm trees. At the center is a grassy hill, which rises from the street in the smooth curve of a perfect bell. A single bench sits at the top, staring away from them down a street on the other side. Suddenly, Zinnia is saying goodbye to Ollie and stepping out of the car with her bag.

Brooklyn checks quickly that no cars are coming and then gets out onto the street. He runs around to the back of the truck. "Don't forget your other bag," he says, meeting Zinnia at the hatch.

She smiles warmly. "I'm not gonna," she says. "These are pretty much all the things I've got left."

He opens the hatch, and she reaches in to grab her other bag. She gently sets both of them down on the curb and throws her arms around Brooklyn in a tight embrace. Unprepared, he feels his breath being forced from his lungs.

"Thank you." Zinnia shows no signs of letting go, so Brooklyn hugs her back, wrapping his arms around her, his face half buried in her tresses. She smells faintly floral. "Thank you so much."

"Are you sure about this?" Brooklyn asks one more time.

Zinnia looks out at the park, empty save for a few bugs hovering here and there, then back at him. "I think I'm going to be okay."

"All right," Brooklyn responds, and this time he believes her.

"You take care of yourself too now," she says. Her concern for him is stronger than her concern for herself, Brooklyn realizes. "I hope you make it to where you're going."

"So do I."

Zinnia stoops to pick up her bags, gathering one in each hand. They look lighter now than they had before, but maybe this is an illusion.

She mounts the path up to the bench, and Brooklyn now notices the brilliant flowers lining the perimeter of the park. They huddle along the edge of the grass in the shade of the elm trees, their colors popping vibrantly against the green: fluorescent shades of pink and purple, yellow, orange, and deep red. Though Zinnia has not looked back, the flowers sway as if waving goodbye for her, gentle and elegant in their passionate hues.

Brooklyn doesn't want to move. He stands behind the truck, with one hand still on the knob for the hatch and the other hanging loosely at his side. He feels bereaved but light at the same time with the understanding that though Zinnia had to leave him behind, they have both been better for their brief encounter. She'll be fine. He is certain of this, for she said so herself. He will do his best to be fine as well.

Brooklyn returns silently to his seat.

"I miss her already," Oleander says.

Brooklyn only nods. He can see her through the window, sitting by herself on the bench at the top of the hill. He wonders how long she'll remain there. Will it be for a few seconds more? Perhaps an entire day. He can't know for certain. What he does feel to be true is that should he ever come back to this very spot—be it decades, or a day, or just a few seconds later—she'll be gone, and he'll never see her again.

Brooklyn starts the car, never taking his eyes off her. Her rounded shoulders stick up above the bench made with slats of golden pine, her bags are barely visible beneath the seat, and her hair—a mass of innumerable curls—bobs freely about her.

Chapter Fourteen

Time moves for Brooklyn like a pendulum. Not like the pendulum in a clock, which denotes passing seconds with precisely timed tocks of its meticulous swings. No, it's the variance of speed that likens the two: the increase in velocity through the curve of their valleys only to come to rest for the briefest of instances when all their kinetic energy has become potential.

For Brooklyn, his time with Zinnia was one of the swift valleys. The hours glided by unencumbered, blurring together in a mesh of inseparable moments, each one the key to understanding the next. He can't relive one moment without another crashing through, demanding to be seen with enthusiasm. The images are vibrant, their colors dynamic. He hopes to hold on to these memories forever. He hopes they don't fade with time.

He now regrets not trusting her right away. His reluctance to join her each time she asked him to exchange premeditation for spontaneity. Of course, his nature is to be more neurotic than adventurous, but the desire to be otherwise both delights and infuriates him. He imagines himself springing from the ground like a wildflower wherever he pleases, able to enjoy the world for nothing more than the sun and the wind. But he knows he cannot be this person. Now that he's had a glimpse of what it's like to be adventurous, the regression that follows is terrifying.

Out of the swift valley of the swing, Brooklyn teeters on the edge of what could be, but the pendulum is losing momentum and coming to a stop. Time crawls like the hazy mountains along the horizon. If he watches closely, he can see them moving relative to himself, but at a glance they are immobile.

He and Oleander drive for almost an hour before speaking.

"She's going to be all right," Oleander says suddenly.

"I don't doubt that," Brooklyn replies. "I'm not worried."

"But you're unhappy now that she's gone?"

"Not unhappy," Brooklyn says, which is partly true. He reminds himself to keep his eyes focused on the road instead of drifting off to watch objects in the distance.

"But you wish she was still here?"

"She was fun."

"I thought so too."

"She was unexpected. I didn't think I'd be around anybody but you the entire time." Brooklyn immediately wonders if Oleander will misconstrue his words. He didn't mean to be insulting. "Sorry, that came out bad."

Sparse clusters of farm buildings peek out from the landscape, while tall crops do their best to hide them from sight. Brooklyn can just see the tin roof of a large barn peering over the stalks.

"Do you wish there was someone else here?"

The question makes Brooklyn's heart sink into his chest, and there it aches. He wants to clutch at the area, to knead the spot above his heart—God, it hurts him—but he doesn't want to draw Oleander's attention to his discomfort. Brooklyn couldn't make eye contact now if he tried.

"Don't say that. I didn't—"

"I'm serious, Brooklyn. I know how limited I am. I just want to know, would having other people here make this easier for you?"

Cars float past on the narrow highway, going in the same direction, though Brooklyn is traveling well above the posted speed limit. He watches them come, appearing close enough to reach through the window, then move slowly farther and farther away.

"No," Brooklyn says. "I don't think anyone would make it easier. Zinnia was different—a surprise, but a welcome change. She wasn't like most people, though." He thinks of all the strangers he has met in passing: the people who sneer and cheat, who give little concern to the world around them. He thinks of the people he's left behind who he'll have to see again when he returns: the ones who talk behind his back, decide what's best for him and what's wrong with him, and discuss why he is distant. The ones who feign concern when they are in front of him, who paint comically overdrawn emotions on their faces when they tell him what he did wrong and what he could have done better, though they assure him it wasn't his fault. He sees these people and thinks, *Why do I hate everyone I meet?*

But how can he not? Zinnia was the anomaly, the exception and not the rule. An old flash of anger comes swift and unprovoked, burning red and hot. But he tamps it down when he realizes that his knuckles are white on the steering wheel.

"You're here with me. That's all I need," Brooklyn says. The words are familiar, calming.

Oleander holds his tongue as if he doesn't believe Brooklyn's sentiment. Should he? Brooklyn has proven adept at convincing himself of the things he wants to believe. The pain in his chest flares in bright throbs that feed the lump growing in his throat.

Garnet shutters. Sheer curtains. A leaning garden shed. Evergreen shrubs blossoming in the yard. Puce flowers opening wide and tacit, with five petals apiece. Brooklyn counted them diligently because it was better to busy his mind doing this than to think about missing someone. Better than cooking meals he'll eat alone at the counter. When the planes passed overhead, he would look up and wonder if Oleander was on board, coming home. Coming back to him. He wondered.

Oleander is with him now. Brooklyn doesn't have to wonder anymore.

"Do you ever think about the people in all these cars passing by?" Oleander asks. "Do you think any of them are doing the same thing you're doing?"

Faces talking. Faces unanimated. Content. Stressed. Far away. "You mean driving across the country?" Brooklyn asks.

"Yeah, you know. Out to change something about their life."

"I think most of them are driving home from work." Brooklyn's answer is sardonic, so he tries a smile. "That, or they're out getting groceries."

"This'd be a far way to travel to get some milk. I don't think we've passed a city since Atkinson." Ollie shakes his head. "You know what I mean."

"Yeah, yeah. I know what you mean."

"But you don't think so?"

Brooklyn shrugs ever so slightly and changes the radio station. The symphonic music switches back to classic rock. "There are probably people traveling," he says, tapping his fingers to a CCR song. "But no, I don't think anyone's doing the same thing I am."

The sign says DAVENPORT.

Brooklyn pulls off the freeway after crossing the Mississippi River into Iowa. The streets are more crowded here, but he's in the realm of the unknown now. He hadn't researched any stops this far from Schoharie, uncertain whether he would make it this long.

With some difficulty Brooklyn and Oleander navigate the streets, searching for potential places to stay the night. Although Davenport seems to be populated enough, it becomes clear that the city is not a strong draw for tourists. Instead it's dominated by a suburban atmosphere. Grids of residential streets fill the land between huddled convenience stores. Brooklyn pulls into one of these plazas to stop at a market. He doesn't feel like eating in a restaurant alone tonight.

Instead he gets a random assortment of foods that don't require cooking.

Then he doubles back, driving alongside the Mississippi River while the remaining sunlight gleams off the water. He finds a cheap chain motel with a lit neon vacancy sign—though it's missing its second *c*—tucked behind a pair of tennis courts and a liquor store.

That night he climbs into the backseat of the Ranger and unfolds the jump seat across from Ollie. They eat the food together, their knees forming a table. Brooklyn doesn't mind the small talk or silly antics, allowing them instead to ease the pain in his heart and relieve the tension in his lungs. They dine on deli meat and cheese, ripping handfuls of bread from a soft roll that tastes surprisingly fresh for having come from a sealed plastic package. He and Ollie share cherry soda from a glass bottle, which Brooklyn removes with care from the sack. As they eat, they melt slowly from a rigid, measured casualness into a tender state of open contentment, a state where Brooklyn is comfortable pointing intimately to the breadcrumbs on the side of Ollie's mouth without second thought.

When at long last they've had their fill and the lights have all come on, Brooklyn takes the paper sack and his duffel bag and heads inside the motel room.

The thin navy-blue carpet exudes the sour stench of nicotine like the vapor from the factory smokestacks across the street. The walls are the pinched yellow of coffee-stained teeth, and half of the light fixture above the sink doesn't work. Still, it is only for one night.

Brooklyn closes the door, and for a few moments he's unable to keep standing on his own and must lean back against the wood for support. Then he reaches over to shut the heavy curtain. He doesn't want to see the truck parked just beyond the latched door. He doesn't want to think that maybe Ollie can see inside this room.

Gingerly, he takes the remaining groceries out of the paper bag and places them on the small table in the corner. He throws his bag of clothes beneath the table, then sits on the bed, turning the television remote over absentmindedly in his palms. He wishes he could hear the

Mississippi River from the room, but he's too far away now, and the mini refrigerator vibrates loudly. After listening to it cycle three or four times, he jabs the power button on the remote and lets the television play.

How does he sink so quickly? Only minutes ago, he was laughing and eating French bread and cheddar with Oleander. Now Brooklyn contemplates his sudden loneliness while his eyes dart back and forth between the muted colors on the screen and the Four Roses Bourbon sitting on the tabletop.

Brooklyn can almost smell it. The aroma seeps into the room beneath the cigarette odor, deceptively sweet with wisps of caramel and vanilla. The man on the television says that Brooklyn needs the four-piece gold-leaf portrait framing set, but he's wrong. That's not what Brooklyn needs.

No. He's a traveler. A man marked with a vexation he is ill equipped to resolve, a thirst that goes beyond mere drink, hollowing the marrow from his bones and siphoning the air from his lungs. Like the stench in the room, his Need lingers on his skin.

He's filled with this poltergeist, which has no other name. He alone can see it. When he closes his eyes, the seductive creature is there. It looks like indigo damask wallpaper and rosette molding on the doorframe. It's like light through the sheer curtain. It looks like dark hardwood floors curling up at the seams, swollen by the seasons.

Brooklyn doesn't recall opening the bottle or taking a drink. The only evidence of what he's done is the sweet-and-spicy finish on the tip of his tongue and the spreading warmth in his chest. But he doesn't remember the drink, so he takes another mouthful. The sound of the amber liquid splashing in the bottle only intensifies his thirst. If he cannot quench the images from his mind permanently, the least he can do is purge them for the night.

He drinks until the edges of his poltergeist are not so serrated. The smell of cigarettes is gone and replaced instead by sucrose and vanilla. Ripe. *So very ripe.* Waiting to be plucked from its chaste trappings and handed over to the senses. Oh, how he misses it. The warmth of it on his tongue. He'd run his fingers over it when the kisses were gone. They were sweet kisses, weren't they? They electrified his lips—transformed from pale, thin lines to full red curves. Flower petals. That's what they became. He misses it in his hands, the feel of glass on his fingers.

He also misses the way his palms conformed to warm skin, as smooth as only a god can make, filling his hand when he curled his fingers. The way it held him too. A strength from reciprocity and symbiosis. The way that skin needed him as nothing else did; it erects the hairs on his arms. He misses interlacing fingers pressed into the mattress. Filling the tight spaces with desire, so much *desire*. How he'd grind his hips to the beat of their hearts, sliding against the body beneath him. Enveloped by that body, *pulled in* by that body. The gasping against the quiet night as he drove himself deeper into pleasure. His sex swollen with lust. And he would lean forward. "Ollie," he breathes, "*Oleander.*" His hands hold desperately to Ollie's hips, thumbs against the small of his back. Heartbeats quicken and so does he, a feverish pace no longer beholden to rhythm. The edge comes rising to meet him. Tension building, building, building . . .

He misses reaching out at night and finding Ollie there.

Reaching out . . .

Brooklyn opens his eyes. There is no one beneath him, only a tan duvet. The heat in his chest freezes to an icy numbness. How foolish he feels now, sitting back on his heels while his fingers slide needlessly over the empty bed and his erection turns reluctantly flaccid. His Need, the poltergeist, has won this night.

Brooklyn swipes the bottle from the nightstand and places it back on the table. But as he turns away, he hears a soft thud followed by the chortle of liquid. In confusion that gives way to anger and frustration, he spins back in time to see the bottle on its side in the duffel, liquid pouring from the open neck into his bag of clothes. The cap, which had not been properly fastened, has been flung off.

With a string of incoherent curses, Brooklyn snatches the bottle and yanks it out of the mess of contaminated clothing. He slams it on the tabletop, feeling betrayed and berating himself. He grabs the cap from the carpet, screws it on correctly this time, and sinks to crouch beside his bag with a defeated grunt.

Not everything has been touched, but the bourbon has wet most of his clothes. Already they smell like ethanol and sickly-sweet flavors. He wipes at the dark patches of wetness, but the damage is done. He can only hope they won't smell so strongly in the morning.

The aggravation sobers Brooklyn enough that he drags himself to the washbasin to brush his teeth, wanting to rid his mouth of the taste of alcohol. Toothpaste forces the taste of mint on him, but it's a drawn-out battle that Brooklyn has the misfortune of enduring. While he brushes, he sits back against the counter, staring listlessly at the duffel bag.

Then he slides himself into bed. The bedside lamp flickers out when he turns the switch, and the room is plunged into a darkness interrupted only by the glowing numbers on the digital clock.

Brooklyn is wondering whether he will fall asleep tonight when sleep enters through the window unnoticed and carries him away in its arms.

Chapter Fifteen

Images of dark ocean waves dissolve when Brooklyn awakens. He stretches stiffly beneath the covers before rubbing his eyes with the palms of his hands. This morning, more than ever, he wonders if this is all worthwhile. Whether he shouldn't just turn around and hightail it back home. Remaining who he is would be much easier than braving the effort to better himself.

In the end, he rolls out of bed and ambles over to the shower, not waiting for the water to heat up before plunging himself beneath the icy streams. The result is painful, but he feels this soft form of self-flagellation is deserved after his weakness the night before. Today, he'll need to stop somewhere to wash his clothes. Had he been thinking more clearly—more soberly—last night, he would have set aside the clothes that hadn't gotten drenched so they wouldn't sit all night in the bag with the reeking items. But he didn't, and now everything smells at least faintly of bourbon.

Oleander is waiting in the backseat with the blanket over him again. He seems chipper, greeting Brooklyn with a "good morning" that climbs down from the crinkles around his eyes.

"I don't know about you," Brooklyn says, cracking his back before climbing into the Ranger, "but I think I need to stay at some classier places."

Oleander laughs. "Well, you'll need to pay up then."

"Eh, who needs to turn their neck anyway," Brooklyn replies with a shrug. His sour mood is only thinly masked by sarcasm.

Iowa's sky is cloudy—not completely overcast, but enough that patches of shadow often cross the apple-red hood of the truck. As he has for the past three days, Brooklyn follows the road absentmindedly. The world unfolds before him and falls away behind him.

Despite Oleander's positive demeanor, Brooklyn withdraws into himself. Images that had sprung forth and burned into his mind last night, both the familiar and those so close to being forgotten, cling to his consciousness. Lost details somehow restore themselves, though he can't understand how. They refuse to leave.

Wide, grassy lands pass him by again, interrupted only by occasional clusters of buildings and highway overpasses. The drive is monotonous today. Tall bronze stalks bend to other tall bronze stalks. To the other drivers they probably appear as nothing more than overgrown fields. Brooklyn knows better. He knows they urge him forward. He must keep going. There is something for him at the end of the road. There is reason in perseverance, and he should not let his moments of solitary drunkenness dissuade him.

He thinks it odd that he has not heard a peep out of Oleander in the last couple of hours, but then he sees that the other man has taken to reading his book again. He must be close to done.

The sign says DES MOINES.

Thinking this as good a place to stop as any, Brooklyn pulls off the highway behind a two-seater with fuzzy dice hanging in the windshield.

"Des Moines," Ollie says. "This is the first big city you've stopped in. I was hoping there'd be more. Are you planning to stay a while?"

"I hadn't really thought about it," Brooklyn says. He has little interest left in large cities. They'd once seemed alluring, intriguing, even beautiful. But his attraction waned as he got older. None of this amounts to dislike or disdain, just indifference.

The light turns green. "I wasn't planning on doing much here," Brooklyn says, "just some laundry."

"Already? It's day four," Ollie says. "Did you forget to pack?"

"Well, aren't you sassy today."

"I have my moments."

"It's the bread and cheese from last night, isn't it?"

"They do say the way to win a man's heart is to give him gluten-based baked goods and dairy products."

"You're weird, you know that?" Brooklyn pulls into a gas station.

"That's why you love me."

The Ranger takes regular 87-octane gasoline. Brooklyn's gaze wanders while the tank fills, though he's careful not to make eye contact with any of the other patrons. An old man trundles into the attached store to pay with cash, money in hand. A mother cleans her Sequoia's front windshield while her car seat–bound daughter watches from inside.

Across the street a group of boys huddle over trading cards, possibly of baseball players, if kids are still into collecting those. They're young enough that their mothers still dress them, evident from the appropriate length of their jeans and their tucked shirts. The lack of jackets suggests that their mommies don't know where they are, though. That's right, they should be in school. They probably said they were going to walk to class with a friend. They probably live within a couple blocks of each other. Obviously, the boys decided to come here instead, to the corner by the gas station and liquor store. Brooklyn imagines they like to stare at their trading cards here because it makes them feel older. After all, this is where the bigger boys hang out. The ones with baseball caps on and cigarettes dangling from their lips . . .

The pump stops. The machine spits out his receipt, and he rips it off cleanly.

~

The large interior space of Jardin Coin-Op Laundromat smells of tap water and cleaning products. The sterile white linoleum floor is lined with rows of identical machines either sitting idle or vibrating with a persistent hum. The washers are to the right, and the dryers to the left. Here and there people linger by their clothes, either reading books and magazines or staring distracted into the distance as they talk into their phones.

He walks down the aisle beside the right-hand wall, sliding past a man sitting on a chair reading in the middle of the path. The man takes no notice of Brooklyn, makes no indication that he will move to let him by, so Brooklyn does his best not to bump the stranger. As he walks back, he recognizes the book cover: *The Bell Jar*.

Brooklyn washes his clothes. He stares down at the linoleum tiles with his hands hanging limply between his knees as he waits. He doesn't think of much, and when the buzzer signals that his clothes are washed, he can't remember having had any coherent thoughts. But this is no surprise; it's happened before, especially over the past couple of years. In some circumstances, drifting is almost better than having to experience every empty minute.

Brooklyn wants to pick the last dryer, the one in the back corner, but unfortunately it's occupied and rattling when he arrives. He skips one and jumps to the next, pushing his soggy mass of shirts and pants into the drum. Before starting the cycle, he runs back to gather the few socks he's dropped. He can't watch the dryer spinning, because it has no window. So he stares instead at the scuffed white paint on the machine's door.

"You must have a massive attention span if you're going to sit there staring like that, love. Damn thing takes near an hour and a half." A stout woman with short, curly gray hair and a conspicuous accent that could be British but isn't comes down the aisle. Over twill pants—the deepest shade of brown imaginable without being black—she has on a burgundy sweater that hugs her likable form in a way that can only be described as comfortable. A tartan scarf loops loosely around her neck. She gives him an airy but warm smile and brushes past him to the place beside the corner machine. "Take it from me, it's why I always bring my stories. You want one?"

She gestures to a pile of tabloids on the table between their row of dryers and the next. Brooklyn can just make out a headline on an issue a couple down from the top, *LOVE CHILD SCANDAL REVEALED!*, but he barely has time to shake his head before she speaks again.

"Of course, Carl never approved . . . s'why I started bringing them here, so he wouldn't see. Messes, all of 'em. I know they may be a load of shite, but you never know, some of them could be true. Entertaining anyway, isn't it?"

Brooklyn is at a loss for what to say. He laughs instead, feeling the need to respond somehow.

"Anyway, thought I had a bit more left of these than I did. Slipped my mind how far I'd read last Tuesday, but can you believe the bloke at the stand—the Shell over there—says they haven't got any new ones. They come out every week, don't they? But he's telling me the ones at the register are the only ones they've got and, well, I've already got those." She gestures with every word, obviously distressed by the event.

Brooklyn watches her with what he realizes must be a vacant expression and quickly changes it to something he hopes looks a little more intelligent.

"Evidently, weekly doesn't mean seven days, even if it has the past hundred years." The woman throws her palms up and gives a disbelieving snort. "Tosser probably thinks I'm a loon, but I know which issues I've already got on me personage—shook the cover in his face to show him! So, anyway, what do you do?"

Brooklyn stumbles at the sudden question. "I—Nothing. I—I'm an author."

"Ooh." The old woman ruffles her feathers. "I could've known—moody and mysterious and such. Sittin' here probably thinking about your next bestseller, wasn't you? And I come barging in talking about my trash." She chortles at the thought. "That's how my friend Caroline was, too—a writer, I mean. Anything gaudy I might've read?"

"No, no, probably not. I was more of the . . . uh, subtle drama type. Realistic fiction, you know?"

"*Drama*." She pronounces an *r* at the end. "Any romances? I absolutely adore romances."

"Some romantic aspects, I guess. I wouldn't have called them romances though." Brooklyn shrugs. "It was more an aspect than the driving force behind the stories."

"Well, isn't that fantastic!" She clasps her hands, and her eyes crinkle with a smile as if he meant the exact opposite of what he just said. "You must be lovely, then. And what brings you here, Mr. Writer? I don't think I've ever seen you out and about, so I'm guessing you don't come to this fine establishment much."

Brooklyn debates what he should and shouldn't tell her, wary of any further probing. Before he's come to a conclusion, however, he hears himself giving her an answer. "I'm traveling. Driving across the country."

"Oh." The woman's brow shoots up toward her hairline. Her eyes are a dark slate color. The dryer with her clothes in it stops vibrating and emits a high-pitched series of beeps. She ignores it. "Isn't that just lovely. It's a wide country, this. You start from the east coast?"

"Well, yes. I started from New York. That's where I lived."

"And to every state?"

"No, just—just a line across, pretty much." Brooklyn laughs, scratching the back of his head. "Just trying to get to the other side."

"Like the chicken, eh?" The woman gives him a wink, then turns away to start taking out her clothes. Expertly she gathers the entire load in her arms, pressing it against her bosom. The clothes pile up over her eyes, but she doesn't drop a single item.

"Carl was always wanting to do things of that sort," she says. "Traveling here and there, jumpin' around and whatnot. It was me who needed convincing. Wasn't practical, see, though it did always sound like fun. But it was hard for him to get this old bitch moving, even when I was a young thing like you. It was hard enough to get me to come out here after we got married—that was a real struggle. Poor Carl. Bless him."

She folds her clothes with quick precision, talking all the while as if her actions don't require any concentration whatsoever.

While Brooklyn had initially crossed his arms and faced his dryer pointedly, he now finds himself leaning against the table and looking at her, drawn into her presence: her amicable demeanor, casual mannerisms, even the rambling way in which she talks. "Where did you end up going?" he asks.

"Bless you too—we never did, love." She lets her hands drop and looks at him, shaking her head with only a trace of melancholia in her smile. "I mean, we went places. Vacations here or there to see family, especially to see my niece once she had Jimmy, my godson. He's a Boy Scout now, you know, top notch, going to be an Eagle in a few years I bet—especially at the rate he's going, 'cause he's smart as a whip, that one. Got some presents in the car for him when I see him next. Heart of gold too. Real handsome lad. Must get it from my side, eh? Anyway, yes, we ventured out here and there, but never the kind of trips Carl wanted to take. No, those were 'too dangerous' or 'too unprepared' for me. And I didn't much like flying. I mean, I still don't, but that was always my go-to response. Nancy up the street always agreed with me, of course, which probably didn't help the matter much. 'Miles in the sky in a tin can? No, ma'am, don't do it, Dahl,' she'd say. She had children though, that was her excuse. But when I say I was an old bitch about it, I mean I was a right hag.

"Ah, and then life passes you by." She finishes the last fold and places her neat stacks—somehow the clothes have been reduced in volume at least threefold—into the white tote bag she's had hidden under the table. She's quiet for a moment but then lets out a cackle that's louder than the running machinery. "Look at me, getting all sappy and yammering on." She reaches out and playfully hits Brooklyn on the arm, with a wink for good measure. "Don't be afraid to shut me up if I'm going to start talking like that, boyo. I'm afraid I'm not as interesting as I think. Why's it you said you were taking the drive, then? Researching for a book, are we?"

"No, nothing like that. Just, uh, needing to clear my head of some things. Get it back on straight." Brooklyn shrugs again, and this time the woman shrugs too, mocking him just a little bit.

"We could all use a bit of that every now and then, couldn't we." She zips up the bag and puts the strap over her shoulder. Then she gathers the magazines in a stack and rolls them up in one hand. "I shan't take a moment more of your time, love." She smiles and nods in gratitude for his company. "I hope the rest of your trip goes well. You sure you don't want to keep one of these?"

Brooklyn shakes his head. He wants to ask her what her name is, but his mouth is slow to respond. By the time he finds the words, she's already past the end of the aisle and headed for the door. The bright light through the front windows silhouettes her short-statured figure. After the last signs of the old woman have disappeared, Brooklyn sits in silence, leaning against the table until his clothes have finished drying. The time seems more cavernous and empty than before. He even looks around once, wondering why there aren't any other conversations happening. None of the other laundromat patrons make eye contact with him.

The dryer signals the end of its cycle. Brooklyn opens the door, takes out the duffel bag first, and unceremoniously shoves his clothes inside. Though not everything had been doused by the spill, he'd thrown it all in as a single load.

He leaves. The red truck immediately draws his eye from across the parking lot. The billowing clouds roll over its windows. He can see dirt building on the undercarriage where the tires spray. A short scratch is etched down the back of the right side, but it's so old he cannot remember when it appeared or how it got there. He vaguely remembers someone giving him a lecture on resale value when it happened— probably Adam—but he can't imagine ever trying to sell or get rid of it. Not while it is his truck. Not even if it stops working.

"Excuse me!"

At first Brooklyn doesn't register that she's calling to him. He keeps walking, staring with a vacant expression at the apple-red truck three spaces away.

"Excuse me!" Brooklyn slows and turns, surprised to see the old woman from inside the laundromat again.

"Ah, hell," she gasps, putting a hand to her chest to calm herself.

Brooklyn, who has had little experience with older folk, panics slightly and wonders if he needs to call someone. "Are you all right?"

She waves away his concern with her other hand. "Just old and fat, love." She takes another moment to regain herself. "It would seem that my beloved car has died. Fifty-some-odd years together, and it finally gave out. Poor timing, eh?"

"That's terrible. I'm so sorry."

"S'all right. The thing was fine this morning, came to life and everything. And then just like that"—she snaps her fingers—"it went kaput."

Brooklyn glances from her to the passenger seat of the truck and back again. "Did you need a jump?"

"I'm quite sure it's not the battery. If my memory's correct—though that is a big if, mind you—I just replaced it last year."

"I can take you to a shop."

The woman shifts the weight of her bag further up her shoulder, finally having caught her breath. "If you could do that, it would be brilliant, yeah." A pause, then a laugh. "But I've actually had a crazy thought, just considering what we were talking about back in there. What if I came with you?"

"What?" Brooklyn can't hide the surprise in his voice. He glances sideways at his truck again.

"What if I—well, you know, would you have me on your trip?"

She is an interesting mix of traits: feisty and yet politely reserved. She'd have never entertained the idea of running off unplanned, but something in her interaction with him has sparked a rebellion in herself.

She continues. "I wouldn't want to be a bother your whole trip—I couldn't last that long in a bloody motor anyway—but if I could go as far as Utah? There are some people I'd like to see there."

The narrow window into the back of the cabin is dark. Oleander isn't visible, though Brooklyn knows he is watching. If Oleander heard anything they've said, then he's probably encouraging Brooklyn not to shrink away from helping people around him. And there is something in this woman's eyes that suggests she's in need of help.

He sees untamed, tightly curled hair, feels the wind from treetops high in the air, and hears the splash of frigid water. An untethered ghost sits between trees in a park until her retreating form disappears.

"I know it's not ideal, shuttling around an old woman like me. I'm not exactly a bundle of fun anymore, but I swear: no knitting, and I'll keep my crotchety moods to a minimum." The woman lays a hand on her chest again in oath.

"What about your car?" Brooklyn asks.

She turns, looking back at a sky-blue Buick parked across the way. Rust has gathered in places on the chrome trim, but besides that it appears to be a proud and well taken care of vehicle. The angled contours shine back at them as if it's letting its owner know that everything is all right. "It's had a long and full life," she says, "but come to think of it, I'm getting too old to find another. I don't plan on being gone too long. I'll find my way back and get it towed then."

"They won't impound it while you're gone?"

"Love, there was a jalopy in this lot that'd been parked here since before JFK was in office. They only moved it last month. He'll be fine."

Brooklyn makes the rotation one last time, looking from the old woman to the two vehicles and back again. He's in no hurry. He has no deadline to meet. So what can it hurt to adopt another passenger? He requests a welcoming smile from his brain, and it responds with a twitch at the corner of his mouth.

"Do you want to put your stuff in the back?" he asks. He can see the woman almost vibrate with excitement. She's instantly thirty years younger.

"Yeah, I've got a few things in the boot I think I'll want to bring along too, if you don't mind," she says, walking with him around to the tailgate.

"I'm Brooklyn, by the way. Brooklyn Durant." He holds out a hand, and they shake.

"Dahlia Dossett, at your service."

Chapter Sixteen

"My favorites!" Kathryn's camera clicks again.

Brooklyn smiles widely for the umpteenth time that night. The overall euphoria has not worn off, but he's grown numb and partially blind to the flashes. He can't help but laugh at her peals of unrestrained excitement, however.

"I knew it! I just *knew* it!" she says. "Didn't I say, Adam? I knew you guys would be the first of our group."

"Quit your day job, Kathryn, and become a matchmaker," Ollie says, teasing her. Brooklyn pulls him a little closer with a hand around his waist.

She winds the camera to the next slot. "I know the ceremony was unconventional and all, but everyone will have to admit that you guys won the 'Best Wedding' prize."

"How do you know?" Adam asks. "They were first."

"But no one's going to beat that!"

"I wasn't aware it was a competition," Ollie says, sticking out his tongue.

"Of course it's not, but it is." Kathryn winks. "The ceremony was smooth, the decorations are fantastic, and everyone who RSVPed showed up."

She looks around the restaurant's patio, the crowd moving in a mesmerizing chaos between the streams of colored lights. Bodies distort soundwaves from the DJ as they cross haphazardly in front of the speakers. "I've been to a lot of weddings—you all know how big my family is and how many marriages we have every year—but this has got to be, hands down, the best one I've ever been to."

"And it's not because you had a hand in planning it, right?" Ollie asks.

Kathryn feigns offense. "I don't know why you'd imply such a thing." She flips her hair over her shoulder dramatically, a perfected practice. "I'm just saying, whoever picked out those centerpieces deserves an award of some kind."

"Yeah, yeah." Ollie rolls his eyes. "You can have the 'Best Friend' award."

"I'm partial to the wine glasses myself," Brooklyn chimes in. From every table, the twisted stems glimmer in response.

Everyone else groans. "If I have to hear one more thing about the wine glasses . . ." Adam lets the sentence dangle.

"Honestly, I thought those were going to get the whole thing called off," Kathryn agrees.

"Made us stronger." Oleander laughs. "It's the details that count."

Brooklyn kisses Ollie on the temple, giving Kathryn cause to emit a few more squeals.

"Oh my God. You two are trying really hard to make me cry, aren't you?" she says.

Adam takes her hand. "Typical."

"I know, I promised I wouldn't." She bats her eyelashes at Brooklyn and Ollie. "But seriously, I love you both so much, and it makes me so happy to see the two of you happy." She rushes forth and wraps her arms around Ollie's neck. Brooklyn lets go of Ollie so he doesn't impede their embrace.

"Thanks, Kathy." Ollie holds her just as tightly. "And thanks for being my best woman."

Adam holds out a closed fist. Brooklyn taps it with his own. "Guess this means I'm officially losing my kayak buddy." Adam laughs.

"Hey, what do you mean?"

"Haven't you heard? Married men only share kayaks with their spouses. It's against the laws of nature to switch."

"Eh, you know it's all symbolic. We're not really married in the eyes of the law, after all," Brooklyn replies.

"Starting already?" Adam shakes his head. "You've got to wait at least twenty-four hours before pulling that one out."

Brooklyn laughs. "I guess you're right. Maybe you can convince Kathryn to start coming along."

"Nah, she'd rather go climbing or something."

"I guess we picked the same kind of people." They watch as Kathryn whispers to Ollie, their embrace finished. The music drifting over from the dance floor is enough to drown out her words.

"Brooklyn, come here please." His grandmother gestures from the doorway into the restaurant. The walls inside are a pale yellow but look gold from the iron sconces. From here, the night beyond the glass is black, save for the glow of the lamps around the patio. Brooklyn follows her, the music fading.

"How are you doing, Grandma?" he asks. Her age gathers along the length of her bones and causes her to tremble slightly at all times.

"I'm old," she says.

"Grandma!"

"I'm eighty-four, Brooklyn. I think I've earned the right to say I'm old."

"Well, you don't look a day over eighty-three."

This makes her chuckle. "Aren't you sweet." She stops at a bench, sits, and pats the seat beside her.

"I'm old, Brooklyn," she says again. He has vague memories of her snatching him from the lawn in her backyard and lifting him high over her head until his hair touched the sun. Of summer days when his parents were working and there wasn't much to do but help Grandma and Grandpa around the house. "I have spent my life looking at the world a certain way, always thinking—*knowing*, I guess it was—that my beliefs are right.

"The world changes," she says, and then pauses for a while, long enough that Brooklyn isn't sure whether she has more to say. "No, that's incorrect. The world doesn't change much. People change. They come to understand each other in ways they didn't before. That's both a beautiful and challenging thing to happen."

Brooklyn doesn't trust himself to speak. His mouth is a thin line on his face. His chest constricts. He sits beside her, not moving, his sweaty palms tucked beneath his thighs.

"What I mean to say is, despite what I may have expressed before, I want nothing but happiness for you and all your cousins." She takes both of his hands in hers while she speaks. "I'm proud of you. No matter who you are, who you love, who you spend your life with. I love you and wish you all the joys I've been lucky enough to have with my family."

Brooklyn had hoped not to cry tonight.

Brooklyn and Oleander have this one evening before they escape for a week of traipsing through New York. They have this evening to begin their union and process what this symbolic marriage means on an individual level. Tonight they don't entertain the notion of what others might think. Tonight is about what this promise of loyalty intends and what it has intended for many lifetimes before their own.

When Brooklyn finds himself near the end of the evening with one hand interlaced with his husband's and the other at the small of his back, he is reminded of the bridge the sun builds across the surface of the ocean, of the smell of fine sand baked in a day that has been bright but cool. He forgets cynicism. At the risk of mawkishness, he forgets the limitations of traditional masculinity. He's in awe of this man who has agreed to spend his life by Brooklyn's side, who contains within him a universe that Brooklyn knows but has yet to fully explore. They dance to a song he cannot place, spinning beneath a sky he does not know, among people he cannot see.

When the time comes for them to leave, they head back to the hotel. Then they make their way to their room, buzzing with excitement and anticipation. Oleander's face glows under the lights in the hallways. The lines of his jaw and cheekbones, his straight and subtle nose, and his skin—many shades darker than Brooklyn's—have all taken on a softer edge that Brooklyn can't shake. Perhaps he's seeing things.

"I'm really glad we chose to do the ceremony and reception the way we did," Brooklyn says when they reach their landing. "I hear all these stories about how people don't even get to enjoy their own wedding because they're running around making sure this and that are ready and perfect. I'm glad that didn't happen."

"I think everyone else enjoyed themselves too. I really think so," Ollie reassures him. "That's got to count for something."

"Greg definitely enjoyed himself."

"Oh jeez, yeah, I saw him hitting on your cousin."

"She didn't look too happy about it."

"And the way he and Carter were throwing back the drinks, I thought maybe they were competing for something."

"Sounds like our friends all right." Brooklyn cocks his eyebrow.

They reach room 514. Brooklyn takes Ollie's arm. "Hey, before we go in, I've got to ask you something."

Ollie grins. "Sure, whatever you want."

"Will you marry me?"

Ollie lets out a barking laugh that's perhaps a bit too loud for midnight. Immediately he claps a hand over his mouth to stifle the sound. He might still be a bit tipsy. "Huh, well, I think I just did!"

"Excellent." Brooklyn smirks. "Then I think it's time I swept you off your feet—"

"Wait!" Ollie suddenly holds up a hand, using two fingers to halt Brooklyn's impending kiss. The movement catches Brooklyn off guard. "I want to go somewhere," Ollie says.

For the first time this evening, Brooklyn falters. Confused, he feels his heart skip a beat or two. "What do you mean? We're literally flying from California to New York tomorrow."

"No, I know, but I mean I want to go somewhere right now."

"Ollie?"

"Come on." And with that, Oleander grabs Brooklyn's hand and leads him back down the hallway to the elevator.

In his confusion, Brooklyn allows himself to be dragged along, his mind racing at the sudden change of pace and direction. Where could Oleander possibly want to go now, at this time of night? They've just gotten married! They should be undressing in their hotel room. There'd been a few hopeful images running through Brooklyn's mind.

The elevator dings and the doors open. They rush inside, and Oleander jabs at the lobby button. For a brief moment after the doors shut, Ollie spins to face Brooklyn and plants a firm kiss on his lips. He wears a mischievous look: eyebrows knit toward the center, lopsided smile firmly in place. Brooklyn has seen this look before. Ollie is consumed now, completely enamored by the idea in his head. He revels in the mystery, determined to surprise Brooklyn and keep him guessing until the last minute.

"Try not to let anyone see you," Ollie whispers as the doors open up again. Someone at the piano in the bar lounge is playing a jazzy rendition of "Amazing Grace." The heavy notes drift through the air like summer heat. A few members of their party linger beside the low fireplace, talking in happy, hushed tones, but Brooklyn and Ollie dart around the corner and out the front door before anyone has the chance to spot them.

Then they're jogging across the parking lot to the side of their truck, a deep scarlet in the pale streetlamps.

"I guess we can't make the limo guy come back?" Brooklyn jokes.

Oleander laughs and shakes his head. Someone has written *Just Married* on the back window in pastel-blue paint.

"Are you going to at least give me a hint?" Brooklyn asks, drawing level with the door. "I mean, if I am going to be driving . . ."

"It's okay, I'll tell you how to get there," Oleander replies simply, and they climb inside.

Brooklyn feels the slightest tug of annoyance, but the effects of the night have not worn off and his overwhelming satisfaction remains in control of his emotions. Perhaps he can use this favor as leverage when they get back to their room.

They leave the lot, and Oleander begins directing Brooklyn. "I used to come here with my friends," he explains offhandedly.

The truck winds through the city streets, encountering little traffic. Before long Brooklyn loses track of how many intersections they've passed and how many turns they've made. He focuses instead on listening to Ollie's directions, trusting him completely. It becomes something of a game, and never once does Ollie make a mistake.

Then the city falls away entirely, and they begin climbing into the hills. The night sky is swallowed by the canopy of trees. Brooklyn feels as though they are alone, the road devoid even of streetlamps to light the way. His headlights fight the darkness alone. He's completely lost track of where they've been and cannot imagine now where they're headed. Seeds of doubt plant themselves, making him uneasy.

"Are you sure you know where you're going?" Brooklyn asks.

"Yeah. We're almost there," Ollie says, smiling. Brooklyn can't refuse him.

Finally, Oleander tells him to pull over where the cracked asphalt widens into a roadside lot large enough for one row of vehicles. The engine dies and is replaced by the hum of crickets and the rustle of leaves blown by a languid wind. The two men get out. The night is cool but warm enough that Brooklyn doesn't shiver.

"Is this where you kill me and steal the fortune I've been hiding from you?" Brooklyn jokes to hide his apprehension. He's not afraid of the dark, but doesn't like that nobody knows they're here. He can't see a thing without the headlights on. He stretches out his arms blindly and touches nothing but empty space.

Then Ollie's warm hand takes his. The skin is calloused and rough—builder's hands—but loving. "Well, who knows if it would go to me now," Ollie responds, tongue in cheek. "There's a rock there, step over it."

"I hope this is really spectacular, otherwise you're going to owe me a little something extra to—"

They crest the hillside, the trees and undergrowth falling away. The earth levels off for a yard or two before becoming a rocky cliff. Beyond, the city unfolds.

Streets cross and curve, folding here or stretching out there in long, straight avenues. They meet at odd angles, yellows and reds and greens and bright whites drawing the eye along the luminous atlas—individual but seamless and unbroken. Brooklyn's breath is taken away. He stands before a star field, a galaxy opening wide as far as the eye can see and deep into the darkness. Against a backdrop of the city, he is finite and the world is infinite, a vast expanse he cannot help but long to be part of. He takes a step forward, though well away from the cliff edge, drops his hands to his sides, and lets the universe consume him.

"We used to call it 'The Edge of the World,'" Ollie says. He stands a few paces back, appreciating the view, though he's more familiar with it than Brooklyn. "When it's bright out, you can see past the city right up to where the Pacific Ocean disappears into the horizon. The sunset on the water is impressive, but I'm partial to the view at night. Pretty cool, huh?"

"Incredible," Brooklyn says. "I don't understand how there's nobody else up here. Do people know about it?"

"A few." Ollie takes his hand again. "Sometimes when we'd come up here, there'd be a couple of people, but never more than that. I think because it's so far out of the city and the road isn't well lit . . ."

"I can't believe it. It's like—it's like . . ."

"Like you're standing at the edge of the world?"

Brooklyn laughs.

"Kind of humbles you, doesn't it? It looks as if there could be as many lights down there as there are up there." Brooklyn points at the human-made starscape below them and then up at the faint lights in the black sky. It's a simple task to tell them apart, but it's far more gratifying to let his mind join the two. They meet at the same horizon, at a point somewhere over the black water beyond his vision. And the lights of one exist as unruly and yet as perfectly placed as the other. One might assume that the stars are a reflection of the city lights in a body of water high in the atmosphere. Who's to say they aren't?

Each light below might be hosting a living being. There might be a family in their living room, playing a game or sitting around the television. There might be people in the parking lot of a store, a traveler pulling into a foreign town, not completely sure of where they've arrived but letting the streetlamps guide the way to refuge.

Who can say that any of the stars above are not serving much the same purpose? There are so many things he might come to know, and so many more things he might never come to know. Acknowledging this satisfies Brooklyn.

"Have you ever wanted to yell into space?" Ollie whispers in Brooklyn's ear, the mischievous grin back. He's every bit as beautiful as this universe.

"What?" Brooklyn asks.

"Have you ever wanted to yell into space?"

"I don't really under—"

"We're married!"

Brooklyn jumps back, alarmed. Ollie laughs as the light wind blows the hair back from his face.

"What are you doing?" Brooklyn asks, but he too smiles at the antics, unable to contain himself.

"Come on, do it with me. We're married, everyone!" Ollie squeezes his hand, and Brooklyn never wants to let go. Ollie leads him forward, out into the vast expanse, out into the starlight.

"Ollie, people are—"

"What people?" Ollie forgets to change volume, and the two of them are caught in hysterics for a moment, laughing hard enough that their sides hurt. "No—" He gasps. "No! Stop laughing. Shout with me. I want everyone to know."

"Ollie!"

"Come on!"

"You look crazy."

"I am fucking crazy! I married this man! Do it with me."

"We're married," Brooklyn calls.

"You've got to be louder than that. I've heard you do better." Ollie sticks out his tongue at Brooklyn. "We're married!"

"We're married!"

"Scream it to the heavens, so everyone can hear. We got married!"

"I'm married!"

"I wanna spend my life with this lunatic!"

"Hey!"

"No, you're supposed to keep repeating."

"Oh—uh, I'm going to spend my life with him, even if he's a lunatic!"

"A lunatic of the best kind!" They laugh again.

Ollie loosens his tie so that the knot hangs down mid-chest. Brooklyn does the same, unbuttoning the top button of his shirt as well.

"You want to see something secret?" Ollie asks. His voice comes much softer now. He has stopped addressing the world and speaks only to Brooklyn.

"I don't know if I can handle much more," Brooklyn replies. He realizes only now that his heart is thudding in his chest.

"You'll be able to take this one, I think." Ollie says. He reaches into the inner pocket of his tuxedo jacket, feeling around for only a moment before drawing out his hand. In his fingers is a small strip of paper folded neatly in half but otherwise without creases. The lighting here is too dark to read what's written on it, but Brooklyn already knows what it says. The short sentence typed in a small serif font comes back to him in an instant.

"No way, Ollie." Is it possible that Brooklyn's smile grows wider? "That's not the same one from Santa Cruz, is it?"

"Yes, way!"

"You still have that? After all this time?"

"Of course." Ollie looks at the paper with affection.

"Why?"

"Because I'm a sentimental fool," he says. Without another word, he slips the paper back into his pocket.

Brooklyn watches Oleander's profile for a moment as Ollie looks out over the edge of the world. Now, there is a sense of completion in the air. A sense that events have come full circle, and he is right where he means to be, where he's meant to be all along. Brooklyn follows Ollie's gaze, staring back out over the starscape. No matter how much money one might have, how many buildings or acres of land might be in their possession, none of these lights or stars can ever fully belong to one person. Still, he feels tonight that a bit of the universe, this collection of stars, is theirs. Not given to them, but perhaps made for them to explore. He squeezes Oleander's hand, and together they look out over their universe.

Chapter Seventeen

Dahlia's car is incredibly clean, nothing besides the normal wear and tear of frequent use. There's no refuse or stray clothing, nothing hung around the rearview mirror or sitting on the dashboard. The only items in the car are the things Dahlia wants Brooklyn to grab from the trunk: a lantern and a small one-person tent, both new.

"They're for my nephew," Dahlia says, "or I s'pose he'd actually be my grandnephew or something like that, isn't he? He's a Boy Scout, have I told you?" Brooklyn nods, but she's not looking for a response. "His own equipment's a right mess at the mo. His parents haven't got a lot of money, so I figured I'd surprise him for Christmas.

"I was thinking that's where I want to go, if you don't mind. If I'm headed west, that's where I'd go, if it's not taking you too far out of your way. A wee place called Duchesne that's in Utah."

Brooklyn consults his mental map of the United States. "Yeah, any place in Utah can't be too far out of the way." He reaches forward. The items are lighter than they look. He can carry them both at the same time.

Dahlia closes the trunk and ambles back to the Ranger alongside him. "Brilliant." Her voice is deep and carries the timbres of age. It reminds Brooklyn of peanut butter fudge—rich and sweet, with just a little coarseness for texture.

Brooklyn sets the tent and the lantern down in the truck bed. Dahlia claps her hands together, and Brooklyn catches a glimpse of her masked anxiety. "Shall we do the damn thing then?" she asks.

"Hop aboard," Brooklyn says. He opens the driver's side door and climbs in.

"Have we picked up someone else?" Oleander asks.

"Yeah. I met her in the laundromat. Her car's broken down, and she wants to come along to Utah, if that's all right."

"She asked you that?"

Brooklyn nods.

"And you said yes?"

Brooklyn nods again. "Is that okay?"

"Why not." Oleander's trace of a smile has more than a bit of pride mixed in. "I think that's a great idea."

The passenger door opens. "—to bless me. These cars are so tall now, I feel like a pipsqueak." Dahlia laughs as she hauls herself in.

"Can you make it?" Oleander asks, appearing around the side of the seat.

"Shite on a shag rug!" She gasps in surprise, nearly falling back out again. "And who are you?"

"I'm Ollie."

She gets back up and scoots into the seat.

"Oh, you're a poof," Dahlia says as if stating his hair color, a hand to her chest. "My apologies for the yelp. Brooklyn didn't mention he was going along with anyone else. I hadn't expected the car to be occupied. Lord above—I'm Dahlia." She holds out her hand around the side of the seat for Ollie to shake, still laughing and catching her breath, but Ollie just nods politely in response. She giggles. "No worries. That was quite the scare you gave me just then. Oh, wasn't that fun? I nearly had a heart attack there, so I did."

"Sorry, I didn't mean to," Ollie says.

Dahlia waves her hand. "Nonsense. The old ticker needed a jumpstart anyway. It was starting to slow." She delights in her dark joke, laughing while she fixes her burgundy sweater.

They leave the lot and head for the highway. Dahlia wastes no time launching into the specifics of her grandnephew and what he likes to do, how he's a "real crafty lad" who has an affinity for building things whenever he gets the chance. He makes his own drawings and uses his allowance money to buy wood and other materials. The shop at his school has all the tools he needs—because God knows his parents can't afford any of those things—and they let him use them whenever he likes—after he'd taken the wood shop class, of course. He made Dahlia the birdhouse in her front yard. She painted it a lovely lilac color, and all the blue jays simply flock to it. Shame she hasn't seen him since she helped them move from Denver. Bright boy, he's graduating in a couple of years, and she hopes he'll decide to go to university for something clever like engineering or computers.

Dahlia says this all rather quickly, and Brooklyn is ashamed to admit that he loses her in a couple places.

Ollie asks Dahlia where she's from and how she came to live in Des Moines. She sighs with a far-off look that tells him much of what he wants to know. But while she gazes many years behind them, she's not melancholy. Rather, she's content, happy with her memories.

"My family is from a northern part of Ireland you've probably never heard of: Donaghadee. Beautiful country, my God! Greenest hillsides you've ever seen. Oh, I used to drive me mam up the wall boggin' my stockings from running in the grass. She'd scold me three ways to kingdom come, but I couldn't help it. You try seeing grass like that and tell me you'd not sit in it."

"Did your family have a lot of land then?"

Dahlia *tsks* with her tongue. "Having land didn't matter much. When I was a girl, I ran where I wanted and didn't give a damn about fences or a bitch chasing me—mind you, that happened a lot. Though I did make friends with many of the neighbors' dogs." She giggles at the recollection, her bosom jostling merrily. "But yes, my father was a farmer. He and my mam raised two kids—myself and my sister. A handful we could be at times, I'm sure of it, but I think as a whole we were never too difficult. We had a brilliant childhood. I think, looking at it now, that my father never wanted us to take the farm. He never taught us much on how to till or when to pick the fruits so they're sweetest. Things of that sort. I fetched eggs and milked the sheep, but nothing much beyond that."

"Why didn't he want you to take it over?" Brooklyn asks.

"I think he wanted us to do other things with our lives. We had land, yes, but my family was far from wealthy. Our plot was small compared to the neighboring farms." Dahlia watches the highway, drumming her fingers on the armrest. "Anyway, my sister is eight years older than me and she moved out when I was still fairly young. Decided to find her way over here. So she up and left. Met her husband, and they settled out here in Iowa.

"As I said, I had a brilliant childhood, and my sister was part of it. Losing her was one of the hardest things I ever went through. It was like waking up one day to find you're missing an arm. Our room felt empty. There was a little less laughter in my world. And keep in mind, you couldn't just call someone that far away back then. You wrote letters, so the fastest you could communicate was every few weeks or so. Drove me mad. I was homesick in my own home.

"Soon as I was old enough, I made the move myself. Left when I was seventeen. Gawkish thing I was, scrawny with big eyes and flaming-red hair—thought I knew a lot, but by myself I was quite timid. Didn't talk much to anyone. Hard to believe, eh?" She elbows Brooklyn in the arm, cackling mirthfully. "Don't know how I found my bloody way without getting lost, but I did. Then my sis's husband introduced me to his friend Carl and . . . well, the rest is history, as they say."

"Was Carl from Iowa too?"

"No, he was from Nebraska. He and my sister's husband went to trade school together. Carl was a pipe fitter—I know, it's not a glorious job, but he enjoyed it." She plays absentmindedly with her wedding ring, a thin silver band with a stone of the palest shade of blue. "You would have liked meeting Carl," she says, as though she hadn't just met Brooklyn and Oleander an hour before. "Everybody liked Carl. He was quite the charmer. Could engage anyone in a conversation no matter who they were or what they did."

"Did you have any children?" Ollie asks.

Dahlia goes silent, though the smile lingers and grows distant. "No. No, we never did," she says finally. "We would have loved children, but . . . seems it wasn't the will of the Lord."

The vehicle rumbles over a rough patch of road, and the cabin sways. Overhead, the sun is bright but often masked by thick clouds that drift across the sky like glaciers in a sapphire sea. Rain might soon be on its way, Brooklyn thinks. The air is far too thick to stay dry for much longer.

A road sign alerts them to their imminent departure from Iowa and their entrance into Nebraska, HOME OF ARBOR DAY. The Missouri River trundles along beneath the highway, wide and placid. To either side of the bridge, it curls off behind rows of trees squatting over the water's edge. Omaha emerges from the grass through stone walls that hold back the hillsides.

Dahlia is quiet, which is not a subtle change. For a moment Brooklyn wonders if she's lingering on the comment about having children, but then he sees her watching the bits and pieces of Omaha passing by with wordless intent.

"Nebraska," she says. It sounds like a breath of air. "You don't know how long it's been."

"Did you ever live here with Carl?"

"No, but while we were courting, we'd come here all the time. Evelyn, my sister, used to live a lot closer to the Nebraska border than I do now. The trade school Carl went to was over there too. And when I settled down in the same town as Evy, Carl would pick me up and we'd cross the state line into Omaha. Date nights dancing at the Old Lounge on Bedford Avenue." She sits for a minute listening to the asphalt carry under the roll of the tires, or perhaps to a band playing live music on a Friday evening while leather booths fill with young and earnest couples too shy to start dancing. In Brooklyn's experience, people can't visit the past for too long without losing their way. Every road, no matter how wide or lively it may be, either ends or funnels down into a trail at some point.

"Jesus, Mary, and Joseph, I'm a right mess. A few hours in, and already I'm blabbering like a sentimental sap," Dahlia says, as if aware of Brooklyn's thoughts. "You boys probably don't want to listen to an old widow rambling on about things come to passed."

Ollie laughs. "I enjoy hearing people talk about their lives. Everyone's got a unique history."

"I'm glad you think so. Those are pretty words at least." Dahlia blindly reaches around to tap the back of her chair in a show of gratitude. "Be careful, Ollie. You keep seducing an old woman like that and she'll have to keep you around. Then you'll get nothing but talk about her life."

"I'm sure there's plenty to tell," Ollie prods. "What kind of dancing did you do?"

The satisfaction in Dahlia's smile shows she's flattered by his prompts for more information. "What dancing didn't we do!"

"Did you have a favorite?"

"Well, I shouldn't toot my own horn"—she puts a hand on Brooklyn's arm and looks back and forth between him and Ollie as though letting them in on a secret—"but I did a mean cha-cha back in the day. When I got going, Carl'd call me 'Foxy Dahl.'"

At that, she and Oleander break into peals of laughter, and Brooklyn can't help smiling.

"Oh, he'd tell me stories about running home after dropping me off. Begging his mam to help teach him to dance just so's he could keep up with me, which was odd because I'd never gone dancing back home. I just took to it like *that*. He'd—he'd . . . I wondered . . ." She drifts away again, and the conflict within her is endearingly obvious. Several times in a matter of seconds, she begins and stops herself from speaking.

"What is it?" Brooklyn asks, bemused in spite of himself at Dahlia's sudden rush of timid, indecisive behavior.

She sighs, her head tilting to the right and her eyes downcast. It's almost as though whatever she wants to say is both embarrassing and sad at the same time. The words themselves seem difficult, like pulling thick, viscous mud from her mouth.

"Well, I—The thought'd just popped into my head. Well, what I mean to say is, I—I don't know that it's a good idea at all, really. Seems silly now that I'm saying it aloud." She takes a heavy breath. "I just had the thought—what if we went to Kearney, Nebraska." She adds the last word hurriedly, as if Brooklyn might be worried about where Kearney is.

"What's there?" Brooklyn asks. He had been expecting her to ask if they could stop in Omaha.

"That's—er, that's the town Carl grew up in. Where his parents lived." At this point, Dahlia has clasped her hands in her lap and sat upright against the back of the chair with carefully cultivated poise. Brooklyn catches her lightly applied perfume for the first time—the faintest smell of flowers. Nothing overwhelming or gaudy, but enough that he can tell it's there.

"Did you know them well?" Brooklyn asks.

"No, not at all, really."

"Why not?"

"Carl's mam died, actually, about a year after we met. Heart problems. And his dad became an old codger. Didn't want to see anyone and was always angry. Eventually, he drove Carl away. He came to our wedding, but refused to be a part of the ceremony and hardly interacted with anyone the entire time. If I were a different woman, I'd've let that sort of bollocks ruin our special day, but as it was, I was more frustrated by how much it weighed on Carl. I think that may have been what tipped the scale." Dahlia smiles again, but it's rueful. "I never saw much of him after that. Neither was it Carl's favorite subject, his whole father business. Threw him into a state every time we had to mention it. So I did my best not to bring it up if I didn't have to."

"I'm sorry to hear about that." In a selfish way, Brooklyn is glad he's occupied with driving, otherwise he wouldn't trust himself to know how to react. He stares at the road ahead of them, at the solid stripes of paint. His hands feel too large, his blinking forced.

"Carl'd been really close to his mother, talked about her often." Out of the corner of his eye, Brooklyn sees Dahlia turn in her seat to face him. Her words come carefully, drawn out and purposeful. "It was a loss that stayed with him. For a long time, he couldn't leave her behind, but even though he loved her, he learned that eventually he had to move on. I think that's why he was okay, while his father wasn't.

"Anyway, I want to go there because I want to revisit where Carl grew up. I heard stories, sure, but I never had much time to piece them together. To map them, as it were, I suppose. Heaven knows I've probably forgotten more of them than not, but visiting will still feel like I'm getting some piece of him back, so it will."

The sun leads the way through Omaha. Dahlia's gaze lingers on Brooklyn a few moments longer, expectant, and then turns away, probably in disappointment. She'd wanted something. He's aware of this tactic—this subtle strategy—and never once has he fallen prey to it. He has no tragedies to confide in her. He's content to comfort, listen to anything she may have to say, but he feels no inclination to reciprocate. Stories are not a right and cannot be traded in equal measure. Using them as such is a cheap trick to foster trust mechanically.

Brooklyn finds himself irritated at first, his teeth clenched and grip tight on the steering wheel. He softens as the minutes pass, though. As always, once the moment is through, he questions why he became annoyed in the first place. Some people seek the misery of others so that their own miseries don't cause them to feel as isolated. Some trade misery like goods and use what they gain to feed upon. Others collect it to remind them how their life could be worse. And still others use it to barter passage across the channels of friendship. There is an unlimited number of ways to use misery, some more innocuous than others but each as innate as the next. He can't blame her. Like anyone else, she does only what she knows.

Brooklyn worries that he's insulted Dahlia by not taking the opportunity to confide in her the way she has in him. But before long she's talking animatedly again, extrapolating on her theories of why she can't stand people who are idiots, and why they're idiots. Also, that she and Caroline have long been friends for this very reason: Caroline understands and completely agrees with her.

Somehow, this topic leads to the last book Dahlia's read and how much it frustrated her. "So, here are these young people, unquestionably human in my mind even if they're manufactured, standing in front of their former headmistress asking why they should be killed when they're obviously human. I mean, you can't see the artwork they've made, of course, because it's a book, but I imagine they've gone and done a few fairly decent things along the way. And the headmistress—the troglodyte—goes on to explain how she's got no say, and they're going to die because that's the lot they've been given in life. Oh my God, Caroline and I cried our lamps out by that point! You'd think the dam had sprung a leak in my kitchen while we were going on about it." Dahlia's decree booms as heartily as her stout stature allows. Brooklyn has no idea what Dahlia's talking about, only having half understood her explanation of the novel.

"I know it's a book and a fictional setting, but how it translates, what it means about the real cruelties in this world, it's just"—she shakes her head in disbelief—"just, well, *fucked!*"

The outburst catches Brooklyn and Ollie by surprise, and they both break out into laughter. Dahlia is quick to join them. "It's the only way to describe it!" she exclaims.

"I guess so," Ollie says between breaths.

"I believe you, Dahlia. I just wasn't expecting that choice of words," Brooklyn chimes in.

"What? Saying 'fuck'?" She giggles, sounding like a schoolgirl experimenting with new words she's not allowed to say. "You know, not all old people are made of milk and cookies, boyo. I'm saggy, but I'm not a gram." She looks back at Ollie and winks.

The sun falls, same as it rose, and turns the sky an auburn-pink. Brooklyn, Dahlia, and Ollie stop in a town called Aurora to have dinner in a small café that feels oddly mistimed, one foot still firmly stuck in another decade. The town bears the atmosphere of the overlooked, the sort of place eyes skip over on a state map, nothing more than a word in fine print. But how does a single word symbolize the lives of the five thousand people living here? The country—the world—is freckled with places like this, and Brooklyn would never know they were there unless he stumbled upon them. Yet the people in this town live their lives as unaware of him as he has been of them. So many people dot the vast expanses of the world that the diversity of their experiences is unimaginable.

The sky is all but dark when they leave to continue the rest of the way. The highway is largely their own, cutting a straight, invariable path through the countryside.

They listen to the radio playing softly, sometimes humming and tapping along, sometimes silent. When night has settled, the headlights of the red Ranger sweep over a green road sign nestled back from the highway near a line of trees. It reads KEARNEY.

"Harmon Park," Dahlia utters, grasping the truck door. "That's where we need to go."

"Where should I get off?"

She points to the first exit approaching on the right. "Here, just get off here. We can find it."

Brooklyn follows the road as it curves off the highway. He turns onto Second Avenue, and the stoplights shine, amplified in the darkness. Second Avenue appears to be the main street, unfolding between stout inns and restaurants, car washes, gas stations, auto body shops, and small banks.

"It doesn't look like much, I know," Dahlia says, "but a place never has to look like much to mean much."

They pass a half-filled lot at the center of a small shopping plaza. Decorations in the windows of one of the businesses remind Brooklyn that Halloween is imminent. Even the trees around the plaza seem to be in theme, their branches growing bare as they drip pale orange leaves.

Then Dahlia speaks again. "His words are coming to life right now—Carl's, I mean. Some of the places he talked about are gone, but some of them are still here. There's the wee drapery his mam's mate ran. Carl'd go there on Saturday mornings when they'd gossip in the shop, and he'd pretend to be a ghost hiding in the fabrics. I wonder if it's still in her family or not. They wouldn't know me, of course, but it's good to see things like that still open."

They drive all the way until the streets start to thin again and the houses die away. Dahlia says, "No, that's not right. The way he described it, the park was in the thick of things. By his grammar school, if my memory's worth a damn."

"Was it off the main strip?" Ollie asks.

"I don't think right off it, but somewhere close. They'd walk to get candy from the general store after class. I'm sorry, can't remember any street names." Dahlia puts a hand to her forehead. "I've only ever gone to his parents' house."

Checking that nobody is behind him, Brooklyn makes a U-turn in the middle of the road, not wanting to wait until the next intersection.

"Did he say anything else? Mention something a lot in reference?" Brooklyn gently prods Dahlia's memory. He hasn't minded the excursions he's taken so far with Dahlia and Zinnia, but he doesn't fancy driving around aimlessly if it can be helped.

"What was one of the stories? Maybe . . . er, shite. Maybe something about a clinic or a hospital? I think he broke his ankle once, or his cousin did. It was a few streets from that. Is there a hospital somewhere?"

"Yeah, there's one of those *H* signs," Ollie offers, pointing to the left.

"Should I go toward it?" Brooklyn asks.

"Sure, try that." Dahlia says.

They find the hospital and spend the next half hour circling it in wider and wider radii. Dahlia's memory fails to grow any better, and while at first Brooklyn's annoyance at the situation bubbles dangerously beneath the surface, he soon begins to feel sorrow and disappointment for her. Dahlia's wide slate eyes betray her mounting desperation, her fear that she could be so close to Harmon Park—this important landmark of her husband's memory—but might not find it. He can imagine the sense choking her, growing thick in her throat like the lump that comes before tears. It would be like having Carl returned to her and then unceremoniously taken away again before she could even touch him.

Then, when Dahlia sounds ready to give in, they pull around the side of a squat brick building, and she places a steady hand on the truck's dashboard. Brooklyn notices again the dull silver band hiding on her finger. The small gem twinkles back at him. Encroaching branches of tarnish that curl around the sides make him wonder how little time it spends off her finger.

"This—this was his grammar school," Dahlia says, her eyes darting back and forth over the half-lit sign standing out near the curb. Her whisper is almost unintelligible, as if she doesn't trust her mouth to move.

The sign, a stucco rectangle embossed with black letters and bordered by brick, rises from the lawn behind a neat semicircle of colorful flowers. It reminds Brooklyn of flowers at a grave, but not unpleasantly so.

"This is his school," Dahlia repeats with more confidence. "Park Elementary. This has to be it. The park is just behind these buildings."

Brooklyn takes this as a cue to pull up alongside the curb, bringing the Ranger to a stop just past the building. The hum of the engine dies, and in its place is quiet. He can hear the cars on Second Avenue rolling past even though they're a couple blocks away. Besides that, not much else breaks the silence.

In this silence Dahlia hesitates. For a moment she is immobile. Then she seizes the door handle and is out of the car in a flash. She stands on the sidewalk and stares first at the back of the school building—faded red bricks that look as though they've absorbed the dust of many decades—and then at the park behind it.

Brooklyn exchanges a glance with Oleander, who nods. Then he gets out as well.

"This is it, Brooklyn," Dahlia says, hands in the pockets of her coat. She glances back at the window of the truck. "He really not going to come out?"

"Yeah," Brooklyn replies. "He doesn't leave the Ranger."

She shrugs, and her attention focuses once again on Harmon Park. A white paved path leads in. Sparse, ornate lights line the path's edge as if calling them into a different world, even though Brooklyn can see where the path leads. It goads them to let it spirit them away. Having the busy road audible but removed somehow tricks his mind into believing that they've found a secret space. This is somewhere others cannot see.

Brooklyn and Dahlia follow the path and leave the truck behind.

"Whenever his mam came up, he'd talk about this park. See, the town had a Mother and Son Day each year at the end of spring. They'd play all the wee games, like burlap sack races and egg tosses. All those cliché things you can't imagine anyone doing anymore. Oh, it was his favorite." Dahlia never stops searching, combing every blade of grass and bench along the way. "He said they never won anything, but they always had a brilliant time. The saddest thing he said was, 'I didn't realize the last time was the last time. And if I had, I would've made it more special.' I find myself saying the same thing sometimes."

"Me too," Brooklyn replies.

The path curves around the back of a gardener's shed, heading straight down the center of the park. He sees a community pool ahead of them, shut away for the season with tarps pulled over the water.

"If he's watching, I can tell you he's got a smile on right now," Dahlia says with a nostalgic grin of her own. "I came, Carl. I didn't plan to, but I made it here."

"Do you think it's the same as when he used to come here as a boy?"

"Oh, I'm sure much has changed. These things are always getting upgrades and whatnot. I imagine much of it's familiar though, like the pond."

Before them is a mirrored surface so still that Brooklyn might have mistaken it for glass. The lamp beside them turns the nearby water ochre. But farther out, the water is a dark green that weaves around minor islands scattered between the shores. River rocks line the edges of the pond, their faces as pale as the moon and as smooth as ice.

Brooklyn is suddenly overcome by the urge to dip his hands beneath the surface. He just wants to see if it really is glass or if he can make ripples. He resists the temptation though and instead puts his hands in his pants pockets.

"The pond was his favorite part," Dahlia says. "He used to hang around this bit because he said it allowed him to feel like he was in a fantasy world. Wee fairies and golems and things, you know. He said he could've sworn he'd seen some of them once as a kid, but as he got older he realized that couldn't be."

"Then reason takes over, doesn't it?" Brooklyn says.

"Happens at some point for most people."

They find a bench by the water and sit there for what becomes another hour. Dahlia tells Brooklyn more stories she'd heard from her late husband about his childhood, and a few about their time together. It seems she hasn't had anyone new to tell in a long while, and he watches Carl come alive in the darkness before her. Brooklyn can see his skin, his full head of white hair, and the black-rimmed glasses that were always a little too wide for his face. He can see the long, thin fingers stretched from playing the piano, and the lines etched around his mouth from laughing too hard and smiling too often. Carl carries himself lightly; he moves with an affable, polite nature, always allowing the other person to go first. He is most comfortable in brightly colored knit button-ups and would take a dinner on the back porch over a five-star restaurant any day of the week.

Then Dahlia draws as quiet as the park. "I may be spending far too much time with him," she says. For a moment the statement makes Brooklyn wonder if he's only imagined the figure of Carl in front of them, or if the man was really there, watching them from across the water. Her descriptions have brought far too much life to his imagination. Carl is not alive. And Carl is not with them now, at least not in a way that they can see. In the absence of her words, he dies again. Dahlia and Brooklyn are alone in Harmon Park.

"No," Brooklyn assures her. "You don't have to stop."

"But I think *I've* had enough for the night," she replies, staring at the ground by her feet. "I think I'm ready to find somewhere to sleep."

She stands. Brooklyn does the same. They walk back along the path in silence, the breeze blowing a little bit harder as if begging them to stay. Without a word, Dahlia takes Brooklyn's arm in her hand and lets him guide her around the corner, back to where the apple-red truck sits beneath the streetlamp.

"Thank you, Brooklyn," Dahlia says. "Thank you very much for this."

Chapter Eighteen

They find an inn with the vacancy sign lit. Oleander's manner is quiet, and his interactions are sparse. The result is a weighty lack of conversation.

When they park, Ollie smiles at Dahlia as she steps down from the passenger seat, bidding her a clipped "Good night." He doesn't make eye contact with Brooklyn or respond to his farewell. Instead, Ollie's chest heaves, and his gaze bores through the glass. He looks almost afraid.

The rejection causes an ache in Brooklyn. He kneads his chest briefly with the heel of his palm, and thinks of this rejection until he falls asleep.

In the morning the wind is colder than it was the day before, the sun not nearly as bright. The clouds are thicker, dragging themselves across the sky on a pilgrimage to the western mountains.

Brooklyn stands in the entryway of the motel, squinting out into the day. If he stares hard enough, the buildings move and the clouds are stationary; they become islands in an otherwise uninterrupted sea. He wills the landscape around him to change, not the sky. The sky is perfect.

The truck stands where he left it, the dark rear windows streaked with dust and dirt from this drive halfway across the country.

Brooklyn will need a heavier coat soon. His hands shoved in the pockets of his jeans, he jogs to the vehicle. He can barely feel the key in his fingers. The cold of the early morning has rendered them numb in a matter of moments. He slides into the driver's seat and shuts the door behind him as quickly as he can.

"I'm sorry," Oleander says.

"Good morning," Brooklyn replies.

Oleander has already folded up the blanket and shoved it back through the rear window. He sits with his legs propped up on the seat opposite him.

"You don't waste much time," Brooklyn says, smiling a little with the corner of his mouth. "I just came out here to see how you were doing before we headed off again."

"When you both came back to the car last night, I was rude. I can't stop thinking about it." Oleander tries to hold eye contact but fails after a few seconds.

"It was barely noticeable," Brooklyn assures him. He does his best not to rub at the soreness in his neck from a restless sleep.

"Maybe, but it was unwarranted. I feel like I've been more like that lately."

Brooklyn doesn't know how to respond. He clasps his hands together in his lap, his fingers interlaced. He doesn't want to lie and say the very thought hasn't crossed his mind, but he's unsure whether he's been guilty of the same behavior.

"I feel unnecessary sometimes," Oleander says. The words are slow. Admission must be difficult. "I'm usually okay on a day-to-day basis, but since we left Schoharie—since we've met other people—I think I may be a little envious every time you leave the truck to go off with them. I shouldn't be, but I am."

"Envious?"

"Yeah, a little."

Brooklyn's brow furrows. "You encouraged me to stop and pick up Zinnia."

"I know—"

"I can't stop myself from doing things or going places or seeing people. That's why I left home in the first place."

"Brooklyn. Please, don't get angry." Ollie reaches forward and puts a hand on one of Brooklyn's wrists. "I'm not blaming you in any way. I'm just telling you why I've been acting cold."

"Could you try to control it?" Brooklyn asks, watching Ollie's hand.

"I know. Again, I'm sorry. I wish I weren't so limited."

Brooklyn wants to be angry. He wants to raise his voice for a great many reasons. But he looks at the man before him and finds that he can't. The reasons are too small and forgettable. The curve of Oleander's eyes, the line of his jaw, the width of his rounded shoulders are too familiar. His hand where it touches Brooklyn's wrist seems to be made of only light and air; Brooklyn can feel it, but he can't concentrate on the feeling.

So, when Oleander slides off his chair, Brooklyn pulls him into his chest, holding the top of Ollie's head beneath his chin. He wraps his arms around Ollie's shoulders. "I know," he says.

Dahlia emerges from the elevator looking as if she might fall over at any moment under the weight of the bag slung over her shoulder. Brooklyn reaches out, and she lets him take it from her.

She shudders and massages her shoulder. "That's a good lad. Didn't realize how much I'd taken, but I suppose that's everything I'd brought to the wash." She giggles. "Didn't feel like that much last night. Suppose I could've taken out only what I needed, but hindsight is twenty–twenty, isn't it."

"I think you may have handed me the wrong bag. This one seems to be full of stones," Brooklyn teases.

"Did you just make a joke?"

"I've been known to do that from time to time."

"Well, that's good to hear, love. We wouldn't want you too serious."
Dahlia pats his shoulder. The gesture feels remarkably maternal. "Is
that you, then?"

They exit the building, the warmth from the heated interior falling
away behind them.

"I thought I was going to have lots of troubles getting to sleep last
night, what with all the excitement at the park and traveling away from
home, but I swear I was out before my head hit the pillow. Didn't even
occur to me that I hadn't brought a toothbrush or anything of the sort.
No, it was like someone had knocked me cold—mind, when I awoke I
was in a state because I could genuinely *feel* how dirty my mouth was.
You ever get that sense? I walked down to the wee store there by the
counter and, wouldn't you know, they had toothbrushes and wee tubes
of paste, luckily for me. I don't think you'd've let me back in the truck."
She buckles the seatbelt.

"I don't think Brooklyn would've minded," Ollie says. "He's the
master of bad morning breath."

"Hey," Brooklyn complains amid cackles from Dahlia.

Ollie continues, "Couldn't kiss him before he brushed."

"You're just laying out all the personal business."

"It's all right, Brooklyn," Dahlia says with a wink. She pats his
cheek. "I won't hear a word of it."

As he backs out of the parking spot, Brooklyn has a sneaking
suspicion that Dahlia throws Ollie a sly glance. The two of them
snicker, and he shakes his head. "I should leave you both here and go
the rest of the way on my own."

"Now, now. You can't do that."

"She's right, you can't get rid of me that easily." Ollie's smirk in the
rearview mirror is mischievous and attractive.

"Oh! Did you happen to see the girl with her mother last night?
They were on the couches when we got there—I don't know what's
reminded me of this. I overheard them talking about this and that, some
winter storms and her friends on a sports team. My guess, she's
probably a softball player. Anyway, her mother was holding a book in

her hand, *The Deepest Shades of Green*—I remember because it had such a beautiful illustration on the cover. I only just realized that the author's name was Durant. Isn't that you?"

Brooklyn's heart had already skipped a few beats when the title of the novel left Dahlia's mouth. After hearing her unexpected question, all he can do is drive toward the highway in silence. He tries to will his organs to recover, but his senses have elevated themselves to a sort of temporal paralysis.

"Yes, it is," Oleander replies for him.

Brooklyn finds his voice again. "My third. My last."

Dahlia nods with understanding.

"It didn't do so well. I didn't think I'd ever see someone with it." The words seem to come from far away, their cadence distorted beyond normal speech.

"Isn't that just like the world to drop you little surprises?"

Little seemed to unfairly restrict the sentiment. "I guess so."

"It's uncanny, something like that: a random woman having your novel in her lap halfway across the country. Sometimes I forget all the people around me have lives. You know? Because I could tell you what's happened to me. If I'm standing in a market, I can tell you the exact sequence of events that found me there: when I woke up, what I had for breakfast, how I decided which trousers to put on, what route I took walking, if I met anyone I knew along the way. And it's exactly that for every single person at that market with me. Something's happened with all of them. I don't think I can ever fully wrap my head around that idea."

Brooklyn listens, appreciating Dahlia's ability to talk without needing much response. But his appreciation is more than superficial— like a fondness for her accent. He enjoys the flow of her words, the rise and fall of her voice. To listen to Dahlia speak is easy because her words grow and bud like fruit trees in a supple orchard.

As they did the day before, the travelers spend the miles of highway lightly engaged in Dahlia's stream of consciousness. The Ranger skirts towns whose names slide by on the highway exit signs without a second thought. They near the junction where Highway 76 splits off southward from Interstate 80, and at once Dahlia sits up straight.

"Oh, we're close to Denver!" she exclaims, pointing at a sign to their left.

"Denver? Like the city Denver?" Brooklyn asks, more out of surprise at her sudden outburst than anything else.

"No, I see me old dog Denver sitting on the side of the road—of course I mean the city."

Brooklyn cannot help but smile. "What's so special about Denver?" he asks. "I've never been there."

"Me neither," Oleander says.

"Before settling in Duchesne, my niece Jackie and her family lived in Denver. It's where she met Roy and had Jimmy. Evy and I came out here to help with their move and we all drove the way through the Rockies to get to Utah. Driving through the mountains was a lovely sight to behold. And I had a brilliant time in Denver as well, in the days leading up. Haven't thought of it since though. Seeing the sign now just brought it all rushing back."

"You want to pass through?" Brooklyn asks.

She entertains the suggestion for a moment. "Nah, it's not that important. Nothing much for me to see there. The sign was exciting, is all."

"If it made you scare me half to death like that, it's got to mean something."

Dahlia laughs. "That's just because I'm bloody senile, boyo."

"Maybe so, but what you just told me doesn't sound like nothing."

"It's not along our way. I think you'd be adding a lot of miles," she says reluctantly, though he can tell the idea is tugging at her like a kitten pulling at a curtain.

"I don't mind," Brooklyn says. "We can drive the same route through the Rockies. I wouldn't say no to some change in scenery." He takes the exit for Highway 76 without further consideration.

Dahlia sighs but then smiles. The corners of her eyes wrinkle. "You're a good lad. I'm glad I found you," she says fondly.

Before long they cross the state line into Colorado and the mile markers count down their approach to the capital. Suburbs ease them into the high-density urban setting, while a wall of mountains capped in white, snowy peaks serves as a backdrop. Clouds curl gracefully through the slopes.

The road is then swallowed by buildings, and the truck becomes one of a thousand other roaming vehicles. Overhead the sun is lost amid the skyscrapers. A sign reads DENVER.

They find themselves at a stoplight and Brooklyn spies a woman in a suit, her pleated skirt pulled high on her waist. She's probably much more put together at the office—one of those workers who rarely take a lunch break, let alone leave for one—but today, she's a bit disheveled. Perhaps her son woke up with a sore throat this morning and couldn't go to school. She couldn't call anyone to take care of him at such late notice—they would already be busy. Sitters are so expensive. So she brought him to the office like she used to when he was a toddler. Brooklyn imagines him sitting at the intern desk she hasn't needed for a while, happily coloring in one of his books. Here he comes now, running to keep up with her. A sandwich should keep him happy. Then she can get back to that review she was making good progress on this morning . . .

"Is there somewhere in particular that comes to mind in Denver?" Oleander asks from the backseat. Brooklyn realizes then that Dahlia's been watching buildings go by through her window. That look of desire has come over her again.

"Yeah, there is," she says.

"We could stop somewhere and find a map," Brooklyn suggests, preferring not to have a repeat of last night's blind scavenger hunt. The woman and her son are gone. They must've rounded a corner somewhere.

"No, see, I've been here before, so I do know where I am." The faltering confidence in her voice strikes a chord of skepticism for Brooklyn, but he lets it slide by for now. Seeing what the last place meant to her reassured him that the search had been worthwhile in the end. "I haven't forgotten everything yet."

"All right, what're we looking for, then?" Brooklyn says.

"It was off Broadway Street. I remember that because Jimmy thought it was where all the plays were. He was much younger then, didn't realize streets in different cities could have the same name and all that. He was confused why we didn't go see a show." Her honeyed cackle stirs the air in the truck. "I tried to tell him, but it took the poor boy a while to understand. It kind of became the running joke of the trip. Yes, but the place was called the Holy Spirit Church, I think. Or the Holy Ghost. One of those two. Catholic place, anyway."

Brooklyn's body involuntarily seizes. His knuckles whiten on the steering wheel, and his back elongates as he sits up against the chair.

"Not comfortable with religion, I see," she says with a gentle grin, taking note of his change in posture.

"It's not religion I have a problem with. I just never know what I'm going to get when it comes to the people," he responds truthfully, and hopes he doesn't need to say more.

"Well, if it helps, I'm not looking to go inside."

And Brooklyn wonders why, then, she wants to see the place. Are they going just to stare at it? He's certain the church is beautiful. Churches in cities like this are always elaborately constructed, made of stone with large stained-glass windows, arches, and pointed turrets reaching up into the sky. They can't compete in height with the glass and concrete buildings around them, of course, but they're tall enough that standing below them is both ominous and impressive. Is that reason enough to go visit one? In Brooklyn's mind, he's already preparing himself for the proximity. He will make subtle, often subconscious changes to his demeanor in the way he walks and speaks, deepening his already gravelly tones. He has never considered himself unmasculine in mannerisms, but the preventative overcompensation can never be helped.

"I don't think there'll be many people there, love," Dahlia says, placing a hand over his arm where it sits on the armrest between them. "It's midday on a Wednesday."

"I'm fine," Brooklyn assures her.

Broadway comes, and they are led down the boulevard toward a cluster of buildings, the tallest Denver has to offer. Brooklyn underestimated the surroundings of Holy Ghost Church: the brick-and-stone building is completely dwarfed by its neighbors, whose pillared bases eclipse the standing height of the single bell tower at the church's forefront. In a symbolic representation of their competing importance in the modern world, the office buildings that share the block nearly engulf the church. A great teal structure curls around the sides of the Holy Ghost as if slowly absorbing the church into its being.

"I think they could've built that one a little closer," Oleander says.

"Yes, well, the space is used efficiently, I suppose." Dahlia laughs. "If there's a spot in one of those lots."

They park without much difficulty, to Brooklyn's surprise, and he and Dahlia nod to Oleander before disembarking into what is a chilly, windswept day. Outside, the bustle of traffic, punctuated by distant sirens, is much louder and echoes like sound in a wind tunnel. Brooklyn and Dahlia join the throngs of people on the sidewalk. Brooklyn resigns himself to the speed of the flow, though it seems faster than the pace Dahlia intended to keep.

"We arrived on a Saturday," Dahlia begins, "and came here that evening. Jackie needed a place to comfort her 'cause she said the idea of moving again, starting over in a new place and all, was frightening. They weren't going to know anybody. It'd be a new house, a new community, a new town to learn. What remained the same amid all the change was a place like this: a church."

The traffic light changes, and they're allowed to cross the street. From their vantage point, the building which threatens to engulf the church hides it from view, but Brooklyn knows what Dahlia means. "I imagine that would be comforting," he admits.

"Jimmy was a wee lad, I think six or so. Didn't really understand what the move meant but could kind of sense it in the way all children can. He was fidgety the whole time. Couldn't stop looking around him like he were watching his back." She giggles. The bell tower is just visible now. "Carl and I took him outside to try and calm him, but as soon as we left the quiet he was on about this and that and not making much sense. Talking about a mile a minute."

"He was going to miss his home," Brooklyn guesses.

"Yeah, but more than that. He said he didn't like moving, didn't like the idea of it. He said, 'Someone's going to take my place, and it's going to be like I was never there before.' Well, what do you say when a six-year-old says something like that? Carl and I, we were baffled. Then Jimmy decided he wanted to leave something behind in every place he went from then on, so that the place never forgot him."

Dahlia seems to choose her words more carefully now, for they come out slow. "I'd be damned if he knew the deeper meaning behind those words, seeing as he was so young. There was no way he could appreciate how the sentiment struck me so. Nearly cried, I did, to see the poor lad struggling that way."

They turn the corner, and the church stands over them now in a glory of beige brickwork and pallid slate. A wide entrance comes to an arch beneath the tracery and scalloped gable. The bell tower stands off to the right, the spire coming to a rounded point beneath the symbol of Christianity. Altogether, the sight is no less impressive or gallant, despite being in the presence of its looming neighbors.

To the left of the church, a group of trees huddles in a triangular patch of earth. In the constant shade of the overgrown branches, the dying grass begs for care and attention. Dahlia drifts toward this area as if magnetically drawn, doing so without conscious thought.

"I ran to the hotel to grab my makeup box, the one I'd taken with me over from Ireland. It was metal and painted mint green with white trim around the corners, so it looked like a little street building." Dahlia speaks while walking out into the triangle, stepping carefully on the soil, ever soft for being in the shade. Brooklyn suspects she counts her steps, arms the slightest bit outstretched on either side.

She chuckles to herself. "Jimmy had nicked a candle from the foyer, the little kleptomaniac. I would've told him to put it back, but I let him keep it because I felt so poorly. Weren't the candles for those who needed the spirit most, anyway? I went back later and paid for it myself. So he put that in first and says, 'In case the place changes.' Then he put in the Matchbox car he'd got with him, the blue one with the windows rolled down on the sides. I didn't have much on me, so I took the pink flower hair brooch and put that in. Carl"—she kneels on the dirt somewhere off center—"says he wants to put something in there too, so he takes off his yellow checkered bowtie and plops it right in."

She starts digging into the soft ground with her fingers, showing no regard for the state of her clothes or hands. At first Brooklyn is taken aback, scanning the area to make sure no church members have seen her doing what he imagines amounts to vandalism. When he doesn't see anybody running forth in alarm, he forces himself to relax and kneels beside her.

The dirt comes away easily, and already the hole Dahlia's dug is considerable in depth. There's not an ounce of uncertainty in her eyes. Before she has to lean forward too far to keep digging, her hands scrape the lid of something metal. She gasps, memory electrocuting her more than any shock that it's still here. Brooklyn sees swaths of pale green amid the brown-red rust, a pastel hue that reminds him of mint ice cream and summer heat. The lid is dented from the weight of the earth but still intact and fairly smooth despite the rust encroaching on it.

Dahlia gets her hands around the sides of the box and removes it from the hole with only slight difficulty. Brooklyn can hear items sliding around inside. Minute windows are painted around the sides of the tin, and there's even a doorway with a two-dimensional stoop.

Dahlia *tsks*. "Oh, I haven't seen this thing in ages," she says, and flashes Brooklyn a wide smile. "Look at it. It's beautiful."

"Doesn't look like it's been touched since you left it," he says, excited by her time capsule.

"No, indeed it hasn't, love. Not by a single soul." She puts the box on the ground beside the hole and takes off the lid, which releases with a *pop*. "Isn't that darling?"

Cut off from the world, the elements, and even time itself, the objects sit inside unchanged. Brooklyn sees them as if he's viewed them before in his mind. The candle is thin and white, about the length of his palm and as thick as his thumb. He can tell it had only been used maybe once or twice by the time Jimmy had taken it, for the wick is black and the tip only faintly indented. The Matchbox car is electric blue and looks like a Ford Mustang from somewhere in the sixties or seventies. There are no plastic windows in the doors, so they look like they're rolled down. Dahlia's brooch is of a many-tiered flower with soft-pointed petals. The fabric is starched and rigid, and the colors are painted carefully enough that Brooklyn wonders if it was done by hand. Lastly, Carl's bowtie—in a rich honey-mustard shade—sits folded with the loop still intact but loose as though it had been hastily pulled over the head at the last minute. But the pleats in the wings are still intact, and the pattern is reminiscent of a man who hails from a homey town in the Midwest.

"The mass ended right as we were burying it, and his mum and dad came out confused as to why the ground between us had been dug up and our hands were all filthy." She looks at her fingers as if that scene were playing out at this moment. Dirt is caked beneath her nails, and streaks of black are embedded in the lines of her palms. "Of course, they laughed when we told them—they weren't strict about those things—and then we went on our way."

"Did Jimmy keep doing it, like he said? Leaving bits of himself wherever he went?"

"I'm not sure. The subject never came up again. At the very least, I never made another one of these with him, and they never moved from Duchesne, so I couldn't tell you." Dahlia puts the tin on her lap while she kneels and runs her hands over the surface, memorizing every kink and crease. "We are strange creatures, Brooklyn, assigning sentimentality to things."

"Are you going to bring the box to him?"

She stares down at the treasures for a moment, deciding. Then she shakes her head. "No, I don't think I will."

"You don't think he'd like to see them?"

"Oh, I think he'd love to see them, but I might just remind him what's here. If he wants, maybe someday he'll come to find the box himself. I think it'd be nice if it's in the ground here waiting. That'd be a much more meaningful adventure for him to have."

Dahlia takes the lid and closes it over the tin again, gingerly placing it back into the hole. The breeze kicks up ever so slightly as she scoops the dirt over the box, burying her memories and a new bit of herself along with it as she goes. Little by little, the mint green box disappears from sight until there's nothing left but a square of broken land bordered by a hill of sparse grass.

Chapter Nineteen

The sun is already dipping toward the mountains in the distance by the time Brooklyn, Dahlia, and Oleander leave. The clouds have begun changing colors, their palette the fragile, warm hues of dusk.

The city falls away behind them, the density of cars thins. The tallest buildings are gone, shrinking steadily beyond the river and the highway junctions. The homes and businesses here are short and have more room to breathe. When the travelers reach the city limits, they begin to climb. The earth has become barren: large red slopes with scant black brush. In the depression off to their left, a thin creek descends the mountain.

The truck whines against the slope, the engine struggling to accelerate. Although Brooklyn wills the old Ranger forward, pushing the pedal down almost to the floor and causing the engine to rev, the vehicle does not pick up any noticeable speed. He places a hand on the dashboard.

"Sounds like somebody's fighting," Dahlia says.

"Yeah, but it'll be all right," Brooklyn replies, palm still flat on the plastic as if the vehicle might be able to feel his encouragement. "We'll make it over."

"Might be a slower go than you were hoping for." She smiles and lays her head back against the headrest.

They ascend into the Rocky Mountains, following the whims of the landscape. When the mountain curls, so too does the highway. They rise together, plateau together, and then rise again. Hidden in the mountains are lakes, canyons, and valleys Brooklyn would've never guessed were so close to the city. When the valley is wide enough, houses appear, strung along the thin roads like Christmas lights. Barren hills give way to cliffs—stark gray outcroppings jutting angrily toward the sky, their weatherworn surfaces rocky and coarse—which give way to impenetrable masses of evergreen trees. The views are at once intimidating and beautiful. Without inquiry, Brooklyn knows Oleander is taken by the display. He has always been partial to the forest and mountains, second maybe to his love of the coast. Oleander had suggested on numerous occasions they visit the Rockies or the Sierras, enamored by the prospect of spending even just a weekend hidden away among the pine trees. They had done so while they were dating, but once they'd settled in Schoharie, they'd never returned. Perhaps this was retribution in some way.

By the time they reach a town called Silverthorne, the night is full and dark and the sky is a wide expanse of uncountable stars. A bright moon leads the way.

In Silverthorne, the buildings all have corrugated steel roofs sloped appropriately to discourage any snow from taking hold. Though many are a dim green or brown that melds nicely with the surroundings, some are painted with bold colors that shine in the darkness. He sees yellows, reds, and even a few violets.

"How far do you plan on making it tonight?" Dahlia asks.

"I don't know. I suppose we should've stayed the night in Denver. I've been on autopilot since we left." Brooklyn smirks. "We're not making it all the way to Duchesne tonight, are we?"

"We could, but that'd be quite the journey." She laughs. "I don't know that my bum is up for that. What says you, Oleander?"

Oleander snorts from the backseat. "You may have found the person with the least say in this discussion."

"Forgot about that tidbit."

"We can stay here if we find a place," Brooklyn suggests. Silverthorne is a gorgeous setting, nestled in a wide valley with the looming snow-capped peaks mapped against the night sky.

"We *could* do that," Dahlia agrees. She surveys the town. "But I've just had another thought."

"Ooh, a thought. I can't wait," Brooklyn says.

"We'll have none of that sass." She laughs, and slaps him on the arm. "Didn't anyone teach you to respect your fecking elders?"

"Yes, yes, of course. I'm sorry."

"That's more like it." Her rosy smile appears in the darkness. "What if we slept outside?"

"Do I have to respect the senile?"

"Brooklyn!" Ollie gasps, but Dahlia cackles.

"What? She's obviously mad."

"And why's that so mad?" Dahlia asks, getting hold of herself with difficulty.

"It's the end of October in the Rocky Mountains," Brooklyn responds. "It's going to be nearly freezing out there."

"Ah, to hell with the cold. We've got a tent," she insists.

"I thought the tent was for your nephew?" Ollie asks.

"Yes, thank you. I thought it was for him," Brooklyn says.

"Yeah, but Jimmy won't mind if I use it once, dammit. Especially if I've got a good reason."

"Does having a crazy death wish qualify?" Brooklyn asks.

"Now you're just overreacting, love."

"Well, you can't sleep out in the cold in just a tent. What about the hard ground? We haven't got any food, just a lantern," Brooklyn argues amicably, though he feels the tendrils of frustration worming their way back into his head.

"It can't be that bad."

"Yeah, it's probably not that bad." Ollie's smiling now, having a bit of fun.

"Hey, choose a side. I'd like to survive through to morning," Brooklyn says.

"Well, what about stopping at one of these stores? They're bound to sell stuff like that." Dahlia gestures out the window at a large A-frame building with a sign advertising sports gear and car chains. Brooklyn marvels at the comedic timing of the universe.

"You're really serious about this, aren't you?" he asks, and the truck grows quiet for a moment.

"I think it would be incredible."

Brooklyn sighs, his eyes drifting over the road before them. This time, Dahlia has no sentimental excuse, no attachment that could persuade Brooklyn into action. This is nothing more than a crazy whim bolstered by her recent streak of spontaneity. Had this been any other trip with another person—say, Jimmy, her sister, or Carl . . .

Brooklyn glances at Oleander in the mirror and sighs inwardly. If this had been any other trip for either of them, the thought would've never occurred. But this *isn't* any other trip.

He gets into the leftmost lane to make a U-turn.

"I was hoping you'd come around," Dahlia says.

"You'd better pray that store's still open, for your sake."

They find a pair of space-grade, insulated, high-tech sleep sacks, which Dahlia dubs "magic bags." She opts to use Jimmy's tent, though they both admit that neither of them has constructed a tent in their lives, much less fiddled with one in the dark. Rather than buying a second, Brooklyn decides he can sleep in the truck bed.

"Seeing as it's already dark, where do you suggest we set up our camp?" Brooklyn asks once they've exited the shop. The night has a certain bite to it, but Brooklyn admits reluctantly that it's not freezing. There's little wind, and the stillness helps.

"I was thinking somewhere along the road outside the town," Dahlia says, opening the bed of the truck so Brooklyn can put the sleeping bags inside.

"Sounds peachy."

"You guys find what you were looking for?" Oleander asks through the sliding window in the back of the truck cabin.

Brooklyn displays the bags for him.

As a final stop, they run into the local market minutes before the doors are locked to grab some dinner. It's nothing more than peanut butter, jam, and bread ("And stuff for s'mores! Jimmy'd never forgive me if he found out I'd been camping and hadn't made s'mores, for Chrissakes!"), but Brooklyn foresees that they won't have the means for cooking. Then the nice, quiet town of Silverthorne disappears into the night all too soon, and they're back on Route 9.

"Not a soul in sight on this Wednesday night," Dahlia intones with a husky voice. "Been working on that one in my head for the past fifteen minutes. I'm a poet, don't you know?"

"Yeah, yeah," Brooklyn says. He can hear the sleeping bags sliding around in the back, and his hands tighten on the wheel. Begrudgingly, however, he knows his anxiety is interwoven with the slightest thread of excitement. *Were this any other trip*, he keeps thinking. Perhaps that will be the motif of the evening.

They wind their way through the woods in the dark, Brooklyn's worries like wisps of smoke around his eyes. Farther and farther they go until all the world is silent and a dirt road appears off to the right, overlooking a river. The relatively flat path is host to only a few trees grouped in small patches. It looks like a campground, or at least what used to be one, though it's unpopulated this evening. The three travelers silently agree to spend the night here.

Brooklyn drives the Ranger down to the lower section, close to the riverbank and the sound of flowing water. The vehicle rolls to a stop and the engine dies, the hum disappearing into the moonlit atmosphere. Nobody speaks; they breathe as the mountain air seeps in through the seams in the vehicle.

"Should I be the first to break out the graham crackers and chocolate?" Dahlia asks.

"And marshmallows. Can't forget those," Oleander chimes in.

Brooklyn smirks. "We didn't buy anything to start a fire."

"Fair enough. I'll eat them unmelted." Dahlia shrugs. "Should we do it?"

She opens the door and slides off the seat. Brooklyn spins around to look at Oleander. "I hope this ends well," he says, and then follows after her.

Even if it's not freezing temperatures, Brooklyn is beginning to regret that he didn't buy a better coat while they were at the store. He might as well not be wearing one, for all the good his does him. The chill worsens exponentially in the passing minutes, so he dives into the back of the truck, searching feverishly. Before long he fishes out his only long-sleeve shirt from his travel bag and shoves it on over his T-shirt. Three thin layers are enough to stave off the worst of the bite. Then he and Dahlia get to work on opening the tent by the light of the lantern.

Though the packaging uses superfluous amounts of plastic bags and tape, the assembly of the tent seems straightforward enough. The process is made difficult only by the dim setting. Elastic cables hold the thin tubular frame taut, and the nylon fabric pulls tight over the skeleton like skin. In less than ten minutes, a cocoon-like tent big enough for someone to crawl into sits proudly behind the truck.

Brooklyn and Dahlia step back, feeling disproportionately accomplished for having completed the assembly. With the tailgate of the truck down, they sit side by side eating their peanut butter and jelly sandwiches. The water trickles by not twenty feet away, slow in this wide section. The river makes peace with the existing quiet, each compromising where they must for the other to be content. The running water sings somewhere below the conscious, writing lyrics in the gap where the mind meets the soul.

"I know we're probably going to make it to Duchesne tomorrow, so I wanted to take this time to thank you, Brooklyn. I've had an incredible experience in such a short amount of time," Dahlia says, staring down at the black water.

"What, me taking you to a couple of places from your past? It was nothing," Brooklyn says, uncomfortable with the gratitude.

"I'm serious. Maybe you can't understand what a wake-up call this all has been, but I think I needed it. I was doing me laundry, boyo, and now I'm on top of a mountain!" She turns to him and smiles. "Plus, I can't wait to see the look on Jimmy's face when I arrive at his door."

"I'm sure he'll be thrilled," Brooklyn says. He wonders why people have an automatic tendency to swing their legs when they can't touch the ground.

"By the by, I think it's great, what you're doing. I think it's a fantastic way to heal," she continues.

"What?"

"Driving from one side of the country to the other, of course. Carrying this box back here. It's not hard to figure out, love. I think it's wonderful that you've the courage to get out here and do what you need to do, to say yes to everything and not hold back." Dahlia's voice carries over the river.

Brooklyn shakes his head. "I don't think courageous is the right word. I think if I didn't—I mean, if I hadn't left when I did . . ." He finds that his tongue is tied, twisted in the brambles of all his thoughts and all the things he's trying to say but also simultaneously keep hidden. For the second time this week, a voice inside him asks why he is speaking to this relative stranger, telling her what he could not say to his closest friends. "I've been terrified this entire time. I've had to be persuaded to keep going, to do anything, the entire way."

"It's all right to be afraid," Dahlia says. "Lord knows, no matter what you go through, some things are never going to stop scaring you. I think the difference is that you're doing something about it. You're *doing* something."

"I've wanted to turn around so many times," Brooklyn admits. "If I hadn't met you, if I hadn't met Zinnia, I think I would have."

Dahlia doesn't ask who Zinnia is. Instead she nods. "People help you along the way. That's part of life."

She reaches out and takes Brooklyn's hand in hers. He looks down at it, seeing the elegant lines that pattern her skin, lines etched by age and time. He wonders how many hands they've shaken, embraces they've pulled closer, stories they've punctuated, waves they've given in greeting and in goodbye.

"You should never have to go the way alone," she says.

Brooklyn glances behind him at the truck's cabin.

The lantern's glow is a silvery-white that feels almost like a mist. But though it's strong and bright right beside the lantern, the glow dissipates quickly into the wide world. Sitting there on the tailgate of the truck, Brooklyn realizes how much bigger everything around him is. The river disappears from sight in either direction, the path winding as it makes its way down to lower elevations. What he can see now is only an insignificant portion of what is tens or possibly hundreds of miles long. Scattered on the bank, the trees reach for a canvas above they will never touch. And in the distance, the mountains surround the valley, standing unimaginably immense. Their peaks and ridges have been formed over millions of years.

Brooklyn feels small. He feels incredibly minute amid the vast expanses.

"When did he die?" Dahlia asks.

Brooklyn's face is wet. "Five years ago." His voice breaks, so he resorts to a whisper. "Just this past weekend."

His heart is heavy. So incredibly heavy. The weight of it is painful, curling his spine forward. He wants nothing more than to lie on his side until the pain goes away. Instead he clutches at his chest with his free hand, feeling tears drip from his chin onto his sleeve.

"We were arguing so much back then. It seemed like every day. We fought about our home, our jobs, the people we knew—anything and everything until it was even the stupidest, inanest reasons you could think of. At a certain point the arguments got to be too much. Ollie told me we were never going to last if we didn't spend some time apart.

He had been thinking. He had thought too long about it, and it was the only solution he could come up with. I hated the idea. I didn't think it could ever work, because it felt like giving up. We fought with each other, yes, but at the same time I never wanted him to leave. I couldn't—but it was clear something wasn't working.

"I didn't want to give him that time away, because I *knew* we wouldn't be coming back. Letting him go would be admitting that we weren't supposed to be together—at least, that's what I thought back then.

"So he decided that if we couldn't agree to spend some time apart, he would just leave." Brooklyn realizes how tightly he is holding Dahlia's hand, but she holds his just as firm, so he does not break the touch. He keeps holding. "I begged him to stay. I promised I would change, even though I'd made that promise before. 'It isn't forever,' he told me. He was just going back to his family in California. I begged him, and he always gave me the same response. 'I won't be gone forever.' So I gave in. I couldn't keep him with me in Schoharie if he was bent on leaving. I drove him to the city, I went with him to the airport. This was back when I could go right up to the gate and watch him board. He left and I sat there. I sat there for six and a half hours."

The taste on his tongue is salty. His voice shakes so much it's unrecognizable in his ears. "He was gone for three months. We wrote letters to each other and called once, but he wanted to emphasize that we were supposed to be figuring ourselves out, deciding what we wanted. But how could we do that from different sides of the country? I already knew what I wanted. I already knew!"

He has to stop here, exhausted from tears and pain. Though she remains silent, Dahlia leans in and wraps her arms around him, pulling him close and letting him cry in a way he hasn't in many years. He leans into her, unashamed, uninhibited, until the aching begins to subside. Until the weight of his heart is not so heavy. She holds him fast and does not let go until his shoulders have stopped shivering and he's quiet again.

Beneath them, the car settles into the night. The mechanics tick as they contract, the cold seeping in through the metal walls of the pipes, chambers, cylinders, and body. Cold that is sharp but comforting. Cold that means rest.

Then Brooklyn straightens up, his eyes sore and nose congested. "The call came from his sister. It was around midnight, but I was still awake, writing. Like I always was when I was too busy for him. She told me he'd been walking home from the store and was hit by a drunk driver. The person took off; she didn't know how long he'd been lying there. When he was found, the paramedics rushed him to the hospital, but that was it. He was already dead."

Shallow breaths. Still limbs. Dahlia holds his hand though. "That was it," Brooklyn repeats. "A few hours and everything was over. There were no memorials or parades, no fireworks set off, no announcements made, no flyers run, no articles printed, no mass emails sent out. We had a funeral, but he wasn't in their papers or on their televisions, so nobody cared. He died alone; not even the person who killed him stuck around. He died, and everybody kept living their lives as if nothing happened."

His voice breaks again. "They wouldn't even let me see his body." Closed black casket. White roses tied together with garnet ribbon, their blossoms perfect but their thorns cut. Amber light streaming through the painted windows onto the chapel floor and the neatly lined pews. "I never got the chance to say goodbye."

They sit in a populated silence, Brooklyn letting the images wash over him. He closes his eyes because it helps. The images haven't faded like paintings; they are rich in color, emotion, and meaning. He does his best to sort them chronologically, but they don't lead him here to this mountain range. Instead they file backward from the moment Oleander boarded that airplane, toward a time when he and Oleander Rhodes were together and happy. Back to when everything felt right and good, and he could say that this was all he wanted. Back through the years they spent together, exploring the worlds without and within themselves.

"I love him," Brooklyn says at last.

"I know," Dahlia whispers, hand still strong. "I know."

Chapter Twenty

"It won't start again." Brooklyn turns the key harder, as if more vigor will get the truck going.

"Again? You mean this has happened already?" Dahlia asks.

"A couple of days ago, but that was the first time." He turns the key, and the engine sputters for a few moments but fails to turn over. "It hasn't struggled since, so I thought it was fine. I guess not."

He sits back, letting his head fall against the headrest. Of course, this would happen when they've stopped in an unpopulated area.

"Try it one more time," Oleander urges. "Please, we can't be stuck out here."

"I'm ruddy useless when it comes to motors, but I agree. Give it one more go." Dahlia turns to Ollie. "Or we can try the American way," she says, and kicks her foot up a bit.

Brooklyn is skeptical, since nothing has changed, but because of their shared interest in moving forward—and their lack of alternative options—he takes hold of the key once more and twists it in the ignition.

The same dry sputtering—and then the engine roars to life.

Brooklyn stares down at the steering wheel between his hands. He breathes a silent sigh of relief, not wanting the others to know how worried he was. When he's sure the truck's running continuously, Brooklyn shifts into gear. The Ranger trundles out of the camp site, bouncing over the unpaved trail. It rejoins the highway.

"Well, that was an exciting way to start the morning," Dahlia says. She pulls at the wrinkles in her shirt, as she's still dressed how she slept. "After an enlightening night, I wasn't sure how the day would go, but I guess that's the universe answering!"

"What does that mean?" Oleander asks.

"Nothing," Brooklyn replies, probably far too quickly.

"Sleeping out under the stars really puts things into perspective," Dahlia says matter-of-factly, her answer much more relaxed and believable than Brooklyn's. She gives only a sly look in Brooklyn's direction, but he catches it.

"It was odd having you close," Ollie says. "I woke a few times during the night, and you were just on the other side of this glass. You're never usually that close. It was nice. Comforting."

"I was surprised you didn't open the window," Brooklyn says.

"I thought about it, but then I thought maybe you'd like your privacy."

And Brooklyn is reminded how different things are now. How close they can be, yet at the same time how cold. So he plants a wayward smile on his lips. "That's the smallest tent I've ever seen, Dahlia. They really meant one person, didn't they?"

"More of a glorified tarp with a frame, if you ask me," she says. "I don't think there's even room to shag if you wanted. I wouldn't've felt more claustrophobic in me own casket. Next time, I'll just pull the bag over my head." She giggles, and then seems to consider the tent again. "I guess it did keep out the wind, so it wasn't a total loss."

"Worth the money?" Brooklyn asks wryly.

"All forty-four dollars, love."

In the mountains, the wind is almost visible. The trees watch as it flits past, turning their heads this way and that, eager for it to run its fingers through their branches.

In the red truck, the trio descends the other side of the mountains, the passing altitude signs marking their steady fall. While the markers pass, Brooklyn thinks on what it will mean when Dahlia leaves. He can already feel the stark sense of bereavement—so quickly it seems to form, especially when he's unaccustomed to attachment—building in his chest as it had when Zinnia requested her stop in Orland Park. Though the sentiment is sorrowful, he becomes angry with himself. This useless attachment to people. This accumulation of sadness. He had encouraged himself to help Dahlia because helping her would be the right thing to do. But why should he encourage himself to fill his life with people when they all leave him at some point?

He doesn't want to be angry with himself. He doesn't want to be angry with Dahlia. She has no part in this. She'd come to him wanting to join his journey, but she couldn't have understood the implications. And maybe she still doesn't fully grasp what has been at stake here. No, she's innocent. If nothing else, her intentions are good. He has a feeling she knows no other way.

This all has to do with Brooklyn allowing her to come along and allowing himself to become emotionally attached. He knows how he is. Hadn't their friends joked that he'd become unsentimental? Hadn't he refused every emotional encounter, opting instead to observe from a distance? Hadn't he ignored the phone calls and the door chimes and the emails that began with "I heard and I'm sorry" until they all went away? He hadn't even said goodbye to their friends, after all.

Does he dislike awkward goodbyes, or is he afraid?

They pass through the town of Hayden, Colorado. Like many other quiet towns along the road, it's akin to a dream. Brooklyn finds himself among the houses, having no recollection of when they began.

"We can't be far, then," Dahlia says absently.

"What do you think they'll do when they see you?" Ollie asks.

"I'm not really sure. Be surprised and happy, I hope. If they can't have me, I'll hole up somewhere else, but I'm hoping they'll give me room and board."

"You think they might not?" Ollie asks.

"I have very little doubt they would. My sister was one of the more hospitable people of the world, and her daughter inherited the same disposition. But I would never want to impose, of course." She sighs.

"She *was* hospitable?" Ollie asks.

"Oh yes, Evelyn passed away some time ago, love. Age took her swiftly and gracefully. She was one of the luckier ones: died in her sleep, felt little pain. It was almost like she knew it was going to happen. Got through the holidays, visited friends and such, and then she was gone, just like that." Dahlia snaps her fingers.

"That must've been terrible to go through," Brooklyn says.

"It was." Dahlia's answer is truthful and blunt at first, but then she shakes her head and shrugs. "Nothing is quite like losing a loved one."

"I don't know how you get over that," Brooklyn says.

"You learn because you have to. If you don't, holding on to them will do terrifying things."

"But if that person was close to you, they become an integral part of who you are. How can a car run if it's missing the engine?" asks Brooklyn.

"It's not easy. Nobody ever said it was." The last rows of homes pass them by, and they leave the town behind. Dahlia watches it disappear in the side mirror. "The only way to do it is to force yourself onward. They're confident words, I know, but they're true, I assure you.

"My sister told me a story once, and I think you might like to hear it. She was not a storyteller, like you, and I'm sure I'll butcher it even further, but I thought it beautiful. At the very least, it stuck with me."

"Go ahead," Brooklyn says.

"All right, let's see. Three figures trekked across a forest land with their guide—oh, it's one of those fantasy stories by the way, Evy *loved* fantasies. So they have their guide, Iam, and they're seeking refuge from a country filled with poverty and despair. As they walked, they came upon the Floodwood River, which stretched beyond where the eye could see in either direction. On their side of the river, an old man sat in his chair beneath an oak tree, watching the water. He kept a gnarled wooden staff on his lap. On the other bank was a young woman clothed in a flowing black dress, and she had with her a great treasure: the most enticing collection of books, food, and elegant fabrics the figures had ever seen.

"As they approached the old man, he dug his walking stick into the dirt and called to them. 'Hello, my friends. Welcome to the river,' he said. 'I am Antiquus, and I've lived here all my life.'" Dahlia gives her best old-man voice and crooks her arm as if holding a staff.

"They greeted him as they should. The woman on the opposite side of the Floodwood River took notice of them and stood at the water's edge to watch. Antiquus continued to speak. 'I see you have spied the woman there on the other bank. Her name is Reliquus, and she has everything you might need to continue your journey. But I warn you, I have seen everyone who has ever come this way, and no one person has ever managed to cross the Floodwood River.'

"Though Antiquus gave his warning, the first figure had stopped listening to the old man. They'd set their eyes upon one of the reams of fabric in the collection on the other bank and had grown deaf to all else. Ignoring Antiquus, the first figure ran forward into the water, sure that their strength and determination would get them through to the other side. But the water was devastatingly cold and the current strong. Before they could make it through, the figure was swept off their feet and taken away.

"Seeing the first figure being carried swiftly downstream, the second became afraid. They thought about all the people Antiquus had seen come this way and—though the figure prized many of the riches Reliquus offered—knelt by the old man's side. Antiquus listened as they vowed to help the old man and heed his stories of the dangers he had seen until the day they died.

"The last figure considered the paths their companions had chosen and the warning that Antiquus had given. With Reliquus in sight, they took their guide by the hand and waded into the river. The water was devastatingly cold and the current incredibly strong. Slowly they trudged through the deepest part of the waterway, where they could use nothing but their toes to hold their ground. But after much arduous travel, they made it to the other side. On the bank, Reliquus welcomed them into her outstretched arms. She offered them the textiles to make clothes and the books to gain knowledge of the new land they'd entered. While no one person had ever made it across, the two of them together had made it to safety."

Dahlia finishes speaking, and the cabin falls silent except for the sound of tires on the road. The scent of pine is subtle and thin.

"Did your sister make that up?" Oleander asks, the first to respond.

"I thought maybe she'd heard it once from our Da. He was always telling fables to sate our curiosities—could've given Aesop a run for his money—but I never did ask her. I was young enough that I wasn't too worried about such things at the time. In fact, I may have pretended I didn't think much of it. As a teenager, I was flippant with the best of them. Story never left me, though, and I still think on it from time to time when I need a bit of a boost."

"People love hearing stories like that, don't they?" Brooklyn says. His words feel vague, and any number of meanings can be taken from his tone, but his jawline is rigid.

"It doesn't hurt," she responds.

Brooklyn lets her words sit on his mind.

"So, who are you?" Ollie asks.

"I would definitely like to be the third figure," Dahlia says with a knowing grin. "And sometimes I am. But sometimes I'm more the second, the figure who pledges to stay on the shore. It's a comfortable place, and it's safe. It poses the least threat to what I am, but that doesn't mean I'm happy there or that I'll achieve any of the things I want to."

"I suppose the moral is to be the third, the Floodwood River's crosser?" Brooklyn asks, a little more harshly than he means to.

"I suppose," Dahlia echoes. "Yeah, something like that."

#

When the sun is at its pinnacle above the cloud cover, when the Rocky Mountains have long since dissipated into pale blue particles and the forests have turned to low, pallid brush, another town sidles up to the highway. Brooklyn can tell it's their destination even before the welcome sign appears. Dahlia has clasped her hands in her lap, and her gaze is unshakable.

"You seem really nervous, Dahlia," Oleander observes gently. "Are you worried?"

Dahlia's eyes remain on the road in front of them while she answers. "I just—It's been a long time since I've come to visit, or written, or even called. You start off with a weekly conversation on the telly to make sure you stay in contact, and someone slips up once. It's all downhill from there. Next thing you know, you're only in contact for birthdays and holidays."

Brooklyn turns off the highway, and the speed limit reduces to a residential thirty-five miles per hour. All of a sudden they find themselves immersed in Duchesne. The post office slides by on their right, its flag raised and waving. The town is small enough that houses border even the main street. Their driveways open up right onto the avenue. Low chain-link fences separate the wide yards but are not enough to break the atmosphere of community, which binds the properties in the same way as the grass growing uninterrupted from one lot to the next.

"Plus, it feels strange coming up unannounced," Dahlia continues. "Modern times don't really allow for such things anymore."

"You'll be a serendipitous surprise," Brooklyn suggests.

"That's the goal, isn't it?" Dahlia sighs, playing absentmindedly with her wedding ring. "Oh, I shouldn't be so flustered. I'm going to look a right mess when I walk up there. Not that I won't already, having slept outside last night. A bloody loon, I am. I'm sure I look off my rocker—squat and disheveled and not at all what I should look like coming around. Would you want to come meet them?" she asks suddenly, as if the thought has just occurred to her.

"What? Go up to the door with you?" Brooklyn asks.

"Yeah, I've talked about them enough. If you wanted to meet them, they probably wouldn't mind."

Brooklyn considers the possibility. He could meet Dahlia's family, the ones whose memory was enough to make her want to travel the country on a spontaneous journey with a stranger. The ones about whom she spoke so fondly and with such vivid recollection. He could see how these mental impressions match the real people. It might be fun.

But something tugging at the back of his mind makes him withdraw. The figures recede from sight behind a phantom shadow.

"I don't know that I should, Dahlia," he says. "Thank you for the invite, but I think your reunion should be between you and your family. No matter how they might react, I'd feel like I was intruding, for lack of a better word." Then he shrugs. "Besides, I think it would be a little weird to show up with a stranger at their door and say, 'This is the random guy I met at my laundromat who drove me across the country.'"

He's surprised by how much this makes Dahlia laugh. Her tension seems to ease a bit, and so does his.

"Well, I could try fighting you, but you've said no and I'll respect that—Make a right here on North Center Street." Dahlia points down a smaller lane. "Oh, it looks much the same as it did the last time I was here. Isn't that wonderful?"

There are no sidewalks. The asphalt curves down into the grass in front of the squat, symmetrical houses. The chain-link fences around the front yards butt against the road.

"But I wish there was something I could give as a thank you for taking me all this way," Dahlia says. "Both of you. Don't worry, I'm not letting you off the hook, Oleander. I don't have much with me though—"

"It's all right," Brooklyn says. "I'm certain I won't be forgetting you any time soon. And I think that'll be thanks enough."

Dahlia takes hold of his arm. He realizes then that she's tired and probably feels much older than she did even just an hour ago. After all, she has seen life and death intimately. She has watched people grow around her from infants into adults, and so too has she seen people evanesce, leaving behind nothing more than a breath of memory. And maybe a small topaz stone in a ring.

Then Dahlia cracks a wry smile, and Brooklyn is reminded of how youthful she can be as well. "That could either be the sweetest thing anyone's ever told me or a snide insult, love." Her barking cackle fills the truck one last time.

"Jesus, Mary, and Joseph," she exclaims. She watches the houses pass for a few moments. They've been a part of this neighborhood longer than most residents. Brass wind chimes hang over porches, as do several flags and numerous rust-colored pots with lively plants.

Dahlia says, "If you could stop here, please."

The Ranger comes to a standstill.

"They're just around this corner," she says. "Unless I've been corresponding with strangers, of course."

"You don't want me to drive up?" Brooklyn asks.

"No. If I remember correctly, it's a dead end on a real narrow lane, so it'll be harder to get out than just parking here."

"It's no problem, really."

"It's fine. I will let you help me carry the bags to the fence though." Dahlia winks and then turns in her seat to face the back, undoing the safety belt. "This is goodbye, Oleander."

He nods. "I hope you find what you're looking for."

"I hope you do too." She looks from Oleander to Brooklyn and back again.

"Until next time?" Oleander grins.

"Yeah," she says.

The air has been getting steadily colder, and it rushes into the cabin without invitation when she opens the door. Brooklyn follows after her with a casual "I won't be long" to Ollie as he leaves. He hops down to the pavement with the sense that—once again—the world completely changed around him since the last time he was outside this truck.

Wordlessly, he opens the back, reaching in to grab the two rolled-up sleeping bags. His bag is still back there, having slid to one corner.

Beside it is the box. He grabs Dahlia's tote, the lantern, and the tent as well. She closes the hatch.

"I'll take that," Dahlia says, grabbing one of the sleeping bags from him. Together they make their way down the lane. The air is heavy with silence.

Dahlia's mind seems occupied, and Brooklyn wonders if they'll reach her family's home before she says anything. Indeed, she watches the road as they travel, perhaps familiarizing herself with the aromatic trees that give the air that scent of homeliness. The clinging apples and thick leaves of cherry trees shade porches. Indigo and fiery, many-petaled flowers bloom in flower boxes along slate garden paths. Plastic straw–stemmed windmills spin listlessly.

Dahlia stops by a gate. "You can drop the bags on the other side," she says. With a little difficulty due to her squat stature, she chucks her load over the fence, and it falls to the grass. Brooklyn lowers the things he carries on the other side.

The house is a pale blue, the kind that makes him think of icing on a cake. On the front porch is a chairlift swing with a plain beige canopy to match the cushions. A few empty flowerpots line the foundation, but besides that the yard is mostly well-kept grass. Brooklyn sees a thick tartan welcome mat in faded yellows and reds sitting before the front door. The curtains are pulled over a large front window, but a sign that looks like it might've been hand-painted some time ago by a child hangs in the center. It says HOME.

"Are you going in now?" Brooklyn asks.

"Soon," Dahlia replies. "I need a few minutes to compose myself, take in the fresh air, spend a little time with the old man who lives on the riverbank." She nudges Brooklyn in the ribs affectionately. "Although, come to think of it, I don't think they're home right now, it being a workday and all."

"After all that, we got you here too early. Sorry. You could stay with us for a bit longer if you'd like. We could find something in town to keep us busy."

"No, don't be silly, love. I want you to get on your way. You've got some important journeying ahead of you," she says. "You need this."

Brooklyn is still for a second and then nods.

"Thanks again, love," Dahlia says. "We've had a wonderful adventure, haven't we?"

"Yes, we have," Brooklyn says. They embrace, and he catches the floral scent of her perfume again. She pulls him tighter, her arms stronger than he would've thought; it's comforting. In this instant, Brooklyn could swear he'd hugged her this way all his life. "You'll be all right, Dahlia?"

"I think I will be," she says.

And then it's time for Brooklyn to go.

He relinquishes the embrace, backing away a few steps to get a full look at her. On the outside she looks much the same as she did a couple of days ago when they left the laundromat together in Des Moines: short, with a touch of approachable roundness. Her hair is the type of gray that matches the storm clouds overhead.

Brooklyn asks one final question: "How did you know?"

She says to him, "Sometimes, we carry our troubles so plainly that everyone can see them."

He nods his final goodbye, not wanting to say the word, and Dahlia smiles brightly in response. Then he turns away and drifts back down the lane, passing the squat houses with their fruit trees, flower patches, and wind chimes. He doesn't look back, not even when he rounds the corner onto the street where the pickup sits patiently on the edge of the asphalt. In his mind he sees her debating in which direction she should walk first, probably muttering to herself and wondering whether she could get one of those tabloid magazines at the gas station she saw on the main strip to keep her busy, just in case it's a while before her family comes back. After all, she isn't sure whether Jimmy still plays American football or has one of those troop meetings today. It isn't anything she minds, though. It will be enough to see their faces when they catch sight of her sitting on their doorstep.

Goodbye, Dahlia, Brooklyn thinks. *I'll miss you.*

Chapter Twenty-One

"Are you going to be okay?" Oleander asks.

"Of course. Why do you ask?" Brooklyn responds, sounding more irritated than he means to. He relaxes his jaw, shakes his head in an attempt to clear his mind, and tries to loosen his brow.

"You're extremely quiet."

"I guess. That's how we usually are, though," Brooklyn says. He was the one who'd grown to hate silence.

"I know." Oleander is close to Brooklyn's ear, resting his head against the shoulder of the seat. "Things have been different. I thought maybe now we would be too."

"It's different when you have three people in the car," Brooklyn snaps. He feels guilty. For all he can see, Oleander isn't offended by his aggression. In the rearview mirror, his expression is passive and distant—almost sad. Is he secretly grieving their loss of Dahlia too? Or maybe there's another reason. Brooklyn can never tell. He was never as perceptive at reading Oleander as he often was with other people. Perhaps this is why he had been so attracted to him, why his thoughts had gravitated to him. And maybe this is what had frustrated Brooklyn most. "I'm just tired."

"You didn't sleep well." It could have been a question, but Brooklyn would never have transcribed it as such.

"Yeah," he says simply.

"A lot on your mind?"

"Something like that."

"Anything I can help with?"

Yes. "Nothing we haven't been over before."

Brooklyn sees no other cars on the road. This lends an uncanny sense of isolation that's not unwelcome. The dark clouds overhead continue to press in, squeezing the landscape from the sky. Oleander clears his throat before speaking again. "I was wondering if I could take you up on the offer you made me a couple of days ago."

"Which was?" Brooklyn asks.

"You said you could get me another book if I wanted. I've read this one enough times. I think I want to read something new." Ollie smiles with the corner of his mouth and, in spite of himself, Brooklyn's heart stirs.

"Yeah. Did you have something in mind?"

"I trust your judgment." Ollie holds his smirk for a moment and then breaks out into a wider grin. "For the most part, you're pretty good at picking things out for me."

"'For the most part,' he says. *For the most part.*" Brooklyn grunts disbelievingly. "When have I ever led you astray?"

"I can think of a couple of books that weren't my favorites."

With a wave of his hand, Brooklyn dismisses Oleander's statement. "I suppose not everybody can appreciate *all* fine literature." He glances back at Oleander, who's watching him intently, an appreciative look on his face. "But yes, I will get you a little something to read. How about when we reach Salt Lake City?"

"Thanks," Ollie replies.

They leave another town behind, one that is nameless to Brooklyn because he misses the sign. They're not too far past it when he catches something else in the corner of his eye. Not allowing his tired mind to think twice, he turns onto a one-lane road away from the beaten path.

Oleander shifts in his seat, but he remains silent. The Ranger trundles along as the way becomes rough with cracked pavement and overgrown yellow grass. Trees squat low to the ground. The road descends at a shallow angle, eventually transforming into a gravel path that ends where the overgrown brush dams the trail.

"Well, it was kind of interesting." Oleander shrugs. His tone suggests that he assumes Brooklyn will turn around now.

Brooklyn unfastens his seatbelt with a muted click like the ticking of a clock. He shuts off the engine, the truck dying instantly, and opens his door. "I'll be back," he says, throwing Oleander an affectionate, albeit distracted glance.

Then Brooklyn slides between the low tree branches, continuing his way down the abandoned trail. He can't hear the highway anymore. The world here is a mixture of dark browns, grays so pale they might be blue, and greens faded by an endless sun. He steps through spindly leaves that give way to his light touch, veils that obstruct the path but don't guard it. His mind is buzzing with intangible thoughts that operate just beyond reach. Gravel crunches beneath his weary boots. And then he hears another sound entirely: the gentle but steady flow of water.

Through the last of the obstacles, Brooklyn finds himself on a shallow bank at the side of a calm river. The water is gray like the sky, and deep enough toward the center that he can't see the bottom.

Brooklyn is overcome with the need to wipe away the muck and perspiration that cling to him from the night before. They are the remnants of a restless night sleeping in the covered bed of the pickup truck, where a collection of scattered memories have settled alongside samples of dirt. They're under his fingernails, in his ears, clotted around his nose, caked in the creases of his eyes, and lingering on his tongue. He longs to be clean.

So he pulls off the long-sleeve shirt and the one beneath it.

Icy wind sweeps off the surface of the river, sending chills across Brooklyn's exposed skin. Gooseflesh ripples his arms, and his dark hair stands on end. Ducking quickly, he pulls off his shoes and socks. The larger pieces of gravel sting the underside of his feet, but they're not enough to stop him. He undoes his belt and the button of his pants and slides them off, depositing them in a crumpled pile on a smooth boulder. Step by step, Brooklyn pads his way over to the water's edge, feeling the sharp pokes of twigs and rocks on his feet but also the soothing caress of coarse sand giving way at his soles.

Before he reaches the water, Brooklyn stops again, his arms limp and hands open at his sides. He looks back at his heap of clothes on the boulder and lifts his hands to his waist. He removes this last item of clothing and feels the air blow uninterrupted over his skin. His body belongs to the wind now, and it leads him with a hand at his back down to the water's edge.

In his nakedness, Brooklyn realizes how aware he is of his hair. On his head, it catches the squalls and bows to them in thick tufts that fall momentarily across his vision. The finer strands on his arms remain stiff and vigilant, marking the peaks of the bumps on his flesh. Sparse, lighter hair splashes across the narrow valley of his pale chest and down his abdomen past his navel. Between his hips, it clumps in trimmed, wiry patches around his penis. The hair on his legs is thin, but bold against his skin.

Clean, Brooklyn thinks, and steps forward.

If he thought the wind was cold, it's nothing compared to the water. In spite of the pain, he welcomes the river, amazed at the way it absorbs his legs without second thought. Beneath the water, the stones along the riverbed are large and smooth. Brooklyn steps from one to the next as he submerges himself. His sex shrivels painfully against his groin, and still he continues. He wades in until the water is just below the bow of his ribs, lapping where the prominent bones show themselves.

Then Brooklyn bends forward, and his head is beneath the surface. The water swirls, noisy and chaotic, displaced by his sudden submersion. Bubbles cascade in impossible directions, gravity lost to this aquamarine nebula. Instantly the icy temperature makes him feel as though he's suffocating. It pinches the skin on his cheeks and makes him grit his teeth to keep from crying out underwater. His lungs scream for air they're certain they don't have. But he denies his body the panicked instincts, instead holding himself beneath the surface and running his hands through his mop of hair. His fingertips massage his scalp, releasing the tension he hadn't acknowledged.

He pulls his head back out of the water. Brooklyn's gasps crystallize across his lips. Now that he's wet, the wind makes the exposed parts of him shiver. He glances at little droplets as they dance and fall away from his skin to the rhythm of his tremors. His hair sticks to his forehead, dripping over his brow. His hands have lost color and feeling. But he hums a tuneless song while he dips his cupped hand into the river and spills what water he can collect in his palm over the top of his head. He does this five times. The sensation is cold and shocking but welcome and satisfying at the same time.

Briefly Brooklyn looks around, searching the landscape as casually as he can. He holds shame at bay—what he would normally feel, naked in the open like this. Perhaps the restless night prior, the tiredness tugging at the skin around his face, the weariness this pilgrimage has collected in him thus far are to blame, but regret is absent. The water is too clear, too inviting.

Inhaling deeply one more time, Brooklyn ascends the riverbank. Smooth stones pave his way back onto the shore. The pieces of himself reemerge: first his stomach and navel, hips, thighs, knees, calves, and finally his feet. He stands, his toes in the coarse sand, every inch of his skin drinking the wild air. Cold.

Brooklyn has brought no towel with him, so he picks up his T-shirt and uses it as best he can to dry off. It rids him of most of the water, but leaves him damp enough that his clothes cling to him when he puts them back on. It will have to do, though. He heads back to the car, exhilaration lining his veins. He feels refreshed, renewed. Spontaneous and, on some level, daring for no one having seen him. He wishes he could talk to Zinnia. He wishes he could explain the significance to Dahlia.

"Did you fall into a lake?" Ollie asks as Brooklyn pulls himself into the truck.

"No, I walked into a river," Brooklyn says, cracking a smile at Ollie's bewilderment.

"Uh-huh." Ollie raises his eyebrows. "Why?"

Brooklyn realizes then that he doesn't have much of a reason. Clipped excuses fall from his lips. "There was a river up there, I was grimy—not that I'm super clean now—and it was irresistible. I don't know. It just felt right. I didn't think much about it. I just went in."

"So you, what, stripped naked and jumped?" Oleander asks.

"That's about the size of it. Yeah."

"I'd have never guessed . . ." The sentence doesn't feel complete. Ollie's voice fades. He looks away. Maybe there's a faint grin on his lips, or maybe Brooklyn can't see him clearly in the rearview mirror.

Something fills Brooklyn's chest that he associates with the sensation of a blossoming flower. It opens, welcoming in air and light. Though he would never say it aloud for fear of sounding sentimental, he hopes the feeling lasts.

The truck starts on the second try, and Brooklyn and Ollie continue their route along the highway.

Chapter Twenty-Two

Either due to his fickle emotions or the changes in time zone, Brooklyn can't tell whether or not he's hungry. He and Dahlia had eaten more of the peanut butter, jam, and bread that morning, which shouldn't have been enough to tide him over for this long, but he has yet to feel any real hunger pangs. In the end he decides to drive through to his stop for the night without getting anything.

The sign says SALT LAKE CITY.

"I guess you took my comment to heart," Oleander says. "You've been hitting all the cities."

"I don't know that this one's quite as big as Denver." Brooklyn surveys the skyline as they descend farther into the basin. Scattered buildings peak above the masses, looking squat for skyscrapers but tall enough that the tips of their rooftops still inspire feelings of grandeur.

Brooklyn shrugs. "I could've avoided Denver, but I wanted to give Dahlia the chance, since it seemed important to her. We have to get back to I-80 though, and I know it goes through Salt Lake City."

"I wasn't saying I minded," Oleander replies. "I've kind of liked seeing a couple of bigger cities in the area. Never really thought much about any places not on a coast."

"The middle gets overlooked sometimes, doesn't it?" Brooklyn says. "I bet none of these people forget, though. It's their life."

"Kind of hard to overlook your own life," Oleander teases. "But I bet they forget about us sometimes."

"Nah." Brooklyn brushes the comment away with a wave of a hand. "Nobody ever forgets about New York."

"Yeah, but I'm pretty sure what they think about begins and ends with Manhattan."

"That I can live with. It keeps them away from the more beautiful areas. Schoharie wouldn't have been the same otherwise."

The suburbs of Salt Lake City's metropolitan area engulf them. Brooklyn can just make out slanted roofs above the highway barriers.

Then Brooklyn and Oleander begin the ritual of driving around until they find a place Brooklyn both likes and can afford. There's no tension in the hunt. He makes a point to keep himself lighthearted, to keep his mind off other things. There are too many farewells he doesn't want to contemplate now. Too many pieces of advice he is afraid to consider. As he forces himself to smile, laugh, and stop resisting Oleander's light humor, he finds himself succumbing to the effervescent mood. Soon he is laughing and smiling involuntarily, lending sarcasm to their rapport. He even considers passing up a satisfactory place in the interest of keeping another of these bubbles of affection intact.

Instead he pulls the Ranger into the lot and stops the truck. Within five minutes he's gotten a room.

"Lakeside Inn?" Ollie says with a smirk once Brooklyn reenters. "It's pretty far from the lake to be considered 'lakeside.'"

"Eh." Brooklyn shrugs. "In this city everything's got to have something with the 'Lake' if they want to get business."

Brooklyn doesn't feel like eating alone at a restaurant. When his stomach finally does begin grumbling, he instead finds a corner market. He grabs a medium-sized tub of an interesting, ready-made pasta salad with a bottle of root beer. The meal isn't much, but his tastes at this point aren't particularly complex. Anything will do.

He parks the truck at the hotel and climbs into the backseat to share yet another meal with the man to whom he was once married. Is still married to? Inside the Ranger they pass the pasta and soda back and forth, reminiscing about old friends, some of whom they haven't seen or spoken of in a great while. Dangerous talk—the kind that could turn sour on a single word.

He wonders why he's given moments like these. Why does he circle around to worlds that no longer exist? Lingering in the past isn't helpful. It doesn't make him feel stronger or braver in the end. Though the taste of the conversation is sweet at first, he knows it will linger past its welcome. So why does he feel a hunger for nostalgia, knowing full well what will come of all this talk?

Oleander hands the tub back to Brooklyn. Brooklyn stares down at their half-eaten dinner, aware that he's again uncertain whether or not he's hungry. "Sometimes, people celebrate the lives of the loved ones they've lost. They bring food to them, dine at their gravesites," he says, chasing a piece of pasta around the tub with his fork. "I'm fortunate enough that I still have you with me, so I don't have to eat alone."

"I didn't want you to feel alone," Oleander replies.

Whether or not the clock is actually ticking, Brooklyn hears it counting the seconds of night until the sun rises. He attempts to iron out the creases in his brow with the heels of his hands. Light filters in through sheer curtains. The sheen is as bright as the glow of an angel or what he might picture around the shimmering, undefined outline of a ghost.

He sees fingers interlocking—some his own, some not—and a warm, calloused palm.

Brooklyn lets his head fall and stares at the ground between his feet. His hands, clenched firmly on his knees, are stiff. The worn denim jeans prevent his nails from cutting into his skin, but he still feels the pressure.

. . .the candid expression of sleep: the loosened muscles of *Oleander's* face, the way the hairs protrude from the skin about his cheeks. He sees pale sheets bunched like flower petals beside their clasped hands. The perfect asymmetry one can only expect from the Unintentional . . .

The harsh light of the incandescent bulb is barely masked by the papery lamp shade. Brooklyn reaches out and grips the neck of the bottle. It fits in his curled hand. He wants it. Yes, he does. His fingers are icy, as are his hands, his face, his throat. This may be the one thing that can warm them. The bottle presses against his skin. He squeezes gently and pulls himself closer. It can't hurt him. Not if he stays here in this room with the curtains pulled closed against the night. Not if he doesn't make a sound. It will feel good. It will hold on to him like a lover and make him forget everything that's ever happened to him.

Until it doesn't.

Until it doesn't, yes. And then maybe he will find himself in a lower place than when he started. But isn't the fall worthy of that fleeting bliss? Brooklyn almost whispers the encouragement to himself. He drags his thumb heavily across the waxy paper label. Won't it be nice to spend those precious minutes in numbness again? Never mind where it'll leave him. What's that saying—it's not so much about the ending as it is the journey? The journey, he is sure, will be passable.

Something drops lightly onto his thigh, no more than the weight of a penny. He hears it more than feels it. That light *tap*. But Brooklyn doesn't move a single muscle. He remains staring idly at the glass bottle in his hand and the deep amber liquid inside.

Then he wipes his eyes, brushing away the collecting moisture. He doesn't want to cry. Not again. But already his eyes are hot and his cheeks are flushed. He swallows hard, resisting the urge to let his shoulders tremble. Instead his jaw tightens, teeth sliding tightly into place. Resolute.

Brooklyn stands, the chair sliding backward on the carpet away from the table. He sets the bottle down, and the thud rings definitively in the dark room. How light his hand feels now, how unbearably empty. Turning suddenly, he goes to the door, grabbing his wallet from the dresser on the way out. The door clicks shut behind him before he gives himself time for second thoughts. He's greeted by mauve carpet and yellow plastic sconce lights.

It's only memories. I'm not there anymore.

Diamond-patterned wallpaper. Elevators with silver doors. Not a single garnet shutter. This is not the house in Schoharie.

I'm here.

The truck is closest to the side exit from this wing of the motel, but Brooklyn ambles past, pointedly keeping his eyes away. He strides around a corner in the hallway. A generic print of a grassy knoll hangs above an empty table. Then he's reached the lobby. He practically sprints through, dodging past a couple coming back from a late outing. The desk clerk says nothing, her eyes glued to her computer screen.

The cold night washes over him like rainwater. The air smells as if it's been swept down from the mountains, filtered by miles of tree branches. He can breathe; his lungs suck in every ounce of air they can, desperate to remove the stench of dependency.

He walks.

He's unfamiliar with the path, but he takes it and wonders only briefly where he'll go.

Chapter Twenty-Three

Brooklyn's consciousness breaks through the surface, and the light also rises.

He awakens to find himself tucked neatly into the double bed. The faded blue comforter is the color of ocean water under an overcast sky. He tries to count the blades of the spinning fan overhead, but they move too fast. Sunlight pours through the sheer curtains. The bottle sits unopened on the table.

Blinking away the remnants of sleep, Brooklyn pulls himself upright. From outside comes the faint drone of passing traffic.

He showers, applying soap to every part of his body twice before he's satisfied. Then he checks his minimal belongings and leaves the room, looking back only once at the bottle of Four Roses sitting on the table.

"You have a good night?" Oleander asks after Brooklyn places his things in the truck bed beside the box.

Brooklyn considers for a moment. "Yes, I did."

"I can tell." Ollie smiles. His lips are full and dark red. "Any reason?"

"I just slept better than usual."

They leave the hotel behind. Brooklyn drives toward the heart of the city.

"So, where to today?" Ollie asks.

"Well, first, I'm going to get you that book," Brooklyn says.

The Friday traffic is cause for a minor slowdown despite it being past midmorning. In the clouded gray light, the Ranger ambles forward until the spattering of modest skyscrapers envelops them. Their windows create mosaics out of the mountains in the distance.

In the hotel room, there had been a magazine detailing the fun dining and shopping experiences in the nearby Salt Lake area. While he'd gotten dressed this morning, Brooklyn had rifled through the pages. One quadrant of a page had been devoted to a bright green bookstore on a corner of a town square. The store was purposely quaint, with colonial grille windows on the second floor and a red electric sign made to look like handwriting. He'd tried to memorize the directions from a map at the back of the magazine, and his powers of recollection were being tested now.

The way is not too difficult. Once off the highway, they take three turns, which Brooklyn remembers by the street names. Before the dashboard clock reads 10:00 a.m., they've parked in a small lot across the lane from the storefront.

"You're going to look rather eager, aren't you? Coming in right when it opens," Oleander teases, but Brooklyn can tell there's a certain sort of shy contentment at the attention he's receiving.

"Eh, it'll make them happy, I'm sure. Employees at independent bookstores are generally excited about having customers."

"Have you decided what you're going to get?" Oleander asks.

"I've got an idea."

"Will you tell me?"

"No, I want it to be a surprise."

"I probably won't know what it is anyway!"

"Then you won't mind me keeping it a secret." Brooklyn smirks.

He steps out onto the pavement, sneaking a backward glance at the blank Ranger windows before heading across the street and through the double doors.

The quiet inside the store is enlightening. Immediately Brooklyn is in his element, aware of how many worlds are at his fingertips. He can smell the binding glue and the stiff spines of unturned pages. Everything is at once new and familiar, old-fashioned but cutting edge.

Before setting off in any particular direction, Brooklyn circles a display table of new arrivals. He feels the fresh covers of hardbound books, their titles embossed in bold capital letters. That was once the most satisfying sensation he knew. He can remember running home as a fifteen-year-old with a new hardbound or two in his hands, eager to get started. Frobisher's was the store's name, wasn't it? The owner kept a chalkboard out front with news of authors coming in for readings and to sign copies. Of course, Brooklyn used the library most often, but it was more exciting when he had the money to buy his own copy.

But he isn't here for himself.

Withdrawing his hand, Brooklyn walks toward the fiction section. The only two employees he can see working the shop are at the register, huddling over a black computer monitor and speaking in hushed tones. Joking. Flirting? They take no notice of him, and one eventually grabs a rolling book cart, no doubt to restock some of the shelves.

It's not long before a couple more patrons enter the store, but Brooklyn keeps his eyes low, perusing the neatly arranged paperbacks on the pinewood shelves. Oleander enjoyed most stories, yes. He read all genres. Once upon a time, he was almost as avid a reader as Brooklyn, just as happy to sit out in the yard in plastic chairs while they tore through stacks of pages. Ollie took almost every recommendation, though he was unafraid to say what he truly thought of them. He'd adored most of the books Brooklyn suggested, but he'd been less impressed with others.

He was harder to please when he was already unhappy. If he read while discontent, then discontent became woven into the pages. Only exceptional stories would break him out of such a state—not that Brooklyn feels Oleander is discontent now.

At last Brooklyn spots what he's looking for. The novel is thick with a greenish-gray spine like brackish waters and a sepia-toned photograph of two youths diving into a foggy bay. The boys are nearly silhouettes, their features dulled by shadow. One is horizontal, diving headfirst with arms outstretched toward the sea, while the other's arms reach out as if he's taking flight. There's only one copy left.

Brooklyn pulls the book out and feels the weight of it in his palm. Is he sure Oleander will like this one? He wants Oleander to like it. He *needs* Oleander to like it, if only to prove he still knows this man. Oleander has never thought less of Brooklyn for recommending a dud in the past—but seeing Ollie enjoy something he finds exceptional is satisfying. Brooklyn can't guarantee the outcome.

A woman wearing a soft-looking sweatshirt comes around the end of the aisle, her pleated floral skirt flowing past her knees. Her hair is so blonde it could be white; perhaps the lighting gives it that slight yellow glow. She gives only the quickest of glances down the aisle in Brooklyn's direction before grabbing something off the end of a middle shelf. Maybe what she selects isn't really what she's looking for. What she wants is farther down the aisle, but then she risks inspiring one of those oddly interactive strangers in hushed bookstores. Brooklyn doesn't think he looks like the type who'd strike up a conversation, but why chance it? After all, who says the novel she picked isn't worthwhile? At least she can glance over it until Brooklyn moves on—as most people do when someone else enters the same row—and then she'll get to what she's really after. It'll only take—

"O'Neill?"

Brooklyn forgets where he is for a moment. He scans the tall shelves to either side of him before his mind makes the leap back to the setting of his nonfiction universe. Where had the voice come from? He lifts his head. He's so wrapped in his extrapolation that this single word jars his senses.

The voice continues, "O'Neill's very good. That one took me a while, though. The prose was so dense, I felt it pulled me out of the emotion, but I guess that means his mastery of language is better than mine."

Brooklyn spins around to find a man standing in the aisle next to him. He's a couple inches shorter than Brooklyn and has hair as dark as fresh tarmac. The stranger stares down at the book in Brooklyn's hand—which Brooklyn now remembers is by O'Neill—and then flashes a strained, heavily apologetic smile at having obviously interrupted Brooklyn's trance.

Much to Brooklyn's own embarrassment, all he can muster in his foggy discombobulation is "What?"

The man laughs, which gives Brooklyn the chance to mentally shake his head and knock himself the rest of the way out of his reverie.

"*At Swim, Two Boys*." The man seems shy, less outspoken now that Brooklyn's facing him. He gestures with his chin. "It was really sad, but I found the narrator's resistance to sentimentality off-putting."

"Oh," Brooklyn replies, looking down at the cover of the paperback.

"Not that you won't like it though. The prose is still beautiful, but I—I had the urge to let you know. I wasn't prepared for it." The man shrugs, his unsuspecting blue-and-white T-shirt wrinkling at the shoulders. "I like my sad stories *real* sad. That's why I picked up this one." He holds up a smaller novel almost entirely a muted navy blue. *A Single Man*. Brooklyn recalls someone mentioning this novel to him before, though he's never read it himself. The man grins innocently. "I've heard this one's exceptionally devastating."

The heavy contrast between the man's eager tone and choice of story subject matter makes Brooklyn chuckle. "Is that ideal?"

"Unquestioningly." The man's eyes are the exact shade of thunderclouds. He seems to reconsider what he's said. "Well, at least when it's called for."

"What do you mean?"

"I don't want to give you the impression I'm only into tragedies, because I'm not. Any kind of story can be a good story, and I'm into the lighthearted ones as much as the next guy." His gaze wanders when he speaks, as if he's looping his words through the air and bringing them back down to Brooklyn again at the end of each sentence. "What I mean is, when I want a sad story, I like them to wreak havoc on me." He grins again, but it's more of a smirk this time. "But that's just me."

"Isherwood does it better for you?" Brooklyn asks, nodding at the novel in the stranger's grasp.

"Well, the jury's still out on that one. At least until I've read it."

"Reserving judgment. I wish other people did the same."

"Isn't that the truth."

Brooklyn glances around. The woman at the other end of the aisle is gone now. Perhaps she took the book she grabbed; perhaps she didn't. He weighs the novel in his hands, debating whether he feels persuaded to set it down or not.

"I'm sorry," the man says, raising an empty hand in the universal display of *I come in peace*. "I didn't mean to make you question your purchase. That is a remarkable story. I assume people want to hear my opinions before I ask. It's one of my worst habits." His laugh is raspy. It's also inviting. "Is it for you?"

"It's for someone I know."

"Ah, well, you know them better than I do."

"He's got a fondness for sentimentality. So, thank you for the warning."

"Don't mention it." The stranger holds out his hand. "My name's Aven White, by the way."

Brooklyn takes the hand; Aven's grip is firm. "Brooklyn Durant."

Chapter Twenty-Four

If Brooklyn hasn't smelled a hand-dipped corn dog before, he has now. Despite the fact that he's never paid them much attention before, Brooklyn finds himself tempted to buy a handful. Maybe the conspicuous, wafting aroma the vendors pump out pulls its weight after all. Brooklyn sates his temptation by grabbing a thick tuft of blue cotton candy. The effect is only temporary.

"Hey! Get your own." Ollie nudges him away with an elbow. "You said you didn't want any."

"I said I didn't want to *buy* any." Brooklyn detaches another tuft and then skips out of the way before Ollie can kick him. Beside them, a group of passengers scream as they're hurled, spinning, through the air. The ride, a rotating pendulum, swings to the right and then back up into the sky. Everywhere, colored lights flash in a synchronized show.

"Stealing another man's cotton candy is a serious crime," Ollie says with the utmost sincerity. "If I weren't already helplessly trapped under your spell, that's the kind of thing that'd get you the boot."

"Especially when that man has as big a sweet tooth as Oleander Rhodes." Brooklyn winks and wraps an arm around Ollie's shoulders. "So, what's left to do?"

"Well, you can't leave the Santa Cruz Beach Boardwalk without doing the Giant Dipper at least a couple more times—"

"Yeah, you mentioned that," Brooklyn says with a jolt of apprehension. They rode the wooden roller coaster earlier that morning, and although he found it somewhat enjoyable, his stomach still clenches at the thought of getting back on. His inexperience with rides is hard to shake.

"—but besides that, we've got to do the haunted house and the skyway buckets."

"And the carousel, right?"

"Yes. And the carousel."

They head for the haunted house first. The ride is not particularly frightening: some dim lighting, objects that clumsily fly out at moderate speeds, and little else. But it's entertaining all the same, and Brooklyn's pleased that Ollie holds tight to him the entire time. While Brooklyn wouldn't normally react to any of the haunts inside, he finds that it's much more fun to scream along anyway and let the amusement ride do its job without resistance. He's learned this quickly from his companion.

They stumble off the ride laughing, Ollie leading Brooklyn through the exit gate by the hand because he's always eager for what's next. The edges of the sky are turning a light pink. It remains cloudless as the warm breeze begins to calm. The two men share a lemonade. When they reach the counter, they both decide to get a corn dog as well.

"Macy won't eat corn dogs," Ollie says after the woman behind the counter hands them their food. "Mom and Dad bought her one here once, and she tried to swallow the thing whole. She threw up a couple of times and blamed the food."

"That sounds like fun." Brooklyn wrinkles his nose.

"Oh, it wasn't. Even though we're older now and she knows who was really at fault, she won't touch them." Ollie laughs.

Then something catches his eye. He stops, grabs Brooklyn's hand again, and leads him along the boardwalk to an open doorway into the arcade. A purple neon sign glows above the arched double doors, made powerful in the dying light of day. But the glow isn't what's attracted Ollie. Just inside the doors is a shallow foyer. On one wall hangs a faded black-and-white picture of the boardwalk in its early days, and on the other—

"It's a fortune teller!" Ollie exclaims.

"It's a machine, though," Brooklyn replies.

"Yeah, but it's a machine infused with the magic of a gifted seer." Ollie wiggles his fingers in the air mystically. He gestures at the mechanical man sitting behind the glass. "Look at him; he's the spitting image of a great psychic."

"Which one?"

"Eh, all of them." Ollie smiles. He leans forward to read a plaque inside the machine's glass enclosure. "Hector Alba."

"How does he get in touch with you? To tell your fortune, I mean."

"Well, you grab that little handle thing right there. And that's how he reaches into the vast unknown and gathers critical information about your future." Ollie finishes the last bite of his corn dog with dramatic flair and darts agilely into the arcade to dispose of the stick. "Go on. Give him a try!"

"Get my fortune read?" Brooklyn asks.

"Yeah, I've got to know whether dating you is worth it or if I should give up now." Ollie shrugs.

"Then shouldn't you be getting *your* fortune read?"

"But you can't get your fortune read twice. I'm hoping he tells you about our future and then lets me know whether or not I get fabulously wealthy." Ollie sticks out his tongue and then smiles nicely in case the previous gesture wasn't charming enough.

Even though Brooklyn's pretty sure the machine can't tell the difference between people and will read someone's future twice so long as they pay, he takes the bait. He fishes a pair of quarters from his pocket and deposits them into the slot. "All right. Here we go."

The machine comes to life in an animated, if stilted, sort of way. The figure in the box does a little routine and makes as if to speak to Brooklyn, who finds himself reluctantly amused. He grabs the metal rod protruding out of the machine, which is meant to help the animatronic man read his energy. Ollie plays along more than Brooklyn, voicing responses to the figure's monologue. In the end the machine spits out a small strip of paper beside the coin slot. Brooklyn takes it. The paper is only slightly larger than that from a fortune cookie.

"Take the ones you love with you on all your adventures," Brooklyn reads in a dramatically skeptical tone. "What a rip-off! That's not even a fortune."

Ollie laughs. "It is too. Well, it's *vaguely* a fortune," he says, taking the paper from Brooklyn's loose grip. He holds it up to read the regal serif script himself and flips it over to see if maybe there's more written on the back.

"That's a statement. A command. I could have told someone that." Brooklyn's not actually upset, given that his expectations weren't high to begin with.

"It's just missing an end bit," Ollie concludes. "Take the ones you love with you on all your adventures, and you will be happy. There. I fixed it. Now it's a fortune."

"Yeah, yeah," Brooklyn says, and puts an arm around Ollie's shoulders, squeezing them gently.

They walk out of the foyer, Ollie not asking to get a fortune of his own as he may or may not have seriously intended. Instead he folds the paper with Brooklyn's "fortune" and slides it into his pocket.

Brooklyn mutters, "It's still a general statement."

"What was that?"

"I didn't say anything."

Brooklyn and Ollie complete the list of rides they've yet to go on. They toss rings at the open mouth of a clown painted on the wall of the carousel—Ollie makes it through the mouth twice and Brooklyn zero times—and ride across the skyway, where they alternate between watching people walk below them and staring out at the gray-blue rolling waves coming into the California shore. Ollie laughs through the entire two-minute ride on the Giant Dipper again and convinces Brooklyn to keeps his hands up, even during the drops.

They progress steadily through a bag of kettle corn as they sit huddled in the cabin of a Ferris wheel that's just large enough to hold them. It turns out that Ollie is talented at catching the kernels in his mouth—or that Brooklyn's really good at throwing them. However, they can't say the same for the reverse.

When the sun has set, the two break away from the rides and settle down on a bench overlooking the sandy beach, their faces flushed and skin warm from the summer heat. The shore is still populated by dozens of groups: families with children who are immune to frigid, brackish waters; twenty-somethings and teenagers making the most of their time away from their studies; and quieter folks reading in beach chairs. Though Brooklyn is no longer on a ride, his head spins, but in a giddy way he enjoys. He's certain human beings weren't meant to be thrown around like that for pleasure, but he's glad they've figured out how to do so anyway.

As a last treat, they buy ice cream—Ollie's a chocolate-dipped vanilla, and Brooklyn's a mint chip in a waffle cone. It nestles easily inside Brooklyn, a light at his core. Maybe it's normal ice cream, but it tastes much sweeter.

The crescent moon is now clearly visible overhead, silvery and almost opaque.

"Did I ever tell you I wanted to be an astronaut when I was younger?" Ollie asks, staring up at the sky.

"Nope."

"I used to be obsessed. Everyone in my family knew, they—Wait a minute, I'm pretty sure I have said this to you before." Ollie stops and breaks his gaze to look at Brooklyn.

"You have," Brooklyn concedes, grinning. "But I like hearing you tell me."

Ollie shakes his head and goes back to his ice cream and the moon. The waves beat a slow and steady rhythm along the shore, receding and gathering into mountain peaks that then rush forward only to tumble and fall just before they make it to land. They were blue before, now as dark as the sky overhead. The families are beginning to pack up, reining in their children though the kids are always reluctant.

Brooklyn wonders if Ollie is finished talking, but as he thinks of things to say, Ollie continues.

"Everyone in my family knew. I was always really excited around my birthday and Christmas because it meant I was going to get a bunch of space stuff, and I couldn't think of anything more exciting than that . . ."

Chapter Twenty-Five

Brooklyn exits the bookstore with the Jamie O'Neill novel he'd intended to purchase tucked in his arm. Aven follows behind with his Isherwood book, his eyes scanning the back cover as if making sure nothing has changed. Brooklyn could easily rush out the door and across the street at a clip that wouldn't allow for social interaction. Instead he walks unhurried and holds the way open for Aven, who smiles and nods appreciatively.

When the door shuts behind them, bell jingling from the doorframe, Aven asks, "So, are you from around here?"

Brooklyn wonders whether or not he wants to tell the truth. Telling the truth has been an invitation for more questions and explanations. He looks down at the cover of the book in his hands and then across the road to where the Ranger's parked. The apple-red truck reflects a sphere of white and blinding sunlight back at him.

"Schoharie," he says. "New York."

"New York!" Aven says. "You're far from home."

Brooklyn smiles and even laughs a little.

"I suppose I am."

"Have you come all this way to visit the great Salt Lake City? Or are you here for something else?"

"Something else." Brooklyn turns away from the bright reflection to face Aven beneath the book store's awning. Perhaps they ought to move away from the storefront so they're not blocking the entrance, although there doesn't seem to be anyone clamoring to get around them. "I'm driving across the country to California. Trying to"—he stumbles over his words—"trying to get out and see more of the world."

"California," Aven says. "That makes more sense. Nobody really comes to Salt Lake City just to see Salt Lake City. Have you ever been to California before?"

"A while back," Brooklyn says. He slides his free hand into his pants pocket. "I went there by myself after I graduated high school and ended up living there for a while, but I moved to New York about nine years ago. Haven't been back there much since."

"It's a beautiful state, isn't it?"

"Yeah, it is." Brooklyn's eyes are on the sidewalk now, tracing the outlines of the cement sections. "How about you? Are you from here?"

"Yes and no. I live here, but I'm not really from here." Aven's gaze never wanders when he speaks; he talks directly to Brooklyn and nothing else. Perhaps this is why Brooklyn cannot keep his eyes from wandering. "I moved here a couple of years ago for work, but very recently I realized industrial banking wasn't my true calling. I left my job last Monday. Haven't really decided what I'm going to do next."

"Oh, I'm sorry to hear that."

Aven laughs. "No need to apologize. I quit."

"Congratulations then?"

"Thanks, I think. It's been one of those things, you know? I thought about it for a long time without *really* considering it, and then one day I did it. I'm still wondering what the hell I was thinking." Aven laughs, shrugs, and shakes his head. "I don't know how many times since then I've wanted to rush over and beg them to give me my job back."

"I know what you mean," Brooklyn responds.

"I haven't gone back, though. Which is good, right?"

Personal questions of this caliber can't be answered with a simple yes or no.

"I hope so," Brooklyn says. "Do you have any ideas about what you might do?"

"I've been thinking about moving back to San Francisco, where my family is. I haven't seen them since I moved here. I think I owe them all some time," Aven says. "I just don't really know how to tell them, you know?"

"They didn't want you to come out here, I'm guessing."

"God, no. When I moved, it was like I'd committed treason." Aven bites the inside of his cheek. "The worst part is asking them to help me move back. I don't have a lot, but I can't exactly carry it with me."

"You have more than you can drive?" Brooklyn asks.

"I don't have a car," Aven says. "Never have. I got my license from practicing with my friend's Civic, but my family didn't really drive much in the city. Friends helped me move out here, and I've been taking the bus ever since."

He smirks and then seems to realize how much information he's dropped on this stranger. Regaining himself, he holds up the Isherwood novel. "Anyway, I think I've probably taken up enough of your travel time."

"I asked," Brooklyn says.

"You probably didn't expect all of that, though."

"I won't lie, I didn't." Brooklyn laughs.

Aven lets the moment stretch until Brooklyn's flash of confidence begins to waver.

"I hope your travels go well," he says eventually, and turns to stroll down the street. He walks as if he has all the time he needs, one hand deep in his pocket and the other curled around the novel. Brooklyn supposes Aven *has* got all the time in the world, for the time being, having quit his job.

Then Brooklyn wants to know if Aven is always so forthcoming with people he meets in bookshops. His unguarded approach to emotional expression is refreshing.

Shouldn't I help this man the way I helped Zinnia and Dahlia?

The thought comes quickly, and he doesn't have much time to come up with an answer. Aven is almost out of sight. Hopping a little in indecision, Brooklyn glances back and forth between the retreating figure and the corner of the parking lot across the way. His mind is incredibly blank, unable to muster up the pros-and-cons list he might've otherwise assembled. Instead he ends up spinning in a circle and almost tripping over himself as he rushes toward Aven's retreating figure.

"Wait!" Brooklyn calls out. "Aven! Hold on!"

After a couple of shouts, Aven realizes somebody is calling him. He looks around in confusion at first and then, figuring out that the voice is coming from behind, spins on the spot just as the crossing signal beckons.

"Brooklyn," he says. Confusion pinches his features. "I didn't take the wrong one, did I?" He looks down to check that he's holding his book.

"No, you're fine," Brooklyn says, drawing level. "I just wondered— well, I was thinking—how would you like a ride? I mean, I'm not going to San Francisco, but I can get you close. And then maybe you could go the rest of the way on your own. You know, you could see your family and tell them what's happened, and maybe they'll come back out here with you and help you move."

He expels this all in stilted phrases, trying to say too much too quickly. He realizes far too late that he's probably made his suggestion more awkward than if he'd asked in a normal voice. So he hopes that Aven's openness will keep him from reacting poorly.

Asking to drive strangers around should've been much easier the third time.

To Brooklyn's surprise and growing dismay, Aven's response is not immediate. He looks back at the crossing light—now with less than ten seconds left on its countdown—and then at a place just below Brooklyn's chin in an unfocused way that suggests he's not really seeing Brooklyn at all.

"I've already made a few friends along the way, a couple hitchhikers who've tagged along," Brooklyn says. "I met a woman named Zinnia, and I drove with her to Illinois. She wanted to clear her head, to start anew. I thought she was a little crazy, but I understood where she was coming from.

"In Iowa I met a woman named Dahlia. She was this little old lady from Ireland, but she wanted nothing more than to see her great-nephew. She came with me all the way to Duchesne—it's a little town in the mountains about two hours from here. You wouldn't be the first, so if you wanted to come with us, I'd be happy to bring you along. More company is always nice."

Aven seems to be churning the offer in his mind, stuck between two responses. Brooklyn's discomfort spirals into dread. He must've overstepped the bounds at some point. Does Aven feel threatened? Is he figuring out a way to politely extricate himself?

Brooklyn raises his hands in the same gesture of backing off that Aven performed in the bookstore. "It's all right," he says, already beginning to turn away. "Just thought I'd ask. I didn't mean to intrude."

"You say you'll get me close?" Aven says.

"Yeah, I mean, I don't need to pass through San Francisco to get where I'm going, but I'm taking Interstate 80 most of the way. There must be a train or bus you could catch where our paths split." Brooklyn realizes that while he hasn't gotten lost on his travels from New York, he's made it most of the way across the country on road signs, the help of others, and the hurried memorization of a US map the day before he left. His memory is imprecise when it comes to the lay of the land. He doesn't even know how much farther he has to go. Maybe a part of him even hopes he'll recognize the way once he's close, though it's been nearly a decade since he was last there.

Aven looks Brooklyn right in the eyes, that unwavering gaze searching him. "I would feel strange not paying you. I don't have much, but I could give you something."

"No, it's all right. I'm heading that way."

"You're certain?"

"No, but when we get to the fork in the road I'll kick you out of the truck. How about that?" Brooklyn attempts a joke, and Aven smiles in response.

"Are you sure that's all right?"

"Yeah, like I said, more company is welcome. Keeps the ride from getting dry."

"And you said 'us.'"

Had he? Brooklyn doesn't remember, although he doesn't know why it should matter. It is true, after all. "I did. I'm traveling with someone else, but I'm sure he won't mind. When the other passengers joined us, he never protested. He even encouraged me to pick up the first."

Aven gives Brooklyn one more look up and down, his lower jaw tugged to the side in indecision. "Would you mind if I went home first, though? Just to get some things for the drive?"

"Are you close? I could drive you there to get your stuff."

"No, no, I'm fine. It's just down this street. I need to pack some clothes and stuff. I hear there are storms coming," Aven mumbles. He seems to be speaking to himself, sorting the situation out in his head.

"Of course," Brooklyn says brightly, eager to have a new companion despite the strands of nervousness tugging at the back of his mind. Ollie hadn't been completely happy about picking someone up the second time around, even if he'd warmed to Dahlia eventually.

Aven feels around on his pants and pulls out a thin blue pen from a back pocket. He opens the novel he's purchased and begins writing on the front page. As he writes he says, "Here is my address. I'll try not to take too long, but there's usually parking right out front. Tall brick apartment building. You follow this road down and then turn left on Linden Avenue. My building's on the right."

He hands the paperback to Brooklyn and, after a brief moment of uncertainty, embraces him in a swift, firm hug around the shoulders. "Thanks. I'll be ready as soon as I can."

Then he's off down the street before Brooklyn can say anything else, not even waiting for the crossing light to turn again.

Brooklyn lingers for a moment, glancing down at the page. The address is written neatly in the bottom-right corner—Aven's handwriting is incredibly straight, with *f*s that dip down below the other letters and curl up like fishhooks. Then he makes his way back to the lot, wondering all the while why he has decided, for the third time, to ask someone along on his and Oleander's journey. Perhaps he really does believe that company helps while away the miles. Perhaps he's afraid of being alone with the glowing embers of his past. Can you love someone and fear them at the same time?

The vibrant red truck winks at him as it comes into view. Brooklyn is startled momentarily by the amount of sunlight it catches from a sky as overcast as the one overhead. He doesn't look through the windows until he opens his door and climbs in.

"Did you buy yourself a book too?" is the first thing Oleander asks, seeing the two novels in Brooklyn's hand.

Brooklyn hands him the Jamie O'Neill novel. "I got you this one," he says by way of answer. "I hope you'll like it."

Oleander takes a long look at the front cover. "Thank you."

But Brooklyn still holds another story in his hand. "I—I met another stranger at the bookstore and, well, they've all been good so far, haven't they? We got to talking, and I offered to give them a ride some of the way."

"You did?" Oleander keeps his eyes on the novel. "To where?"

"San Francisco. Well, I'm not taking them all the way there, just until I-80 splits off, but I figured we're headed in that direction anyway. And since it's been fun with Zinnia and Dahlia, I thought we might keep it up."

Oleander's silence is telling. "Yeah, I did like them both," he finally says.

"It's only for a short while, and then it'll be just the two of us for the last bit." Brooklyn smiles.

Oleander nods and shrugs. With the windows closed and the truck off for so long, the air tastes stale and recycled.

"So, who is it?" Oleander asks. "Where are they?"

"His name's Aven."

"A man?"

"Yeah. He was a banker, but I guess he figured out it wasn't for him. Quit his job and wants to see his family again in San Francisco. He asked if he could go home and pack some things, so I told him we'd pick him up there."

"And you trust him?" Oleander asks.

"Well, I believe him. As best as I could judge, he was telling the truth. We didn't know much about Zinnia or Dahlia before we picked them up."

"Yes, but we could see that Zinnia needed our help—we passed her car and everything. And Dahlia . . . well, she was an old woman, and it didn't really seem like she could've done much to hurt you."

"Dahlia was pretty feisty." Brooklyn tries to interject a laugh. "I don't know. She probably could've kicked my ass."

"But most likely not."

"Are you saying I shouldn't have agreed to help him?"

"I'm saying you should be careful who you offer your services to. Helping people is nice, but you're offering to drive him a long way, and that gives him ample time to do something."

"You're the one who convinced me to pick up Zinnia."

"You reminded me of that when you offered to bring Dahlia."

"Well, I've already told him we'll help him, so I'm not about to back out now. Besides, we have his book—I don't steal."

Brooklyn starts the truck, feeling the engine struggling to turn beneath him. He holds the key in the ignition anyway. *We're almost there, friend*, he thinks. *You can make it.* And the Ranger rumbles to life.

Following Aven's brief instructions, Brooklyn heads down the street adjacent to the bookstore. He glances again at the address written in the book, his eyes swinging from cross street to cross street until he finds the one named in the neat handwriting.

Aven's already standing on the curb, a duffel bag strapped across his torso. He's looking around as though unsure whether or not Brooklyn meant it when he offered the ride. His hands grope at the strap, twisting the black nylon around his fingers and then untangling it again.

"Is that him?" Oleander asks, spotting the stranger standing at the edge of the sidewalk.

"Yeah," Brooklyn says.

"You said you'd drive him to San Francisco?"

"Part of the way, until our roads diverge."

"Where's that?"

"I don't know." Brooklyn sighs. "I'll tell him we can't give him a ride after all if you really don't want him coming along."

Oleander considers. The emotion behind his gaze is unreadable. He watches Aven repeatedly step up to the curb's edge and back away while he and Brooklyn wait for the light to change so they can make a left turn. Aven appears neither aggressive nor plotting; if anything, he seems nervous and apprehensive. He fidgets with his duffel bag. Despite what Oleander might want to believe, Brooklyn thinks, he can't force Aven to be suspicious.

"You don't have to do that," Oleander says just before the light turns. "You shouldn't go back on your word."

Brooklyn makes the turn. As Brooklyn and Ollie pull closer, Aven notices them and lifts a hand in acknowledgment. Relief breaks over his face. "I thought maybe you'd taken off with my book," he says with a laugh as Brooklyn comes around the back of the truck to open the camper hatch. "Just beside the box there?"

Brooklyn nods. "Yeah, it was actually just an elaborate scheme to get two books for the price of one."

"Clever." Aven stands back to let Brooklyn close the hatch again. "I hope I've brought enough. I just kind of shoved a bunch of clothes in there."

"It looks like it'll be plenty," Brooklyn replies.

"Thanks again."

"Don't mention it." They go around to their respective sides of the vehicle.

"Aven, meet Oleander. Oleander, this is Aven," Brooklyn says.

Aven nods and smiles brightly. The effect is such that Brooklyn notices how white his teeth are.

"Nice to meet you, Oleander."

"You too," Oleander replies with feigned enthusiasm that Brooklyn notes, though it's almost indiscernible from the real thing.

"You don't have to sit back there. I can switch with you. I really don't mind," Aven offers.

"No, it's okay. I always sit in the back," Oleander responds. "You can sit back here with me if you want, but I'm going to stay."

Aven laughs, perhaps not understanding that what Oleander says is true. He climbs into the cabin and pulls the seatbelt over his shoulder.

"You ready?" Brooklyn asks.

"Yeah, I think so. Ready as I'll ever be."

"Then let's get going," Brooklyn says, and pulls away from the curb.

Chapter Twenty-Six

Brooklyn worries that having Aven along will taint the atmosphere of the drive, especially if Ollie's initial hostility carries through. In addition, Aven seems to be wrapped in the consequences of what his spontaneity will mean for him. He's quiet as he stares out at the passing landscape of overlapping buildings. He knows these streets. And if he has never owned a car, he probably knows them better than many Salt Lake City drivers. He knows the way they smell and feel, which ones get him to his destination faster, and how the route might change depending on the time of day. He knows the stretches of even pavement and the creases where the tree roots have made the sidewalk uneven. This was where he, at one point in time, found independence and a home. And now he's taking the first steps to leaving it behind. Brooklyn sympathizes, but he hopes this silent Aven doesn't take the place of the talkative one who struck up conversation in the bookstore.

"Brooklyn says you're from San Francisco," Oleander says, and Brooklyn could almost turn around and kiss him then and there for breaking the silence.

"Yeah, I lived there for most of my life. My family's still there. And I guess I'll be joining them soon. Maybe permanently," Aven says, and grins.

"I'm from the California coast too, but a little south," Oleander says. "I visited San Francisco a few times. Beautiful city, the hills and all that, although it's not as sunny and warm as the postcards make it out to be."

Aven laughs in agreement. Brooklyn is reminded of wind gusting in a thunderstorm.

"I can't deny that," Aven replies. "I spent my childhood in fog. There were days when you couldn't see the lines on the road because it was so thick."

"Sounds like a big change from here." Brooklyn gestures with his head at the view outside his window.

Aven nods. "Everything about the cities is different."

"Is that why you left?" Ollie asks.

Aven twists all the way around in his chair to face Oleander. For the first time, he gives Oleander a good look with direct eye contact, and this causes Aven to stop for a generous moment. He seems distracted, only managing to find himself once a bounce from a large pothole breaks his gaze. He shakes his head, perhaps wondering how he became mesmerized, but his tone afterward is hesitant and layered with flakes of confusion.

"I—I guess so," Aven responds, looking down at his legs and back at Oleander sitting behind him. "I was still used to city life but found my hometown to be suffocating. Thoughts like that seem pedantic now—I know, the romantic suffering of a twenty-something from a middle-class family—but the feeling was enough to drive me away."

"I find it amazing that someone can feel suffocated in a place like San Francisco," Brooklyn says.

"I had too small of a picture, I think. If I had seen the whole city instead of my tiny corner of it, I might not have felt such a strong urge to resist."

"What do you mean?" Brooklyn asks.

"I mean that I lived in the house that my father grew up in, which he and my mother inherited the moment they married. We share it with my grandparents, who live in the bedroom on the first floor. They own a restaurant down the street, and I went to school three blocks away. And not the long blocks, mind you." Aven speaks like these facts once bothered him but have taken on a new meaning since then. "I shared a room with my brother, and my older sister was right across the hallway. When I got to high school, I started working at the restaurant. I got up every morning, went to class, bussed tables, did homework, and went to bed. Every day. Rinse and repeat. Everything around me felt so *small*. You know? My life encompassed a five-block radius when I lived in one of the most famous cities in the world. Maybe my view of the place was just too restricted, and that's why it didn't fit. I didn't want the world to feel so small. It bothered me. Do you know what I mean?"

Brooklyn does.

Before long, the Salt Lake City area dissolves around them.

Once the dam of Aven's apprehension breaks, he returns to a sprightlier form. Perhaps he's compensating for the nervousness he still feels, but he proves lively—his interest genuine and his tone carefree. He takes them through the memory of his family's reaction when he announced that he was leaving for Salt Lake City and recounts how they coped with a missing brick in their solid wall of familial proximity. He tells Brooklyn and Ollie how his curiosity leads him to talk to strangers, giving the impression that he is forward, but he has difficulty keeping up social interaction in the long run. The people at his company in Utah will miss him, he says, but none of them will maintain contact now that he has gone.

"What's wrong with you?" Oleander asks, joking—or then again, maybe not.

Aven laughs. "Hopefully nothing too serious. I had friends there, and we'd go out and entertain ourselves. I guess it's just harder to keep that up when you're not around somebody every day."

As Brooklyn has found for much of the country, the city gives way to long spans of open land. Nevada is barren in contrast to the verdant fields Brooklyn is used to seeing along the route. The crusted dirt is layered with wiry patches of grass in shades of brown or washed-out green. The coarse foliage stretches for miles into the distance until the soil and the plants blend together into a solid mass. An austere beauty grips the large desert basin.

Aven asks to turn on the radio, and Brooklyn is relieved that much of their music tastes overlap. Aven's singing voice is decent—much better than Brooklyn's, at any rate—and Brooklyn doesn't mind when Aven and Oleander duet poorly to Billy Joel's "Vienna," complete with a vocalized interpretation of the piano bits by the newcomer. Oleander's initial distrust of Aven appears to fade. He can't help himself. Ollie is malleable to the amicability of others; he dislikes few people. This is one truth that's always held.

The travelers drive on, encountering few towns along the way. Most that they see are sprawling plots of land dotted with flat rectangular houses. Brooklyn marvels at how different life must be here than in many of the other small towns he's passed along the road, even Schoharie. To choose life here is to prize solitude and isolation.

As soon as the towns come into view, they're gone again.

By the time the travelers decide to break for lunch and fill up the gas tank, Brooklyn has forgotten any worries about whether his decision to give Aven a ride was right or wrong. There is no right or wrong, only what did and did not happen.

"Any preferences for where we stop?" he asks.

"How about Battle Mountain?" Aven reads from a freeway sign. "That's an intense name for a city."

"Must've had some historic event there," Brooklyn guesses.

"Or it's the settling ground of Vikings."

"Land Vikings?" Oleander asks with a raised brow.

"The world is ever changing," Aven says.

"Ah, yes, of course." Oleander rests back against his seat.

"You want to take a look?" Brooklyn asks.

Billboards spattered along the highway usher them into the setting of a modern Western. The sidewalks are dusted with red sand blown in on the wind. Old cars parked in a dirt lot nestle between square buildings with awnings over their windows.

They find a gas station, beside which is a deli. Convincing Aven that Oleander doesn't want anything takes some time, but when Aven and Brooklyn are away from the vehicle, Aven doesn't ask much about it. They order sandwiches wrapped in thick, waxy paper and smelling of cooktops drenched in grease. Despite the fact that Brooklyn's not sure if he got what he ordered, the sandwich isn't half bad. He and Aven stand beneath the portico awning and take hushed guesses as to what the different chunks of ingredients in their food are, struggling not to choke while stifling laughs.

"Down the street from my office was a place this deli reminds me of. Norton's, I think, was the name. Total hole in the wall. It had windows so tinted, half the time you couldn't even tell if it was open or not. My coworkers used to love eating there, but I always turned it down because it looked absolutely disgusting," Aven says, crunching his empty wax paper into a sodden ball. He looks at the slick stains on his fingers with amusement and wipes them off on his jeans. "I swear, sometimes I could see little things crawling around in between the bread slices."

"That must've been the secret ingredient. Maybe your coworkers were onto something."

"Maybe," Aven says. "People swore up and down on that place. I guess you can't actually judge food on how it looks. This wasn't half bad."

"It goes the other way too. I've made some pretty beautiful things that tasted like shit," Brooklyn says. "Just ask Oleander."

Aven laughs. "Yeah?"

"We still ate it, because we didn't want to waste food, but sometimes it was *really* difficult. I tried experimenting a few times, and the results were horrendous."

"I can imagine." Aven laughs.

"Is it that obvious?"

"Not at all what I meant." Aven laughs again. It comes easily to him. "You needn't worry, though. Despite hailing from a family of restauranteurs, I myself inherited next to no talent in the kitchen."

Aven offers to take Brooklyn's empty wrapper, sliding them both into the trash bin at the corner of the portico. "While my siblings were off making turkey Florentine sandwiches for school lunches, I mostly stuck with ham and cheese."

"Sometimes simple is better."

"Who's laughing now, though? While they're still working at the restaurant, I went off to see the world. I made it all the way to Utah!" He winks.

Aven and Brooklyn don't walk for long, but somehow their short stroll reminds Brooklyn how much more of a journey he has, and how many more hours of driving that means. The last stretch of the trek will undoubtedly be the hardest.

They return to the truck, but Brooklyn isn't quite finished with Battle Mountain, Nevada. He wants to stop for more than just a lunch break, his legs increasingly antsy from the days of travel.

"Back on the road," Aven says.

"Actually, do you mind if we go somewhere to walk?"

"A walk?" Oleander asks from the back, his tone sharp and questioning.

"I'm not ready to get back on the highway," Brooklyn explains. "Nothing long."

"Sure," Aven says.

In the rearview mirror, Brooklyn can see Oleander staring out the window, expressionless.

"How great would it be to say you went to Battle Mountain High School?" Aven asks once they've continued further into town.

"As long as they've got a good mascot," Oleander says.

"Imagine if it was the Hummingbirds or something." Aven looks around as though hoping to see the high school. "They almost have to be a warrior of some kind."

Instead they pass signs for a college. "You could go to college here," Brooklyn suggests.

"Are you trying to say I need more education?" Aven asks.

Brooklyn laughs. "I only meant you might be too old for high school."

"They probably get people from all those smaller places we passed," Oleander says.

Another sign welcomes them to the rodeo grounds. Brooklyn pulls the Ranger over to the side of Old River Road. Seatbelts click, and Brooklyn and Aven step outside. The breeze whistles through the low brush, and Brooklyn understands why the trees are so few beyond the city limits.

It looks like rain is coming. The swollen clouds are dark enough now that, looking up, Brooklyn wonders how they can hold everything back. They hang low in the sky, bulges of growling mass roiling in the air. Brooklyn never thought he could describe a cloud as taut before, but he finds the word appropriate. They're almost green, like the sagebrush at his feet.

"You want to see where this goes?" Aven asks.

Brooklyn nods and leans into the truck. "We'll be back," he says to Oleander, but this feels like an unnecessary clarification. Is Brooklyn cruel to leave Ollie so often? Ollie is always waiting, watching the clouds go past from the other side of the window. He's convinced Brooklyn before that he doesn't mind. After all, Brooklyn needs to breathe, eat, sleep, and live. But, all the same, Brooklyn wonders what he is doing to Oleander every time he leaves him behind.

"I might've been wrong," Aven says, his hands in the pockets of his jeans.

"About what?" Brooklyn makes himself turn away from the vehicle.

"This place might not be as intense as the name suggests." Aven waits until Brooklyn draws level with him, and then they head down the road. "The name is a bit of a misnomer. It's pretty flat, at least compared to the mountains out there."

He points off in the distance.

"Yeah, I'm kind of seeing that too."

While Aven's talk has been easy thus far, in this moment it almost seems forced, like he's looking for things to say. He lingers between words, searching for the next one and leaping to it halfway through a breath so that he almost runs out of air before he can finish.

"Maybe the battle was so incredible that it completely leveled the mountain," Aven says. "Or it hasn't happened yet—the name is a precursor, and the ensuing struggle will end with a mountain of corpses." He kicks at the dirt, and a cloud of dust floats before them.

Brooklyn wrinkles his nose. "That's a little morbid."

"Only a little? Should I extrapolate?"

"That's all right, I don't really need more details."

"As you like it." Aven winks. "Not a fan of death?"

"Is anyone?" Brooklyn counters.

"No, I suppose not."

They walk past the curve of the fence where the rodeo ring ends and the last strands of the town get left behind. Before long the asphalt fades. In its place is a dirt path that continues on in a straight line between the starchy branches of ground cover. The road before them is so lightly traveled, it threatens to bleed into the surrounding landscape—a sprout here or there gives the illusion that their little path has disappeared.

Old River Road earns its name when the sound of lapping water distinguishes itself above the wind. The weathered path gives way to a truss bridge that may have been black once but is sun-bleached a green-gray color. Nature has a way of bringing all colors together so that nothing seems out of place for too long. The two men come to a standstill at the bridge's edge, and Brooklyn watches the water drift by underneath, its undulation like a heartbeat. He sees the bottom of the bridge reflected in the water.

"I'm going to get a boat," Aven says. The statement is startling in its bluntness. It feels like it doesn't belong.

"What?" Brooklyn asks, confused, though he doesn't tear his gaze away from the current. It doesn't smell like a river. It smells like rainwater, a storm maybe.

"I want to buy a boat. I want to learn how to sail." Aven crosses his arms and leans back against the first of the vertical truss members.

"Okay, sure," Brooklyn says.

Aven smiles. "I really mean it. I want to learn how to sail a boat."

"Is that your plan when you get to your family?" Brooklyn asks. "To be a fisherman or ferry boat driver or something?"

"I'm not really sure. Maybe not as a job—just in general. It sounds out of the blue to say, but it's something I think about every once in a while. I'm telling you now so that I'll have to do it." Aven raises his eyebrows as if to champion his proclamation, and then he turns and takes a few steps out onto the bridge. "I want to stand on the deck enshrouded in morning fog—because, let's face it, I'll be by San Francisco—breathing in the briny air, waiting for the sun to break through."

"Sounds nice," Brooklyn says.

"I hope it will be." Aven reaches the center of the bridge, some fifteen paces from Brooklyn. The clouded sky behind him somehow lightens his hair so it doesn't seem as black as it did before. He smiles sheepishly back at Brooklyn as if the confident words make him giddy. "Just me on my boat."

"All by yourself?"

"Yep."

Brooklyn laughs. "I thought you were going back to be with your family."

"Well, I haven't got the boat yet; that'll take a while. And yeah, I'm going back to see them, but that doesn't mean I'm going to be around them all the time. I'll take them out with me sometimes, if they want to go."

"You like being on your own, don't you?" Brooklyn's eyes fall to where the dirt beneath him ends and the bridge begins. This side is jagged, alternating between crumbling away and being filled by the dust that blows on the wind. The steel side is measurably straight, undamaged save for the peeling bits of paint giving way to patches of rust. He can line his feet up so that his toes balance over the edge and he's perched above the minute crevice in the path, almost touching the squared steel on the other side but not quite there.

"I don't mind it, no," Aven replies. "I've spent a lot of time on my own, especially in the past few years." He says this all matter-of-factly.

"But you wish sometimes you didn't have to be," Brooklyn ventures. "That's part of the reason you're going back?"

"Solitude provides a sort of occupation. You find ways to fill your time with the different parts of you. But you should never mistake occupation for company." Aven flicks something invisible off the railing. "It took leaving my job to realize that. You can enjoy your solitude, but when you've got nowhere to spend the night, you realize the most basic need for relationships: someone to fall back on when the going gets tough. Realizing that everyone around you is no more than an acquaintance can change your perspective."

"Yeah, someone to fall back on," Brooklyn says vacantly.

Aven stoops to pick up a twig from the ground. A few leaves still cling to it. With a cavalier flick of his wrist, he tosses it over the side of the bridge and watches it float downstream. "You loved him, didn't you?" he says once the twig makes it around the bend out of sight. "You loved him extraordinarily."

Brooklyn says nothing.

"I suppose you still love him, or he wouldn't be here." Aven rests both hands on the railing, his arms stiff, and leans out a tad over the water as he tries to find his reflection in the ripples. "I didn't understand at first, but I can see it now."

There are creatures in the crevice staring up at Brooklyn with eyes too small to see. *There is nothing in the crevice, nothing looking back at you from down there.* Really, he should just step completely onto the steel. So he does.

"I couldn't tell whether or not it was really him or just you. But it's him. He's still here." Aven keeps talking, filling the silence. "He must have loved you extraordinarily as well. He never leaves."

The breeze is picking up, causing Brooklyn's clothes to cling to him on one side of his body and billow out on the other. He walks until he's level with Aven. "In one way or another," Brooklyn says, "he never has."

They depart from Battle Mountain as the light wanes. With some difficulty, the trio find their way back to the highway and follow the sun toward the Sierras far off in the distance.

Since Brooklyn and Aven's return to the vehicle, Oleander has remained reserved. He listens to their conversations but is otherwise unengaged. Even when Brooklyn or Aven directs words toward him, he answers with a minimal response but smiles reassuringly, as if to say, "I'm happy, just quiet." And this is enough to deflect inquiry.

Brooklyn feels guilty for leaving him to walk the streets of another unknown place, but he already knows what the answer will be—especially given Aven's presence. So he does his best to keep including Oleander, because that is what Ollie wants, though he won't admit it.

The sign says WINNEMUCCA.

Brooklyn exits the interstate, and they find a promising motel. The small lot is empty save for a black sedan here and a blue SUV there. Brooklyn sees that the lights are on in one of the rooms, but the rest of the windows are dark. Perhaps the other guests are out.

Aven goes into the lobby to check the vacancies.

In his absence, the truck is silent. Brooklyn hears himself breathing. Then there is rustling as Oleander searches for his newly acquired book beneath Brooklyn's seat.

"Are you going to be all right in here? I mean, I don't have to stay in a room. I could stay in here with you."

"We've been over this before, Brooklyn." There's that not-quite smile again. "I stay here every night. I'll be fine." Oleander sighs when he sees that Brooklyn doesn't seem satisfied with his answer. "I wouldn't want you staying in here with me anyway—it's ridiculously uncomfortable. Just imagine what it would be like with two souls instead of one. That would be complete torture." He laughs a little. It sounds genuine enough to be infectious.

"I slept in the truck bed the other night. You didn't seem to think it was torture then."

"Yeah, but it was a terrible night for you. I listened to you toss and turn. And you had a sleeping bag. You've got nothing this time." Ollie shakes his head. "There's no reason to stay the night in here, except maybe to torment yourself."

"That's not true."

"Well, I don't want you here. You sleep. I don't do much of that anyway. Really, it's better for you to take a room." Ollie raises his eyebrows and lifts the book to just over the tip of his nose.

Brooklyn smiles. "Thanks," he says, still not entirely convinced but accepting. The thought of a bed is undeniably more attractive than the back of his truck, but his guilt eats away at him. "I don't forget about you, you know, when I'm out and about. I just . . . I know you're in here all the time."

"I know." Oleander squeezes the bridge of his nose with his right hand, his eyes shut tight.

"I don't forget that—"

"I know. I know, okay?" A flash of irritation.

"Ollie . . ."

"Please, Brooklyn."

"I just want to make sure you don't feel like I'm abandoning you."

"I know, Brooklyn. And I don't." Ollie sighs. "We have this conversation far too often. Every time I have to tell you the same thing: your apologizing doesn't make it any easier."

Brooklyn's immediate urge is to apologize again, but he bites his tongue, not wanting to leave Oleander tonight on bad terms. Lines crease Ollie's face, stitching together his brow and pulling the corners of his mouth toward one another. "I just don't know what else to say."

"Why do you need something to say?"

"Silence hasn't always helped us."

The car is still again. Brooklyn takes low, steady breaths. *In and out. In and out.*

Aven emerges from the lobby, backlit by incandescent bulbs. His breath crystallizes in the dark air, the white vapor trailing upward through the swathes of light beneath the streetlamps.

"Maybe I'll find a way to make it easier for you," Brooklyn says.

"Yeah. Maybe."

Chapter Twenty-Seven

Brooklyn is torn by two competing urges. On the one hand, he wants to sprint toward the finish, to end a journey that—though it's had its share of ups and downs—has felt arduous in length. On the other, he's afraid for the ride to be over and seeks to slow the pace to something less than breakneck speed.

To pass the time, they resort to playing games, having each other pick which out of two foods they'd rather give up forever or which animal they'd rather be reincarnated as. Talk remains simple this way, vapid but inoffensive. Brooklyn finds the miles pass quicker this way.

Then Aven's eyes alight. Facing forward, he points ahead to where a tall, mud-colored sign stands erect alongside the road. "Can we go there? *There*, to Nixon."

The sudden pointing causes Brooklyn to swerve into the next lane, prepared to exit without question. Aven apologizes for the outburst, which has thrown Brooklyn off guard, but they laugh about his reaction while entering another sprawling town.

"I don't see Nixon written anywhere," Brooklyn says, trying to read one of the signs as they pass by.

"It's not, but I know it's this way. I passed through here when I moved to Utah," Aven says.

"Didn't you move out there years ago?" Oleander asks, skeptical. "You still remember which exit it is?"

"Yes, I remember. My best friend drove me to Salt Lake City, and for a long time we debated going to this lake out here, Pyramid Lake. We saw it on the map, and thought it might make for a fun detour. Perhaps a way to make the drive feel more like a road trip and less like an extended goodbye. We debated right up until the moment we passed this exit." Aven's eyes scan his surroundings, replacing the interior of the Ranger with that of his old friend's car, Brooklyn muses. Perhaps a sedan. The blue-gray upholstery fades into tan leather beaten by years of heat and abuse from bodies throwing themselves down repeatedly on the seats. Cranks to lower the windows sprout beneath the armrest on the door. A crack runs along the top of the windshield over the space where the window tinting turns the sky an absurd turquoise.

"Did you end up going?" Brooklyn asks.

"No, I decided at the last minute that we couldn't stop if we were going to be the first ones to Utah. Otherwise our other friends wouldn't've been able to get into my place. That was the logical decision. We said we'd come back one day when he visited. But we never did," Aven says. The sedan is gone; they're in the Ranger again.

"Are you sure you want to go with us then?" Oleander asks. "You don't want to wait for him?"

"No. It's—well, we lost touch," Aven says. His tone suggests to Brooklyn that this is a lighter version of events, but Brooklyn gets the idea that Aven has a lighter way of putting many things. He speaks of his own experiences with emotional pragmatism.

Brooklyn sees the exit coming around the bend. "Let's see this Pyramid Lake," he says as they split from the highway. "Do you know where to go from here?"

Aven stares ahead for a minute, racking his brain. Apparently unsatisfied with what he finds, he dutifully answers, "I know it was north of the freeway, so you should turn right after this, but I'm not sure what comes next. I'm hoping there are signs."

Brooklyn holds to this one instruction, which takes them along a narrow road. Eventually they wind up in a town labeled WADSWORTH, with signs advertising the way to Nixon and the lake in question.

They're instructed to take Route 447, a narrower road baked a golden brown by the sun and carved smooth by the incessant winds. Brooklyn listens to his companions who reminisce about summers spent lakeside, about houses in the mountains that look out into seas of evergreens. Though they've never met before and come from separate places, their experiences growing up share many similarities. California has lent them sandy ocean beaches as well as towering mountains blanketed by pines.

Nixon unfolds along the winding curls of the Truckee River. Like many of the towns the travelers passed, the homes are spread sporadically, some bunched in tight groups while others go without a neighbor for long stretches. The residents don't bother with fences; the properties coexist with one another where the land changes or footpaths carve their way between buildings. Sidewalks are unnecessary. The asphalt ends where the dirt begins.

"How do you think someone ends up living in a place like this?" Aven asks. He then adds, "Sorry if that sounded ignorant."

Brooklyn turns onto another numbered route, following the signs. "Well, I'm sure a lot of them lived their whole lives here, so they kept hanging around. Their parents are here, and their kids will live here."

"Yeah, but how do you find your way here in the first place? I understand smaller towns centered around a major populated area, but there aren't any big cities all that close." Aven watches houses pass with porches adorned in patriotic bunting.

"For some people, this is exactly what they want. They seek out somewhere low-key and out of the way—someplace private, simpler, with quiet neighbors who are like-minded."

"Don't they ever want to leave, though?" Aven asks.

"Some of them probably do," Brooklyn says. "There's got to be at least one teenager who hates this place and dreams about living in San Francisco. They've got a couple of friends, probably not a lot, but they're not holding out for anybody because they know one day they're going to move on. Maybe they make it to the big city and decide it's not for them after all. So rather than go back and face the 'I told you so's they're bound to encounter, they go off and find another small town hidden somewhere in a valley." Brooklyn shrugs. "Maybe that's why they end up here."

"That was the most specific and yet vague, hypothetical I think I've ever heard," Aven says with a knowing grin.

Brooklyn shakes his head. "It's not about me. I just like making up stories for people."

"It was convincing enough."

"Some of them probably stay for the beauty," Oleander says. "I never really thought of deserts as beautiful before—just a bunch of dust and heat—but it's got its own aesthetic. When I think of nature, my mind always goes to green forests or oceans full of life. This is something entirely different."

And then Pyramid Lake appears before them.

Brooklyn has never been to a desert lake before. He expects the water to hide behind curtains of foliage, to wait in the shadow of a bend in the hillside until it unfolds in a wide, flat valley. But this is not true for Pyramid Lake. In fact, the shore barely has a declivity. The water sits almost level to the road. Only the breeze shows the lake surface for what it truly is, drawing ripples where the wind and the water kiss. If he hadn't realized the lake was there, Brooklyn might have tried to walk across it and known no difference until he felt the wetness tugging at his feet.

He pulls the red truck over to the side of the road, certain that nobody who minds will come along. The engine comes to a stop, and because Brooklyn is too distracted to move, Aven is the first to venture out. He drifts amid the sagebrush, drawn toward the water's edge as a moth to flame. Brooklyn exits the vehicle and follows Aven, hopping at a faster pace in order to catch up.

"Would you look at that: I'm here," Aven says.

He and Brooklyn walk until they're a foot or so from where the dirt transitions to lake. The water line barely moves, oscillating a few inches or so but no more.

"Is it what you thought it would be?" Brooklyn asks.

Aven crosses his arms over his chest, sweeping his gaze over the flat surface. "You know, I can't say I ever expected anything. The idea was a whim, a dare almost, to ourselves, and then the chance was gone before I knew it. It was more about the company than the destination; I think that's true of any good road trip. And maybe that's what I was trying to create at the time. But I hadn't thought about it much since; it's been years since Pyramid Lake crossed my mind. Now I'm here and, well, there it is."

"You going to jump in?" Brooklyn asks.

Aven smiles and chuckles briefly. "I've jumped into plenty of lakes before. I think I just want to look at this one."

He sways with the breeze and then, to Brooklyn's surprise, gets down and sits in the dirt. The brush moves to accommodate him. Some of the taller plants are almost at eye level with him. His legs crossed, he picks a piece of grass and fidgets with it, passing it back and forth between his fingers.

Brooklyn watches him for a while and then joins him on the ground.

"I'm going to find something I like to do," Aven says, pulling the blade of grass taut between his thumbs and index fingers. "I'm not going back as a failure. I'm going to find something that I like to do, and I'm going to do it well. Then I'm going to get a boat and learn how to sail it."

Brooklyn smiles.

"I'm serious!" Aven wets his lips where the wind has dried them. A tuft of hair finds its way to the middle of his forehead, but he doesn't brush it away. "Oh, and I'm going to read about a million books along the way."

"Yeah?"

"Yeah. I'm going to read all the saddest books I can, because emotions are great. I'm going to work hard and be happy about it. And I'm going to sail on a goddamn boat."

Brooklyn laughs.

"That's right, a goddamn boat!" he yells louder, making Brooklyn laugh harder. A few cars drive past, headed swiftly toward Nixon. "I don't think they heard me," Aven shouts. "Dammit, I'll be a sailor if I want!"

Brooklyn reaches out and pushes him gently on the shoulder, but Aven makes a show of it and falls back onto his elbows.

"I think everyone in a five-mile radius heard you. We get it," Brooklyn says.

"Well, okay then." Aven grins. "Took you all long enough."

Aven flicks the grass onto the water. It floats in place, bobbing. The normal yellow blade is no smaller or larger than any other piece. But now, as it sits on the water, slowly making its way back to shore, it idles at the edge of something immeasurable in comparison. A lake one thousand times larger than it. A million, maybe. An expanse consuming much more space than the blade of grass.

Without help, it will simply float back to land.

"All right, I've told you my plans. What are *you* going to do, Brooklyn?" Aven asks.

Brooklyn can't remember Aven saying his name before, but the sentiment is comfortable. He wants to lean forward and snatch the blade of grass from the lake before the waves push it to the shore. "Find resolution."

And the first raindrops fall.

Chapter Twenty-Eight

When Brooklyn and Aven determine that the rain is not going to clear any time soon and is, in fact, beginning to worsen, they hustle back to the truck. Aven laughs the whole way, hurtling through bushes instead of going around them. He shakes his head so droplets fling from his hair. The dark spots on the soil chase their pale shadows, but they manage to get into the Ranger before they're too wet.

"This damn thing," Brooklyn mumbles, turning the key for a second and third time before the engine comes alive.

"I didn't think it'd start raining so soon," Oleander says, staring up at the sky. "Looked like it would hold off a bit longer."

"Mother Nature is as untamable as they come, isn't she?" Aven is all teeth. He can't mask his enjoyment.

"Hopefully it's not too bad getting up into the Sierra Mountains," Brooklyn says, looking in the direction they'll soon be headed. He swings the truck around toward Nixon, headlights bobbing on the road. The scent of first rain on dry, dusty ground seeps in through the vents.

"Do you have snow tires?" Aven asks.

"Well, they're labeled all-weather," Brooklyn responds. "I'm not sure how much that counts for, but I'd rather not get caught in anything."

The storm has other ideas, however. Heavy sheets of rain fall, pelting the windshield with large drops that render the wipers next to useless. Their progress slows, Brooklyn cautious by instinct. Aven and Oleander fixate on the dark clouds hovering above.

They reach the city of Sparks, Nevada and follow Interstate 580 alongside Washoe Lake. In the wake of the weeping clouds, night descends early. The trees, perpetually blown sideways by the gusting winds, bow frenetically in the storm.

Brooklyn thinks of a squat linen armchair a red so deep it could almost be brown. The chair sits beside the bed, angled toward the curtained window. Plump, carved wooden feet are reminiscent of ripened pumpkins and winter days. He remembers the way the cushion seems to curl up around him when he sits down, to hold him better. The chair is wide enough that he can bring his feet onto the seat beside him and watch the blustery day while the stillness settles inside the house. Wallpaper with delicate blue pinstripes that cascade down from the ceiling to the baseboards. The droplets tap gently on the windowpane, and he hums along to himself, not certain of the melody—but it feels *good* to sing along. *Tap, tap, tap, tap, tap.*

In Carson City a caravan of vehicles gathers around them, trekking through the rain. The solemn yellow headlights and brilliant red taillights cut through the downpour. These phantom colors are all Brooklyn can see of the other cars.

The Ranger winds through the city streets, through the lit signs for businesses saddled on the main drag and tempting any customers still outside. The road turns onto Highway 50, and up the mountainside they go.

The temperature drops. With each minute, Brooklyn feels the cabin growing colder until finally Aven breaks the silence to ask if he can turn up the heat.

They climb, following the taillights. The lines on the road fade to dim suggestions. Up the incline, the highway careens this way and that. It's steeper than any road he has traveled thus far—at least it feels much steeper, impossibly so—and Brooklyn wonders whether he feels the truck struggling again or if this is only in his mind. The Ranger should have strength enough to make it, but given its recent history seeds of doubt have already taken root. Should he have stopped over in Carson City?

But his determination to make progress had taken over when they left Pyramid Lake, and he opted to keep trudging on. Now that they're crawling through the storm, turning back is no longer an option. The chill is enough now that the rain turns to hail and then to snow. Outside, the flakes scurry like scattered dandelion florets in the wind.

"There's a place just before you get to South Lake Tahoe that my parents used to rent in the winter. It's on Santa Claus Drive. As a kid, I thought that was the greatest name for a street," Aven says, dreamlike. Brooklyn gets the sense Aven talks now only as a source of comfort, combating the mounting unknown with the memories that come to his mouth before crossing his mind. The words do more to warm the truck than the heater, and so Brooklyn lets them be.

"The house had five rooms," Aven continues. "A kitchen— everything was laminated: counters, table, floor. All the most awful yellow color you can imagine. A bathroom just large enough for two people to stand inside to brush their teeth. A living room with couches that sagged in the middle when you all got together. And two bedrooms: one for my parents, the other for me and my siblings.

"For a while, we spent every Christmas there. I bet my parents thought they were clever, because of the names of the streets. Each was something Christmassy: Snowflake Lane or Candy Cane Court—real cheesy like that. It was always storming when we were driving up, and my father would threaten to turn around and call it off. Every single year. 'Janette, we're not going to make it. Look at this.'

"My mom would talk to him and calm him down, and in the end we always drove the rest of the way. I don't think we skipped a single year, and some years were pretty bad. But coming around the corner and seeing the house looking just like we'd left it, even though I'm sure other people also stayed there throughout the year, was one of the best feelings. We'd help my parents shovel the driveway when we were old enough, pile the snow on the side of the property. We'd run inside to turn the heater up higher. And then it was Christmas."

The cars have slowed further, their pace little more than a determined crawl up the mountainside. Snowflakes cascade through the bright headlights and dance in swirling drifts. Staring off into the darkness, Brooklyn can almost imagine that he, Ollie, and Aven are floating through space with stars spinning around them.

"How beautiful," Ollie says. "It sounds like you have some fond memories there."

"Someday I'm going to see if that house is still around." Aven raps the backs of his fingernails on the window, mimicking the sound of falling rain. Snow is silent when it falls. "I want to see if the same people own it and still rent it out. I hope they do, because when I have a family, I want to take them there."

Aven describes some of his Christmases on Santa Claus Drive: the hunts for Christmas trees that scrape the ceiling, busy nights of decorating, the special treats they only got then, the courageous snow battles, and his father teaching him how to drive in the snow the winter after he got his license ("I nearly destroyed the house across the street trying to back out of the driveway."). Brooklyn and Oleander interject stories of their own, highlighting the similarities that permeate their respective experiences. And as the years accumulate and the men realize they can't quite place when exactly the holidays changed, they cross the summit, and the caravan builds speed again.

"We continued most of the traditions even after moving away, though," Brooklyn says, glancing in the mirror at Oleander, who nods. "I mean, we still used to get a tree every year and put up decorations."

"Did you visit family? I'm assuming they weren't in the same place."

"We took turns spending different holidays with our parents," Oleander explains. "If we had the money we'd do one for Thanksgiving and the other for Christmas."

"That's a good way to do it." Aven smiles. "I'd agree to that."

"It worked well," Oleander says.

Through the shadows of the trees to the right, the dark water is visible. Lake Tahoe is large enough that the other side is enshrouded by night. The lake feels like an ocean, reaching out for eons. Brooklyn tries hard not to watch it while he follows the road in and out of tunnels bored through the mountainside. The red taillights lead him as the flurries intensify and clots of snow infringe upon the pavement.

"I stopped when I was alone," Brooklyn says in barely more than a whisper, as if he's not sure he wants Oleander to hear.

"Stopped?" Aven asks.

People turn off the highway, taking roads to the places where they'll spend tonight. What had seemed like a crowd before is thinning without notice. The street darkens.

"I stopped getting Christmas trees. I stopped putting up lights. I didn't make warm drinks or watch ridiculously corny, optimistic movies." Brooklyn's hands are white and stiff on the steering wheel. He drives mechanically. "I didn't call anyone or fly to anyone's home. I didn't buy anyone gifts. I didn't wish anyone a happy holiday. I stopped."

Oleander remains silent and still. His presence is so diminished, he might not be there at all.

"Didn't anyone try to come get you?" Aven asks.

"They did. Some definitely did," Brooklyn says. The last car ahead of them turns off the highway, and suddenly they find themselves alone. "I just didn't want anyone around after he was gone. I had him to myself then."

"Had him to yourself?"

"When you remember someone, you remember a certain person. They're all the things you ever said to them and they ever said to you. They're the places you went, the cities you visited, the flights, the drives, the meals, the movies. That's how they keep you company when they're gone." Brooklyn digs the nails of his thumbs into the steering wheel, burying them in the worn leather. "Anyone else's memory of them— it's of the same person, but it's not your memory. It's a hand-me-down. Even if a memory involves everyone in the same room, how each person describes it will be different, and their memory changes yours. It starts to chip away at your memory until yours isn't authentic anymore. It's a collection. I didn't want to talk about him to anyone. I wanted to preserve what I had left."

"But maybe their memories could add dimension to him," Aven says. When Brooklyn doesn't respond, he says, "You know? Maybe they could offer glimpses of him that you didn't know or had forgotten." Aven's hand hovers above the center armrest for a brief moment. Then it drops back to his side. "You have your memories, which contain half of him, and maybe others have the rest of the pieces."

Brooklyn's gaze is straight, though every one of Aven's words mulls behind his eyes amid an innumerable kaleidoscope of others. Maybe as many words as there are snowflakes falling from the sky.

"I don't want to share the memories I have," Brooklyn says.

"That's fine. I'm just suggesting that maybe you could—"

"I know what everyone thinks I need." Suddenly Brooklyn is filled with anger.

"Brooklyn, I—"

"I am fine, and I don't need anyone—"

"You're not understanding."

"I understand perfectly well!"

"Brooklyn, watch out!"

The bend in the road comes swiftly, slicing through the black landscape as sudden as an apparition. The insufficient streetlamps swathe the snowbank and surrounding trees in a grim yellow glow. In his agitation, Brooklyn hasn't prepared himself for this turn. He slams his foot on the brake pedal and yanks the wheel to the left, hoping the truck might respond despite the frozen conditions.

The tires struggle against the road, sliding instead across the surface. The anti-lock brakes pump against Brooklyn's rigid calf. But the ground is slick with new-fallen snow compacted by traffic and frozen over by the night's low temperature. The car fishtails on the icy pavement. The wheels slide.

Then, the impact.

Snow erupts into the air, soaring like a tidal wave over the vehicle. The windows turn white, enveloped in an unbroken mass of blankness. Brooklyn thinks briefly of flying through a cloud. The world around them is erased.

A muffled thud emanates from the right side of the truck. Crumpling. And then everything is still.

The white falls away from the Ranger's side mirrors, and the windshield wipers—still powering through—eventually begin to clear away the debris on the windshield.

Heavy breathing. Someone sounds as though they're hyperventilating. It takes a moment for Brooklyn to realize he's listening to himself. He looks over at Aven, who is uncurling his arms from around his head. He appears calm.

"Ollie?" Brooklyn spins in his seat, pulling against the locked seatbelt. It doesn't give, and he is forced to fumble with the buckle until it releases.

Oleander sits up, a bruise already forming on his cheek and a small cut on his lip.

"Are you all right?" Brooklyn asks.

Oleander seems dazed, his eyes unfocused. He lifts a hand to his head. "Yeah, I'm all right."

"I'm so sorry!" Brooklyn exclaims to them both. His heart hammers so heavily in his rib cage it's almost painful. "I'm sorry! I wasn't paying attention. I should've been going slower. I don't know what happened. I should've been—I wasn't—I didn't see it coming at all—"

"Brooklyn!" Aven says, and Brooklyn stops rambling. "We're okay."

Brooklyn notices the narrow window beside Oleander. The glass isn't damaged, but all that shows beyond is the dark, plated trunk of a pine tree. Not thinking twice about the cold, Brooklyn throws open the door and dives out into the night.

Snowflakes pelt his exposed skin. He has trouble seeing through the flurries and has to duck his head this way and that to get around to the other side of the vehicle. The nearest streetlamp shines resolutely down on him while the Ranger's headlights stare straight into the darkness.

He begins clawing snow away from the truck, pulling the powder free in heavy sweeps. A large dent mars the side of the vehicle at least a foot in height and half a foot in width where the apple-red sheet metal curled around a tree trunk. Some of the paint has been scraped away, leaving matte gray streaks in its place. The vehicle must have slid back after the collision, standing now a few inches from the trunk. The tree itself seems miraculously undamaged.

"Brooklyn!" Aven's shout reaches Brooklyn's ears for the third time in as many minutes. Aven sounds as though he is hundreds of feet away instead of only a few, the wind howling over his words.

Aven throws an arm around him. "What are you doing? You're going to freeze out here!"

"I—I had to check the truck," Brooklyn replies, out of breath. His voice is high and hoarse when he shouts.

Aven looks back at the damage. "I think it's going to be fine."

"No, I need to see—"

"Brooklyn!" Aven has both of his shoulders, and Brooklyn has no choice but to look at him. "It's not so bad. It's going to be fine."

Brooklyn takes a moment to consider this and then nods in agreement.

"You need to get back inside," Aven says.

Only now does Brooklyn realize his clothes have grown damp from the snow. His skin is cold and he shivers. His shoes are heavy and sodden.

Now feeling the full force of the storm, Brooklyn hobbles back around the front of the Ranger. The truck drenches him in the powerful yellow glow of the headlights, and for a moment everything is too bright to see. Then he's at his door, sliding behind the steering wheel. His body is numb yet somehow in pain at the same time. His lungs restrict, and he struggles to get the breath he needs. Wet hair clings to his forehead and around his ears. He cannot stop shivering. How can he be so cold? He was outside for only a few minutes.

"Are you okay?" Aven asks. His voice is warm.

Brooklyn clings to that warmth. "Y-yeah. I think so."

"We need to get to the closest inn or hotel," Aven says. "Maybe I should—"

"No. I'll be fine," Brooklyn says, adamant again.

Aven looks him over for a minute, skeptical, but the color is now returning to Brooklyn's skin.

"Please, Aven," Brooklyn says. "I'm fine."

Somehow, after all that, the engine still idles. The truck eases off the bank, sidling back onto the road at an excruciatingly slow pace. As though running on its last legs. From inside the cabin, the world is quiet. The wind does not howl.

Chapter Twenty-Nine

Short peach carpet on the floor. The shade is almost the same color as Brooklyn's toenails, the kind of mixture of pink and beige that fades from memory the second he looks away. The haricot curtains are only a few shades darker, purchased perhaps in the hope that they'd give the room a dash of elegant design without any chance of offense.

Brooklyn runs a hand through his hair, feeling the still-damp strands part around his fingers. He presses the back of his hand against his cheek; his skin is warm. Alive. His chest rises and falls when he breathes. His eyes close and open when he blinks. His heart thrums inside him of its own accord.

He drops his hands to the bed beneath him. The sheets are soft enough, maybe a bit too starched, but they smell like laundry detergent. They're whiter than the snow outside, creased along the edges where they're kept folded in between uses.

Clothes, still wet from the elements, hang in the bathroom over the shower curtain rod. They've stopped dripping, but he knows they won't be dry until morning. The light from the nightstand is tinted blue by the lampshade. He's had the television on but muted for the past hour.

Earlier, Brooklyn had paced the room, his eyes combing the walls and lingering on the shapeless masses in the texturing without registering them. He's never paced before. The act always seemed unnatural to him, a calculated habit made popular by stories and films. But as he slowly wandered the room, aimlessly moving back and forth among the furniture, he realized that not all pacing is done in a straight line.

Soon, however, he'd realized wandering did nothing to help calm his mind. When the carpet began to chafe on the soles of his feet, he sat down.

At no point during the collision had he feared death. Brooklyn is certain of this—the thought never crossed his mind. This alone is a fact that Brooklyn hasn't the energy at the moment to explore. What does concern him is the fear that he'd be unable to continue his journey. As the Ranger slid into the bank, this thought barreled its way forth and has since stood unshakable in his mind. He's afraid that the truck, which has carried him all this way, will not make it through. That it's damaged to the point that he'll have to either get it repaired or find some other way to move forward.

Even the thought that he might need to finish the journey in a different truck distresses him. But could he wait out the time it might take to fix any damage? It could take days. Weeks, even. He's known friends who were without their cars for up to a month following an accident. He'd have to wait. He couldn't move on without the Ranger. And this notion feels both silly and rational.

Brooklyn's second fear is that he hurt Aven. He can't imagine being responsible for injuring this man, who trusted him. Already Aven's company feels invaluable to Brooklyn. And for the first time, he considers that while driving any of the passengers along his way, Brooklyn had held their life in his hands.

He drops his head into his palms, pressing them against his forehead. His body aches. Homesick not just for a place but for a time and state of being. He feels as though instead of leading the way, he's been dragged through the thousands of miles to get to this inn on the eve of what could potentially be his last day.

Only one more drive to determine if he'll find what he's looking for.

Perhaps this is what frightens him more than any thoughts of death or damaged vehicles. What if he *does* make it the rest of the way only to find that the journey has not helped? What if he is unchanged? Brooklyn doesn't know if he could handle this outcome.

He has rarely wished for company, but now he wonders what Zinnia or Dahlia might say, were they in the room with him. He knows he can't be like them. He can't make himself into their image. Zinnia, with her confidence and zeal. He doubts she's ever been troubled by choosing what's healthiest for her. And Dahlia: resolute, calm, but lively. She had regrets and had experienced loss, but she found her way. She discovered what it meant to move on.

How can he? He's neither of them.

Brooklyn almost misses the knock on the door.

He looks up, unable to tell if the sound came from his own imagination. The stillness that follows impregnates the air. The sensation is akin to having someone press pillows to his ears. But the starched white pillows are still arranged at the head of the mattress.

More knocks.

Brooklyn stands. In a few short steps he crosses to the entryway where the plastic sconce sends a dim fan of light over the ceiling. The door is heavy, solid, but it swings open.

"Hi," Aven says. He flashes a nervous smile, embarrassed to be bothering Brooklyn. An oversize sweater clings to his shoulders, looking as though it has lost a long, arduous battle with gravity. Yet, it also looks like it was meant to fit him this way.

Surprised and still somewhat lost in thought, Brooklyn doesn't return the smile. While Aven's gaze holds, his flickers away. Time ticks in through the door from the hallway. Brooklyn can't see the source of the noise, but it's just as well that it remains out of sight.

"What's going on?" Brooklyn asks. He doesn't mean to sound suspicious, but worry has too strong a hold on him.

"Nothing. Nothing's wrong," Aven says. He shoves his hands into his back pockets. The hotel appears to be empty. Though it's not yet ten o'clock, the hall is as still as a photograph.

"Oh," Brooklyn says.

"I didn't mean to scare you."

"You didn't."

"I'm sure you were probably watching something."

"I wasn't. It's been muted."

Perhaps someone is moving the clock farther away, or perhaps it was never there at all. The ticking fades, replaced by Brooklyn's pulse in his ears. His instinct, then, is to close the door. It's not that he dislikes Aven White or his company. Rather, some part of Brooklyn doesn't want to relinquish the isolation he clings to after trauma. When he is alone, he doesn't need to know how to relate to someone else. Isolation is comfortable. It's natural. Interaction is not.

"Did you want something, Aven?" Brooklyn asks kindly instead.

Aven gives him the same brief and guilty smile as before. His figure is diminished by the sweater. It looks as though he and the worn piece of clothing have spent a good many years together, and the loss in elasticity like sagging skin is the result of their time. "I did."

"Yes?"

"And now I'm thinking better of it."

"It's too late for that," Brooklyn says. "It'd be unfair to say nothing now."

"You might be right. I hope you don't take this the wrong way." Aven inhales, and then the breath sweeps out from his lungs. "I was wondering if you might be comfortable with me driving tomorrow."

"What?" Brooklyn asks, more out of surprise than outrage.

"What I mean is, I don't know if you've done much driving in the snow, but I have. And you've come all this way from Schoharie, driving every day. Maybe you want a break for just a couple hours."

"Oh."

"Not that I'm suggesting you aren't capable of driving in the snow." Aven holds up his hands in a show of peace.

"Of course not." Brooklyn smirks, distracted now from his prolonged emotional turmoil by the discomfort Aven feels at making his suggestion.

"You're a pretty good driver—I mean, you're a good driver. Not just a pretty good one. I don't know why I said that, I just—If you want someone else to take a turn for a bit, I am comfortable driving in snow," Aven finishes. He deflates further within the sweater. "I should probably go now. Please don't leave me here because of that."

Brooklyn laughs. "I'm not offended," he says, leaning against the open door.

"You aren't?" Aven asks, relieved.

Brooklyn shakes his head, but the grin fades. Gravitas flushes his cheeks.

"Does that mean you'll take me up on my offer?" Aven asks.

Brooklyn can't find his words. He can feel his tongue in his mouth, the smooth surfaces on the backs of his teeth. He's aware of the breath entering and exiting his nostrils. But he cannot form speech. To his recollection, he and Oleander have never before let someone else drive the red Ranger. They haven't done this on purpose. When they went on trips with other people, they always took a smaller vehicle with better gas mileage to save money. Brooklyn used the truck a few times to help friends move large furniture, but he was always behind the wheel. And after Oleander was gone, driver exclusivity had been a subconscious decision he'd only come to recognize later, predicated on the sense that letting anyone touch the steering wheel other than himself would be wrong. The Ranger was *his* truck, and therefore *he* would drive it.

But was this a rule he should cling to? It was only one accident, but he'd allowed himself to get distracted. And it was true: he wasn't the most comfortable driving in the snow. Sure, it had snowed many winters at home, but back there the land was flat. Driving after a storm meant traveling half a mile down the street to the store.

This isn't the case here. He envisions the heavily graded roads like the one leaving Carson City, when the rain had first frozen over. He still feels guarded and territorial about the Ranger, but look what he's done. There is a dent in the side of the truck now. The paint has been torn away. He's responsible for that. Maybe, for just a few hours, it would be all right if someone else took over.

Brooklyn doesn't know how long they've been standing there. When he reconnects with the world, Aven is staring at him with a quizzical and expectant look on his face. Does Brooklyn trust him to be the first *other* to drive? He has no reason to believe Aven isn't capable. Aven has talked about learning to drive in the snow only miles from this very hotel. But what would giving Aven control of the truck mean?

"Brooklyn?" Aven asks, and steps forward.

It's just one step, but Brooklyn backs away. He takes his shoulder from the door and turns, retreating into the hotel room.

"I won't be hurt if you say no," Aven assures him.

"It's probably a good idea," Brooklyn says. The words are difficult, and he has to practice with his lips before saying them. "I think you should. At least until we're through the mountains."

He turns back. Aven is standing just inside doorframe, his hands still shoved into his back pockets. "Only if you want me to," he says. "If you're not feeling comfortable driving after the incident . . ."

"No, I understand," Brooklyn says. "It looked like the snow was coming down pretty good out there. I don't think the streets will be cleared up soon, but I have to keep moving. You should get us through the mountains."

Aven gives a half-smile. "I'd be happy to."

"Just be careful with that truck. I've had it a while now. It's what's keeping me going." Trying to break the nervousness causing his hands to tremble, Brooklyn laughs. "I'd tell you to be as careful driving it as I would be, but I think we both know that's not a good example anymore."

Aven returns the laugh. "No, I guess it's not." He traces the walls and the ceiling with his eyes. Then he stands up straight, pivoting to leave.

"Did you want to come in?" Brooklyn asks.

Aven stops, perhaps too quickly, and turns back around.

"I can stay for a while," he says. He comes away from the door, looking around the room. If not for Brooklyn's bag lying open on the dresser, it might've appeared unoccupied. The bed is still made, with only a dent in the sheets where Brooklyn had been sitting. The curtains are still drawn, blocking out the canvas of darkness beyond.

Aven walks over to the table in the corner beside the window and sits down in the wooden chair. He folds one leg beneath the other, resting his hands on the veneer tabletop. Brooklyn opts to sit on the bed where he'd been before. The room's heavy door swings shut with an audible click. The silence that develops is amplified by the enclosed space.

"Were you watching something?" Aven asks again, pointing at the television, which is still muted but flashing scenes from a bad cop drama.

Brooklyn shakes his head. "No, I was going to, but there wasn't really anything on."

"Too much on the mind?"

"Something like that." Brooklyn grabs the remote control and jabs at the power button. With a quick flash of white the screen goes dark, and he sees a dim reflection of himself sitting on the bed.

"What kind of things?" Aven asks. He runs his fingernails along the smooth surface of the table, tracing the grains in the wood.

"Just things, you know?" Brooklyn says. He feels like a teenager being pried at by a counselor. They both know that he doesn't want to continue this particular conversation. Already he regrets asking Aven to stay.

"That's a very broad spectrum," Aven says, and raises his eyebrows. The effect is charming but doesn't persuade Brooklyn to any degree. "Were you thinking of places? Where you're headed, where you've been? Or maybe people? Friends you left, friends you still have?"

"I know what you're doing," Brooklyn says before Aven can continue. "I'd much rather you told me about something else you want to accomplish. What do you think your family will cook first when you get there? It'll be a much better conversation. Believe me."

"Well, I don't think so." Aven interlaces his fingers and looks back at Brooklyn. He has a toothy, crooked grin. Why is his gaze so hard to hold? "I do too much talking. I'm always saying things without thinking first. But I think you've got a lot that needs to be said. More than I do, at least."

"Nothing *needs* to be said."

"There's a man waiting in a truck outside who might disagree."

"You think that's my fault?" Brooklyn asks, at once defensive. "Believe me, I didn't choose for him to be there. That's why I drove all the way to California in the first place. I'm helping him move on."

Aven is silent, his eyes searching. Eyes as gray as thunderclouds. Brooklyn has described eyes like Aven's in fiction before, but he's astonished at their vivacity now that they're staring back at him. He supposes sight is humankind's most valuable tool for navigating their vibrant world. Perhaps this is why Aven's eyes are so memorable and so striking.

"I'm sorry," Aven says. "There I go again—saying stupid things. I didn't mean to cross a line."

Brooklyn doesn't respond and instead fiddles with the remote in his hands.

"He's lucky to have you," Aven says. "Not many people would show the same dedication that you do."

"I have to," Brooklyn replies.

Aven's brow creases. "You're obligated?"

Brooklyn shakes his head. "No, but . . ." The flush of embarrassment returns to color his cheeks. "But he was my chance, you know? I love him. I have to do this for him. I wouldn't be able to live with myself."

"Your chance?" Aven stands. Uncomfortable on the stiff wooden chair, he instead leans back against the table, his fingers curling around its edge.

"What I mean to say is, well, it sounds childish, but he's everything to me. What you said before, about me loving him extraordinarily—I do. And once you've experienced that, you can't really go back, can you? I can't imagine loving anyone else like that." Brooklyn feels his heart hammering again, and heat swells in his face. His eyes burn, but he holds back, determined not to cry.

"Do you think you can't love again?" Aven asks.

"I know I can't," Brooklyn says. "I wouldn't want to stop loving him for anyone else."

"Do you think you'd have to stop loving him?"

"I don't think I could be in love with more than one person."

Aven is silent for a moment, his head bowed. Other than his breathing, he's completely still. Brooklyn is prepared for a pitying look when Aven lifts his head again. He almost wants to skip to the part where he tells Aven goodnight and he's left alone. But Aven's face contains no sympathy.

"I have always thought of love in the same way as words," he says, his cadence deliberate and thoughtful. "You can use words to write a book, spend years adding textures and layers to the characters, carving out mountains and valleys, filling every conflict with detail and nuance. You might spend your life lost in the world you've created and the words you've written, always expanding and expounding upon the pages. But maybe you don't. Maybe you finish the story. And maybe you start to write another.

"They're both a part of you. They can both be very real to you. And just because you've started another doesn't make the first one any less beautiful. They're both stories made of words, but they're different. And the differences are what makes it possible to move on from one that's finished to one that's new."

The heater hums beneath the window, blowing the curtains. The lamplight casts blue hues over the fabric. Figures dance unrelentingly. Smooth, elegant earthen patterns ripple across the surface like waves.

When the minutes accumulate, Aven stands, his sleeves pushed up over his forearms, bunched at the elbows. "Perhaps I should go," he says. "It's getting late."

Brooklyn nods, still not looking up.

Aven hesitates, and Brooklyn wonders whether he'll walk with the other man to the door or remain where he is. As Aven passes, Brooklyn follows, keeping a few paces behind.

The light in the room's foyer casts shadows on their faces. Aven pulls the door open. In another moment, Brooklyn will be alone again. He'll sit on the bed and wait for sleep to come. He'll turn off all the lights, hoping this will speed the process, though it doesn't often help. When he's alone again, he'll stare into the darkness, painting moving pictures on the walls that tell stories of the people he sees walking on the streets, their lives loosely intertwined but otherwise independent. When he is alone—

Aven leans forward across the threshold, and his lips meet Brooklyn's. For the briefest of moments, the barrier between them is demolished, and they stand together in a place unencumbered by shadows or snow. Water eddies beneath them, while the ticking of time assembles pieces of a world built on words that Brooklyn cannot imagine and hasn't the ability to say. Not yet at least. By the time Brooklyn realizes what's happening and feels himself give in, Aven pulls away.

Aven utters a soft goodnight and ambles onward, without another lingering moment, into the hallway of the small hotel.

Chapter Thirty

When light filters through the curtains, it does so with finality. Brooklyn cannot remember awakening, though he was asleep. Remnants of confused dreams dissipate like water vapor, swirling away between his fingers when he reaches out to grab at them. He sits up.

The room is frigid. He'd turned the heater off before he slept, frustrated by how often the unit cycled to maintain the temperature. So, after a quick spot of mental preparation, he darts from the bed into the bathroom, grabbing his duffel bag on the way. He showers, washing away the last bits of sleep and dislocation from reality. They run in rivers down his face, spine, and legs to be carried down the drain.

The soaked clothes from last night are dry—although they feel frozen from sitting out overnight. He puts on a fresh pair of pants, along with his now icy long-sleeved shirt and jacket.

This hotel doesn't offer breakfast, but they do have two large coffee dispensers in the lobby: one decaffeinated and one regular. He takes a regular and gets a packaged muffin from the convenience store attached to the entrance. He deliberates getting one for Ollie as well.

His heart flutters. How will he face Oleander Rhodes now? Should he tell Ollie what happened last night? Would Brooklyn be able to act normal if he didn't, or would he be incapable of avoiding suspicion?

Not that it matters much, Brooklyn tells himself. Aven had been the one to do it; it was a bold move on his part and nothing else. Brooklyn hadn't asked him to—and really it shouldn't count as a kiss. If his memory is correct, it was more of a brush or a peck. His lips had barely made contact with Aven's.

But you kissed him back, a voice inside Brooklyn says. He dismisses the thought.

No. He shouldn't be worried. He could act as though nothing had happened, because nothing *did* happen. And if Oleander does notice something is off—which he won't—then Brooklyn can mention that trifling detail about last night's conversation.

The icy air bites at Brooklyn's face when he walks outside, whisking away the steam coming through the plastic lid. His shoes crunch on the fresh layer of snow in the parking lot, leaving a trail. Only when the world is at its coldest can he see where he's been. He treks around the side of the building, surprised with each step by how malevolent the gusts of wind can feel. They're almost berating him, punishing him, pushing him backward. He bows his head, not to pay them respect but to hide his face. His defensive posture does little good.

Then he's at the Ranger, fumbling with the keys in fingers he can scarcely feel. He mutters under his breath to keep his teeth from chattering. He should brush the snow from the top of the truck and the windshield, but he can do that later when he's had the chance to warm himself. He's not prepared for how cold this morning is.

Finally, he finds the correct key and throws open the door. "It's a good thing you can't tell how cold it is, because it's absolutely—"

The wind howls past his ears. The cup hits the ground with a muffled thud, and the snow is soaked through with muddy-brown coffee. Brooklyn can't find his heartbeat. His insides have instantly and completely knotted themselves into a twisted mass.

The truck is empty.

"No," is what he manages first.

Brooklyn slams the door closed, the harsh collision echoing off the trees and the hotel's fake log cabin siding. Patches of snow slide off the

Ranger. Then he yanks the door open again as if meaning to tear it from its hinges.

Still empty.

He repeats this endeavor, no longer cold or numb, his throat dry but his face flushed and hot. Each time he opens and closes the door, the cabin of the vehicle remains vacant. And then he throws himself inside, maneuvering through the tight space as if Oleander might be hiding: squeezed beneath the seats or curled under the blanket in such a way that he's not visible. His books remain, but he's nowhere in the back of the truck and isn't hiding on the other side of the connecting window either.

Brooklyn goes outside again. His breath is ragged, and his hands tremble as he lifts them to his mouth. He throws himself to the ground, but nobody hides beneath the vehicle. The asphalt under the shadow of the truck is clear even of snow. He runs around every side of the truck, but they are all just as vacant. Just as clear and empty.

"Ollie!" he cries. Somehow the word sounds foreign in his mouth. His tongue slides strangely across the back of his teeth and curls against his molars. The two syllables reverberate against the sky and come back to mock him.

"Ollie!"

A trio of birds, still around in this cold weather, take flight from nearby trees.

"OLEANDER!" Brooklyn's throat feels as if it ruptures. He doesn't care what time of morning it is or who might hear.

Rapid footsteps crunching toward him.

"What's wrong?" Aven asks, jogging up with his coat zipped just below his chin.

Brooklyn's lungs burn. Ire rips through him like lightning, and he wants to run over and shove this man down. But the urge clears out almost instantly, and he shakes his head, confused and scared and worried.

"Ollie is gone," he says. Were he calm and alert, he might've been surprised at how childish his voice sounds—high and desperate. He gestures in defeat at the truck. "He's not in there. I can't—I can't find him."

"What? I thought he couldn't leave?" Aven runs over to the vehicle in disbelief. He checks through the window. "How—"

"He can't leave!" Brooklyn stumbles forward, and Aven takes his wrists, holding Brooklyn up and steady. "He can't!"

"But—"

"I DON'T KNOW!" Brooklyn shouts, dry sobs stealing the air from his lungs. He gasps for breath, his eyes wide. "He can't leave!" Brooklyn repeats. "He has never left! He has to stay there. He's always been there!"

He could sink into the ground, straight down past the snow and into the asphalt. The weight of the Ranger presses down on his shoulders, curling his spine forward as he strains beneath the weight. Panic sucks the life from him, spinning every word he knows inside his head in a vortex so turbulent he cannot distinguish a single coherent phrase. His limbs do not obey him; the muscles are unresponsive when they should be rigid, tensed. He can't blink away the dizziness. Can't shake himself out of the stupor overcoming him.

"Brooklyn, stay with me. We'll find him," Aven shouts from a great distance. His chest is in pain and he tries to knead it with his palm, but Aven's hands grip tighter to Brooklyn's wrists to keep him up. "Brooklyn, we'll find him. He can't have gone far."

The muffled slam of skin on glass catches their attention. Palms slide against the inside of the smooth, tinted surface.

Brooklyn throws himself at the vehicle. His hand slips on the door, but he manages to grab it the second time and throws it open.

Oleander falls forward against the driver's seat, gasping for air and drenched in water. His hair clings to his forehead, strands reaching down for his eyes. He coughs, his gaze lost as though he can't see the two men staring in at him. Maybe he is blind. His hands search the empty space beside him.

Brooklyn climbs into the driver's seat, making to grab Ollie in his arms. He can't. Their skin remains separated by empty space. Like light traveling past a solid surface and only brushing it with illumination. He tries again and again, aware somewhere in the back of his mind that they've touched before, but now he's failing and unable to help it. They can't touch each other. They can't feel their skin connect.

Oleander's crying, still coughing between breaths. His hands and eyes search, but they are growing still as the minutes wear on.

"I'm right here," Brooklyn says under his breath. Under the wind and the pale gray sky. "I haven't left you. I'm right here. I'm still here."

He means every word he says.

Chapter Thirty-One

Brooklyn stares beyond the glass, wondering if this is how Oleander feels watching the country slip past him. As feet turn into miles, the headache subsides until Brooklyn reaches a numb stasis. As per his request, the radio pours vacant music into the space. Nothing that sticks. He doesn't want the truck to feel empty, and appreciates the presence of music for filling that need.

They climb out of the Lake Tahoe Basin, their slow progress limited by the speeds of the snowplows that clear Highway 50. Again, they find themselves in a string of many cars: people who have stayed the weekend and are heading home on this Sunday morning before the traffic gets worse. He finds the landscape a strange portrait of muted colors: the stony sky above, the blanket of white snow covering nearly everything in sight, the bark on the evergreens, and their fraying needles, which appear colorless amid the dreary backdrop. Even the cleared road is a stark black.

Only the hood of the truck—a deep apple red—extending beyond the windshield contrasts the color scheme.

"Where were you?" Brooklyn asks when he feels his heart rate return to normal—or as close to normal as it will be for now.

Oleander thinks for a moment, his brow creasing in the middle. "I—I was nowhere. I don't really know."

Brooklyn can't decide how to respond, but he senses that Oleander isn't done, so he waits for him to continue.

The memory seems to come with difficulty for Ollie. Or maybe he doesn't want to say. Perhaps it's something that feels deeply personal, and therefore he's reluctant to describe the experience aloud.

"I thought I was swimming," he says, tracing invisible lines on the narrow backseat window. The glass fogs where his skin should touch, crystals forming over the area, and then fades back to normal. "I thought I was submerged in a large black ocean with nothing around me but empty darkness, and I was swimming through it toward a blinking light—a lighthouse maybe. It was very dim. It didn't penetrate the black space around it, but it was there. I know it was there. And because it was the only thing that existed in that space, I swam toward it. Unsure, ignorant, but comforted by its presence. Thinking about it now, I should've been afraid. There was nothing below me and nothing above me. A void, except for that barely discernable light. But I wasn't afraid. I was drawn through the vast ocean."

He pauses and lets the last of the lines he's traced on the window fade. The Ranger continues to follow the cars up the mountainside. The pace is much slower than they've been used to traveling, but it's consistent, and perhaps that's better for the time being.

"How did you find your way back?" Aven asks.

"I didn't," Oleander says. "At some point, I sort of understood. That sounds strange, but I looked around and realized that I wasn't breathing even though I was underwater. And then I thought that I should be breathing. It wasn't right. I was going to suffocate.

"I thrashed around for a bit, panicking. My lungs burned, and my head felt like it was going to split open. But I calmed down enough to orient myself, and I started to swim upward. There'd been nothing but darkness before, but after I swam for a while, kicking as hard as I could, I saw the surface. I could tell it was there even though there was no light above. Just blackness below and blackness above, but I could sense myself rising and getting closer. I thought I might not make it, that I would pass out before I did, and I wasn't sure what would happen then.

"When I should have breached the surface, though, I opened my eyes and found myself in here. Just as I always am." Ollie shakes his head, as if telling the story has disoriented him. He looks around, almost surprised to find himself still in the Ranger. "I wasn't in pain anymore; I couldn't feel anything at all again. That's when I knew I was back."

Oleander presses his palm against the window, and when he takes it away his imprint is left on the glass. The fogging is imprecise, and his fingers bleed together near the palm, but it is unmistakably a hand. His hand. It fades as all the other impressions have.

"I'm sorry," Brooklyn says. His guilt is enormous, though he cannot pinpoint exactly how or why he is responsible. What exactly had changed that transported Oleander to, well, wherever he had been? Brooklyn doesn't want to believe that the correlations he's drawn in his own mind are correct. They can't possibly be. They don't make sense.

Oleander says nothing.

Though Brooklyn had sworn to himself that Aven would only drive until they left the snow, he ends up letting him drive for much longer. He finally realizes how many miles he's gone this past week: through so many cities and small towns, along so many streets and highways. And though they were spread out over many days, they now feel heavy as he sits in the passenger seat. He's never been so tired of driving in his thirty-some-odd years of life. He also feels much older than he should. His body is tired from sitting in this confined space for so many days in a row. But he doesn't feel ill will toward the Ranger; the dark gray upholstery is as comforting to him as a wool jacket in the wintertime. The way the chassis creaks around him as it ambles down the interstate is the voice of a loved one in his ear.

As the travelers dip down from the mountain and out of the clouds, the snow melts and is replaced with a world of vibrant color again.

California towns line the road, meshing with the curves of the highway as it winds from the summit to forested foothills and then down into the state's central valley. The thoroughfare widens, and the fleet of cars thickens. Though the sky remains overcast, pockets of pale, wintry sunshine peek through.

Great wind turbines rise over the buildings, dotting the rolling hills of farmland soaked in fresh rainfall. The turbines rotate, their massive blades catching the currents of the wind blowing past. The sides of the freeway are lined with signs advertising shopping outlets and a variety of eateries. One advertises ANDERSON'S PEA SOUP in a less than desirable green font. Clusters of neutral-toned buildings accumulate alongside parking lots, which are brimming with a sea of cars.

Aven pulls off the freeway, taking an exit that brings them adjacent to a residential area. The sign says FAIRFIELD. A high school across the intersection hangs banners inviting community members to student-run events. He parks the truck in a small square plaza. Even though there are few patrons present, Brooklyn senses that these businesses are unique to the neighborhood. Their signs are not quite as flashy, their names unrecognizable.

"I thought we might stop here for lunch," Aven explains.

Brooklyn glances behind him at Oleander, wary of leaving him alone in the vehicle again. Is it safe to do so? He can't be sure now that Oleander will be there when he gets back. The idea distresses him.

"I'll be okay," Oleander says, encouraging. "I'm not going anywhere."

But Brooklyn wonders if that is a promise Ollie can make. Uncertainty stays Brooklyn's hand on the seatbelt buckle. "What if you do?" he asks.

"I won't," Oleander says, once again with more certainty than Brooklyn can muster.

Brooklyn nods, and he and Aven exit the Ranger.

The small café serves sandwiches and salads. The entrance is through a covered porch surrounded on all sides by planter boxes overflowing with lush plants. They're all the same. Between almond-shaped leaves blossom minute flowers, their petals spread wide in subtle proclamations of beauty.

The two men pick a seat by the window, as close to the truck as the interior of the café allows. Brooklyn finds himself watching it, glancing every few seconds to make sure the vehicle hasn't disappeared. He knows he shouldn't. He tells himself Oleander's vanishing was an anomaly, that it won't happen again. But he doesn't trust himself to know for certain.

"Are you going to be all right?" Aven asks when they've received their food. The question pulls Brooklyn back to the table, though his focus is foggy and evanescent. "Will you be able to drive the rest of the way?"

"What?" Brooklyn asks, before comprehending the words. "Yeah. I'm good," he says, then grins unconvincingly.

Aven takes a bite of his sandwich.

"I'm still a bit shaken by this morning, that's all," Brooklyn says, starting to eat his own food.

"It's been an eventful twenty-four hours," Aven agrees. He keeps his eyes down.

"I'm sorry—"

"Don't apologize," Aven says, interrupting Brooklyn. He smiles too. "I didn't just stop here because I was hungry."

"Is that so?"

"My stomach controls most of my decisions, but not all of them." Aven laughs.

He is beautiful.

Brooklyn looks back at the truck. It hasn't moved.

"I want to help you," Aven says.

Sunlight reflects off the windshield for a few moments, and then the patch of open sky gets enshrouded once more by another cloud.

"You have helped," Brooklyn says, "and I'm going to get you back to your family."

"No, I mean, I want to help with you. I know we're pretty much strangers—"

"I don't need help," Brooklyn says.

"This is what I've observed," Aven says firmly.

They both pause, looking around the café to make sure they haven't disturbed anyone. The café's only other occupants remain unmoved in their own conversation over chicken Caesar salads. Aven continues in a lower voice, "You and Oleander are still emotionally intertwined, and—"

"Aven, please," Brooklyn says even more firmly.

"I just don't want to see you hurt," Aven urges.

Brooklyn sets his food down. The wind outside moves the front door so that the entrance chimes sound every few minutes. The employees aren't fooled anymore; Brooklyn doesn't see anyone respond to the sound. "So, what's the other reason we've stopped here?" He can guess, and the resultant emotion that churns his insides is confusing, to say the least.

"This is my stop," Aven says. He pauses for a while, his sandwich still frozen in midair. He sets it down. "I can catch a bus here to San Francisco. This is about where the highways split. I think you mentioned going south of where I'm headed, so you'll probably want to take 680 to avoid bay area traffic."

"I didn't realize it was coming up so suddenly," Brooklyn says.

Aven shrugs. "There's only so much highway."

"Are you sure you have to leave here?"

"It's going to start impeding your progress if you continue in my direction." And Aven does look sorry that this is the case.

"I suppose I'll have to give you back your book. I don't think Oleander's read it yet, but I'm sure he won't mind. We can always find it somewhere else. I remember the name. It sounded interesting, so of course I'm going to want to read it too—"

"You should visit me sometime," Aven says. His hand comes forward, maybe to touch Brooklyn's. But then he seems to think better of the gesture and withdraws, placing his hand instead on the tabletop beside his other elbow. "I would like that. Perhaps when you've found what you're looking for. Would you want to see me too?"

"Aven," is all Brooklyn can say.

Brooklyn can see from Aven's eyes that this was not the answer the other man was hoping for. Brooklyn fishes for another response instead, but he's unsure of the truth. "I do. I just don't know if I can."

"You could tell me where you're headed," Aven suggests.

Brooklyn repeats Aven's name and then sighs. "You're right: we're pretty much strangers. We barely know each other. You don't even know where I'm from. How can you ask where I'll be?"

Aven thinks for a moment. "If I search where you were, I'll get nowhere. But if I go where you'll be, I'll find you." He smiles, and the hurt inside of Brooklyn grows stronger. "That's why I'd rather know where you're going than where you've been. If you can't tell me, then at least I'll let you know where I'm going to be."

Aven stands and borrows a pen from the vacant host's podium. Coming back to the table, he tears off a piece of his napkin and begins writing on it. "Just in case," he says as he scrawls the words. "Then I'll leave it up to you."

He hands it to Brooklyn, who takes the slip of paper and gingerly puts it in his pants pocket. It feels substantial, with hyperawareness soaked into its edges.

"Thank you," Brooklyn says. "I wish I could give you a better response."

"It's an honest response," Aven says. "I think I know how it'll turn out, though."

"You do, huh?"

"Yeah, I think I do."

Brooklyn cannot help his grin. Aven's lips are just across the table from him. And try as he might, he can't help himself remembering what they felt like. It was a kiss after all.

"To hope," Aven says, lifting his glass of water.

Brooklyn shakes his head before doing the same with a sadder smile. "To hope," he repeats.

~

They finish their meal, Aven determined that their last conversation not be bogged down with sobering words. They laugh and smile, making up stories about where they'll be and who they'll be ten years down the road: Aven obviously lost at sea on his sailboat, and Brooklyn somewhere in South America when he decides driving from coast to coast in the US isn't enough. They talk until Brooklyn realizes that it's been a while since he last looked at the truck. It's still there.

Then, with sighs, they rise from their seats and leave the little café with the blossoming white flowers on the patio. They embrace, Brooklyn clinging tighter than he means to, and Aven opens the passenger-side door to say goodbye to Oleander and retrieve his book. Oleander wishes him a safe journey, and Aven returns the sentiment.

Aven assures them that the bus depot is just around the corner, so Brooklyn starts the vehicle without him inside. Aven waves at them both, book in his hand and duffel on his shoulder. Though Brooklyn can't see the tiny white flowers from this distance, the wind blows their vines so that it appears the leaves wave them away alongside his friend.

The Ranger passes through the exit of the plaza's parking lot and down the street toward the highway on-ramp. Aven is lost from sight.

Chapter Thirty-Two

Weariness hangs over the vehicle at this last stretch of the journey. Both Brooklyn and Oleander know where it ends, how far there is to go. Oleander has no more questions, or maybe he does but feels they're not worth voicing. Mystery has flown from the cabin. While the separate parts have seemed grand and monumental, the journey itself has passed quicker than either of them anticipated. And now there's nothing left between them and the finish but highway.

For a long time, California is one large section of sprawling civilization blending together. The cities have no end and are distinguishable only by exit signs and the height of their buildings. A great deal of time is spent surrounded by people, cars entering and leaving the highway in droves. The vehicles fade as soon as they are out of sight, as do the names of the cities he passes.

When the population thins, so does the road. Nature converges on the truck once more, and the sprawling cities turn to stretches of solitude. There's not much left to say, so the two men don't say much at all.

The sun is descending. The clouds turn the colors of October leaves: warm hues of umber and magenta and violet. Wind rustles the redwoods, which shake their branches over the road. They bid the travelers safe passage before the world opens for the last time and Brooklyn and Ollie leave the forest.

The sign says APTOS.

It's a small town, the majority of which cannot be seen from the highway. The houses fold into the foliage, which includes stout trees burning red with the remnants of the summer sun they've collected in their veins. Brooklyn no longer guesses his way. He knows the roads to take, for he has driven them before. Though it's been many years, the paths are etched into his mind as deeply as those of his own hometown. There is the high school. The fire department. The funeral home.

Finally, there's the ocean. He knows before he sees it. The Pacific is as close to life emulating a painting as Brooklyn can ever remember seeing. The water is too many combating shades of blue-gray. Birds hover in the distance above waves too evenly capped with white. And the rolling clouds bathed in unbelievable hues make Brooklyn almost want to wait for another day. He doesn't want to risk ruining a breathtaking evening such as this.

He's the only one parked in the lot. The beach is abandoned on this late autumn evening, a Sunday. The engine dies and the truck is silent. Everything is much too still, much too weighed down with the emotions permeating the air. Brooklyn feels them pressing against his chest. Breath comes heavier than he's used to. For a moment, he can only sit there, his hands hovering over the rigid steering wheel, feet planted on the floor beneath him, seatbelt hugging his chest. What have these hands done, and what will they do?

He turns in his seat. Oleander stares back at him, his face a mixture of fear and sorrow. His lips are parted as though frozen mid-sentence, but they say nothing. He's trembling, his arms limp at his sides.

"I love you," Brooklyn says, and leaves the vehicle.

The air is frigid, but it doesn't mask the briny odor of the ocean. Standing here, Brooklyn believes that even were he blind and deaf, he'd be able to find his way to the water. Down to where the world ends, the ocean tethered to the sandy shore by the coastline. Half stumbling, Brooklyn makes his way around the back of the Ranger. He fumbles with the locks before pulling open the canopy and the tailgate. He must hoist himself up into the bed to grab the box from where it's come to rest.

The box is simple. Three sides contain nothing but polished brass dully reflecting the dying light of dusk. While the brass is plain, there's a simplistic elegance to the flat surface. Running his fingers over it is akin to sliding his hand over a river rock chiseled smooth by thousands of years. The fourth side has a peaceful scene of the ocean shore painted on it. Waves lap against the light yellow sand while the sun sets on the edge of the world. There's a pier on the left that reaches from the sandy shore into the water. And maybe, far out at its end, you might be close enough to touch the horizon.

The box is heavier than Brooklyn remembers.

Not trusting himself to look back at the truck, Brooklyn walks out onto the beach. Sand flies into the wind and gets carried away in swirling gusts that disappear almost instantly. His heart throbs inside him, and his teeth grit against the cold from without and within, but he doesn't stop. He ambles down the shore until he's at the water's edge and the waves, rising with the tide, lap ever closer to his feet, beckoning him forward with each pull.

Brooklyn stops, almost toppling over. His head is calm, but he can't quiet his heart. It takes precedence, beating loud and brash when the waves would prefer it to roll slow and rhythmic.

Reaching down with one hand, Brooklyn pulls off his shoes and socks. He places them behind him and then rolls up the legs of his pants. Now he feels the wind on his skin, unbelievably icy on his feet. He grits his teeth when he steps into the water, pain rising over his legs. But on he goes until the tide is up around his calves.

Now Brooklyn is still.

Standing in the ocean, he hugs the box to his chest. Wind gusts around him, blowing his hair and flying up through his shirt and jacket. The static of the waves mixes with the lilting of the quaking trees far behind him.

With one trembling hand, Brooklyn opens the latch and lifts the lid of the box. He realizes he's been holding his breath, keeping the thickness in his throat at bay. The lid folds back on cleverly hidden hinges, opening unto the world.

Delicately he lets the ashes pour out.

Bereavement tugs at Brooklyn's chest. He wants to chase after the ashes. This was a mistake; he never meant to let them fly away. He longs to gather them all back inside the brass box, but they're already dispersing into the world. Some fall into the great ocean, and some fly through the air. His throat releases a strangled cry, but he clenches his mouth shut and the sound dies. Standing alone in the water, he watches the last remains disappear forever, and something cavernous and disparaging rips open within him. Brooklyn clings to the box, holding it to him like a lover's hand. He stares at the wind as if he might be able to glimpse something fleeting. Something he might've forgotten.

He stands at that spot until there is nothing left. He is alone in an ocean.

Then, much slower than he came, Brooklyn leaves. He backs away through the water, the tide pulling at his legs, begging him not to go, pleading that he take just one more look. He asks it to stop, fighting his way back to shore. *I am only a man*, he thinks. *Please, let me go.*

When he's on land again, he grabs his shoes and turns his back to the water.

Let me go.

The truck isn't locked. He slides himself into the driver's seat, his eyes shut tight against the world. Bereavement still clings to his bones like flesh. Perhaps it was always there, but he only feels it now. Somehow, he can't remember life without it.

With the door closed, the rolling waves grow faint. He hears no birds or whispers in the leafy canopies. There's nothing but an uncommunicable silence.

Before he can think otherwise, he reaches to the ignition and turns the key. The engine retches. Nothing.

He tries again, and this time the truck kicks but the engine does not turn. Frustrated, Brooklyn grips the steering wheel tighter with his other hand. Nothing.

The third time he receives no response at all.

"Did I ever tell you I wanted to be an astronaut?"

At first Brooklyn wonders if he's heard correctly. He opens his eyes. The steering wheel is before him: a circle of worn, fraying leather. He lifts his head. The ocean is still there and the sky is the same, though the sun is so low on the water that any minute now the colors will be gone.

Brooklyn's hands quiver, as does his voice when he speaks. "You may have told me before."

Without looking, he sets the brass box down on the passenger seat. It sits with the painted side facing forward.

"Where will you go?" Oleander asks in a whisper.

"I don't know," Brooklyn says, shaking his head. He slumps in the seat, releasing the steering wheel and the key, which is still in the ignition.

"You don't know where you're going?" Oleander asks.

"No," Brooklyn responds. "I—I don't know."

"Are you going to him?"

"I don't know."

"Answer me."

"I really don't know!" Brooklyn raises his voice, turning in his seat. Oleander stares back at him, not angry but with a fire burning in his eyes all the same. The bruise on his cheek is still brilliant and bold. Brooklyn's resolve falters a step.

"How can you not know?" Oleander asks.

"I just don't, okay? I had one destination, and that was to get here. Drive to *your* hometown and spill *your* ashes into the ocean. That was all I had planned. And now we're here, all right. I don't know what I'm going to do next."

"So that's it, then," Oleander says, crossing his arms over his chest.

"What?" Brooklyn asks.

"That's it! You drove all this way here, and now you want to leave me."

"Ollie, how can you say that?"

"Well, it's the truth, isn't it?" Ollie shrugs defiantly. He raises his hand toward the windshield. "I appreciate the gesture. But after all that, you want nothing more to do with me. You just want to leave me behind."

"Ollie, you're dead!" Brooklyn shouts. "Everybody knows it. Our friends, our family, Zinnia, Dahlia, Aven, you and I. We all know it."

"Then why am I still here?"

"I don't know!"

"It seems you don't know a lot of things."

"Is that my fault?"

"Well, it certainly isn't your strength."

"What am I supposed to do, Oleander?"

"Nothing. Just leave me here!"

"Ollie—"

"Just leave me here!"

Oleander raises a fist and smashes it against the back window as hard as he can. He hides the shock in his face when the window cracks, lines radiating outward from the point of contact. For a moment they stare, their chests heaving, suspended in an enclosed space rife with crackling electricity.

And then Brooklyn releases a long gasp of air, and his figure diminishes, shrinking against the skyline behind him.

"Ollie," he says, struggling to hold his strength, but it's like holding water in his fist. "I'm sad."

His voice breaks on the last word.

Oleander softens. He turns away from the damaged window, looking back at the man who loved him even after death. Who has held his memory so close, it's like he never died. That man is crumpled in the front of the vehicle, deflated and spent. He has done everything he can think of, and now he's at his wits' end.

Brooklyn tries to breathe slowly, but a steady stream of tears runs down his face. His throat is sore, and his eyes burn. He has no means of stemming the thick droplets falling away from him.

"I need to let you go," Brooklyn says. "I love you and I have missed you *so much*, but I have carried you so close to me that I don't know how to—to live. I can't keep spending every moment thinking about you and wishing you were here with me. *Really* here with me. It's stopping me from experiencing what's still good about life. What I can still do. What is still waiting out there for me.

"I'm not forgetting you," Brooklyn continues. "But I need to move on."

For a while, they say nothing to each other, but stare intently into the other's eyes. Brooklyn wants to memorize each part, to imprint into his mind the lines that pattern Ollie's irises, as if this detail is the most important. This is what he wants to carry with him. And he doesn't break his gaze for a moment, he doesn't waver.

Then Oleander lifts a hand and points at the glove compartment. "I think you still keep tissues in there if you want to clean up."

The two of them burst out laughing, a heavier flow of tears raining down on Brooklyn's cheeks and curling under his chin. He wipes them away but reaches into the compartment to find the tissues.

"Unbelievable," he says through his tears, shaking his head. "You can't even be serious for this."

Brooklyn blows his nose and wipes his eyes again with his sleeve.

"I love you," Ollie says.

"I love you," Brooklyn says in return.

Then he opens the truck door again and steps back out into the world, knowing that when he returns—if he returns—there will be no one waiting for him. He has his shoes in his hand, and when he goes around to the back, he grabs his duffel and places the box inside. It seems a little unceremonious to be traveling with it in such a way, but the box is more of a symbol now than a vessel. Its former contents are a part of vast expanses.

Maybe he'll return to the vehicle; he doesn't know. At the least, Brooklyn will have to call someone to tow it away, but in any case, he won't be keeping it for much longer. He can return to this circumstance later, though, when the time is right.

Brooklyn walks along the shore, following the quay, which separates the sidewalk from the beach below. The wind has weathered the stone, dying it the palest of grays and planting seeds of grasses that crawl out between the bricks to the point that the layers almost look natural. The sand, cold and moist, squishes beneath his feet as he walks, pressing into the space between his toes. It's glorious. He imagines walking along this beach over a decade and a half ago and wonders if he had these same thoughts then.

A dark woman, dressed all in black, passes Brooklyn by. They smile at each other, and she almost seems to know him.

As the stranger disappears, Brooklyn stops to look around, surprised that he's the only one in the vicinity. He hops up to sit on the edge of the quay, places his bag down beside him, and rummages inside. With the light contents, it should be easy to find what he's looking for, but it takes him a few moments before he removes a small black notebook and a ballpoint pen.

Brooklyn writes, oblivious to the wind and ocean spray, for the better part of half an hour. Nothing substantial, but enough to awaken something long dormant inside him. When he looks up, he's surprised—but then again, not so surprised—to see someone sitting on the pier extending out from the end of the quay, looking as though he's been there for hours.

The boy is young, probably seventeen or eighteen, and has dark wispy hair that tries to sail away each time a gust blows. He sits above the place where the water meets the shore, swinging his legs listlessly back and forth. He stares down at the space beneath him, probably wondering something silly like "How would it feel to be a sea creature?" Yes, he's got an earnest gaze, tainted with a healthy dose of sarcasm and maybe an unhealthy dose of growing cynicism, but for now he is eager and excited. He's from a small town somewhere nobody's ever heard of. Tired of feeling like he's missing something and being trapped in a place so small and restricted, he's come out here. The famous beaches of California. Maybe he's deciding that this side of the country is where he'll go to college or make his living. Maybe that will satisfy him.

But the boy cannot fathom what the ocean has in store.

Another boy walks onto the beach. He's a local—Brooklyn can tell by the short pants he wears beneath his sweater, even though the cold outside is undeniable. He's got lighter hair than the first boy and walks taller, with a bounce to his step that can only be part of his personality. Without fear, he approaches the first boy and sits down beside him on the inland side of the pier.

Brooklyn is surprised that he can hear them talk so clearly.

"It does that all day, you know," the second boy says, nodding at the surf below them.

The first boy smirks but keeps watching.

"What're you doing?"

"Well, there's this bird down there swimming around the pillars, happy as a clam," the first boy says. "I've never seen one like it; it's real colorful. And it just keeps swimming around there." He looks up at the second boy. "All by himself."

The second boy looks down and, sure enough, the bird floats around below. "That's a funny thing to be staring at."

"There's no ocean where I'm from," the first boy says. "I'm not used to seeing something like that."

"So, you aren't from around here." The boy with the lighter hair smiles. "I knew I hadn't seen you before."

"Is it that obvious? Maybe you just forgot me."

"No. Trust me, that wouldn't have happened. I come down here a lot. And usually I see the same people, but I haven't seen you before. You've got incredible eyes," the second boy says unabashedly.

The first boy blushes, embarrassed by the compliment. He wouldn't agree—his eyes are dull and colorless, not vibrant like the other boy's, which are green and bright. "Thanks."

"So, why're you here?"

"Just wanted to see more of the country," the boy with the darker hair replies.

"You come with anyone?" the second boy asks.

The first shakes his head. "I do most things on my own."

"That's all right. So do I. You get things done faster that way." He nudges the other boy with his elbow.

The first boy laughs and lets his gaze fall back down to the water.

"You must be a big fan of the Santa Cruz Beach Boardwalk if you like piers this much," the boy with the lighter hair muses.

"What's that?" the first one asks.

"Oh, I already forgot, you're not from around here." The second boy pulls his legs up onto the wooden planks and sits cross-legged, facing his new acquaintance. "It's a seaside amusement park. Really fun. It's got corn dogs, fortune teller machines, the Giant Dipper, and the carousel with the rings . . ."

The first boy laughs. "I see. I haven't been to one before."

"Well, there's only one Santa Cruz Beach Boardwalk," the second explains.

"No, I mean an amusement park."

The boy's mouth drops open in bewilderment. "What? You've never been to an amusement park before? Not a single one?"

"They don't really have any where I'm from."

"It's settled, then," the second boy says, crossing his arms.

"What is?" the first one asks, laughing again.

"We're going to go to the Boardwalk," the second boy replies, nodding as though to close the deal. He smiles widely, and there is no refusing this disarming grin.

"All right then," the first says, clearly not convinced.

"I mean it." The second boy stands as though to prove his mettle.

"All right."

"No, I mean it," the second boy repeats. "Say you mean it too."

The first boy bites his lip, trying not to show how happy he is that this stranger came to talk to him. He stands as well. He's a few inches taller than the second boy. "I mean it: we're going to the Boardwalk."

The second boy holds out his hand, and they shake. The wind gusts but does not ripple their clothes nearly as much as it should. It's almost as if they're standing in a separate wind, their lives drawn on another landscape.

When they can't hold it in any longer, they both laugh. Youth lights their faces, preserving them in an untouchable state. Neither boy recognizes the affection that the other already feels nor foresees what will come for them now that they've met. What it means to live and to fall in love. This sandy shore will forever be the place where they met. Where the redwoods sway in the distance and clouds gather in the darkest shades of blue, having finally relinquished the warm and vibrant colors they held for so brief a period in time.

"I'm Oleander," says the second boy.

"Brooklyn," says the first.